Also by Megan Frazer Blakemore

The Water Castle
The Spy Catchers of Maple Hill
The Friendship Riddle

———

The Firefly Code
The Daybreak Bond

The Story Web

Megan Frazer Blakemore

BLOOMSBURY
CHILDREN'S BOOKS
NEW YORK   LONDON   OXFORD   NEW DELHI   SYDNEY

BLOOMSBURY CHILDREN'S BOOKS
Bloomsbury Publishing Inc., part of Bloomsbury Publishing Plc
1385 Broadway, New York, NY 10018

BLOOMSBURY, BLOOMSBURY CHILDREN'S BOOKS, and the Diana logo
are trademarks of Bloomsbury Publishing Plc

First published in the United States of America in June 2019
by Bloomsbury Children's Books

Bloomsbury books may be purchased for business or promotional use. For information on bulk
purchases please contact Macmillan Corporate and Premium Sales Department at
specialmarkets@macmillan.com

Library of Congress Cataloging-in-Publication Data
Names: Blakemore, Megan Frazer, author.
Title: The story web / by Megan Frazer Blakemore.
Description: New York : Bloomsbury, 2019.
Summary: When animals in Alice's small Maine town tell her the Story Web is in danger,
threatening the fabric of our world, she knows she can mend it by being honest
about why her father is gone.
Identifiers: LCCN 2018045330 (print) • LCCN 2018051375 (e-book)
ISBN 978-1-68119-525-4 (hardcover) • ISBN 978-1-68119-526-1 (e-book)
Subjects: | CYAC: Missing persons—Fiction. | Storytelling—Fiction. | Animals—Fiction.
Classification: LCC PZ7.B574 Sto 2019 (print) | LCC PZ7.B574 (e-book) | DDC [Fic]—dc23
LC record available at https://lccn.loc.gov/2018045330

Book design by Danielle Ceccolini
Typeset by Westchester Publishing Services
Printed and bound in the U.S.A. by Berryville Graphics Inc., Berryville, Virginia
2 4 6 8 10 9 7 5 3 1

All papers used by Bloomsbury Publishing Plc are natural, recyclable products made
from wood grown in well-managed forests. The manufacturing processes conform to the
environmental regulations of the country of origin.

To find out more about our authors and books visit www.bloomsbury.com and
sign up for our newsletters.

For Henry

Chapter One
ALICE

(A long, long time ago when she was small)

When Alice Dingwell was only five years old, she followed a silken strand of thread from her backyard into the woods. It was silver, almost clear in places, and from time to time she lost it in the mottled light that streamed among the oaks and pines of the forest behind her house. She ran her finger along it as she walked and felt its sticky pull. The thread wove around tree trunks and into a gully where the stream gurgled in the spring. On and on and on into the woods she went until none of it was familiar anymore. Not the moss on the ground, nor the lichen nor the boulders on which it grew, not the lady slipper orchids nor the patch of wild blueberries. This was the part of the forest she had been warned against ever entering, where the bigger kids claimed witches, ogres, and sprites lived. Still, she was not afraid.

The strand dove under the branches of a willow tree and

popped out in a clearing. There, stretched between branches high and low, was the biggest spiderweb that Alice had ever seen. Big enough to catch her if she were foolish enough to step inside a spider's home. It was nearly as tall as the oaks and pines and stretched from one to another across the clearing. Drops of water hung like pearls from the threads and glowed iridescent in the light that filled the clearing.

Alice's father found her in the woods long after the sun went down. He hugged her close, and she felt his familiar, rough wool jacket against her cheek. On their way home, he told her that it was a Story Web, that each strand was a tale. The strands laced together, crisscrossing one another to make the fabric that tied the world together. "It's a precious, fragile thing, this web of ours. It's what connects us. Few have seen it, and those of us who have must be careful to protect it."

Her father was full of stories. As time went on and the memory became hazy, she began to wonder if the web had truly existed. Maybe her father's story was so vivid the web only *seemed* real.

She was wrong to be doubtful.

There is no such thing as *just a story*.

Chapter Two

ALICE

(Now, more or less)

Alice didn't follow spiderwebs anymore. She did not go down wayward paths. She went where she was supposed to go and rarely ventured into the forest. She did not believe in magical webs. She did not believe in magic of any kind.

So it was a surprise when she turned invisible after the back-to-school social. It was a strange kind of invisibility—as if she had disappeared completely, while, at the same time, was closely watched by everyone. They sidestepped her in the hallways and turned their heads on the street. The other kids never spoke to her anymore and generally went about their business as if she were a houseplant or a harmless bug in the corner of the room.

She was even invisible to Izzy and Sadie, who skipped right over her in Mrs. Zee's closing circle. Mrs. Zee said,

"Time to scoot, little newts." Lewis said, "See you soon, raccoons." Brady Sykes said, "Hit the road, toads," and smirked. Before Alice could share her new idea for a goodbye, Sadie said, "Goodbye, butterflies." Which is what she always said. Izzy jumped right in with "Be sweet, parakeets." A real ironic one, Alice thought. Izzy and Sadie used to be her best friends. Her group, her squad, her everything.

That was before the fall social.

Before the smoke alarms went off.

Before her dad went away.

Weird Melanie cleared her throat. "Time to switch—"

There was a collective gasp. Was Melanie going to say "witch"? Everyone knew the stories about Melanie's aunt, the witch in the woods. She'd cut off your toes and feed them to her birds. She'd cast a spell on you and turn you into a crow. She was why most kids in Independence never went deep into the forest.

But Melanie said, "Little twitch."

"A twitch isn't an animal," Izzy said.

"And it's not plural," Sadie added.

"No rejections," Mrs. Zee told them.

"Mrs. Zee?" Lewis asked. "I think we skipped Alice."

"Oh," Mrs. Zee said, blushing a little. "I guess we did." Even she wasn't really seeing Alice anymore. Before Alice could share, Ms. Barton from the front office came on the intercom and said, "Walkers may now be dismissed."

Alice jumped up from the circle, grabbed her backpack, and raced out the classroom door.

There were benefits to being invisible. Back when she was friends with Izzy and Sadie, it could take her twenty minutes to get out of school with all the goodbyes and call-me-laters. Now, she just gave a wave to Ms. Engle, the librarian, and was out the door.

Alice's mother worked at the hospital two towns over and didn't like Alice sitting at home alone after school watching television and eating Lucky Charms. So, Alice had two choices: the ice rink or the Museum. Most days Alice went to the Museum, which was less a museum and more Henrietta Watanabe's antique shop.

According to Alice's father, Henrietta Watanabe had been a spy. "A *British* spy," he'd told her. "Back in World War II. Like Peggy Carter," he said.

In the *Captain America* comics, Peggy Carter had been a brilliant secret agent. There weren't a lot of women in comics, and Alice liked her best of all. There was nothing especially special about her—she wasn't from some other planet like Supergirl, didn't have a mutation like Storm or Rogue. All her strength came from her alone.

"But even cooler," her dad went on. "Mrs. Watanabe would dress like a man and fly fighter jets behind enemy lines. She'd pose as a simple housemaid, pretended not to speak a word of German, and gathered all their secrets."

Alice thought this was highly improbable.

That was the thing about her dad, where everyone else saw drab or old or strange, he saw glitter and shine. Like the Museum. It was dusty and dark and nearly impossible to walk through without tripping over something, but her father called it heaven.

When she arrived, she caught a glimpse of his way of seeing things as the afternoon sun hit a chandelier in the window and fractured, sending out rainbows on the sidewalk. She gasped. Then a cloud passed over, and Independence, Maine, went back to being as dreary as ever. She saw her own reflection in the glass, and the cloudy sky made her white skin look gray as well.

In the doorway sat a small mouse. It rubbed its whiskers and looked up at her.

"If I tell Henrietta, she'll put out a trap," Alice told it. "You'd better run along."

The mouse cocked its head to the side and blinked slowly. Then it ran right over her shoes and disappeared into a hedge in front of the town hall building.

Alice opened the glass door, setting the bells to jingle, and took her seat at the counter next to Clarice, a mannequin that was always dressed to match the season. Today she had on her witch costume, even though it had been more than a week since Halloween.

Henrietta stepped through the beads that separated the

back room from the front. She dressed the way Alice had always imagined Mrs. Whatsit did in *A Wrinkle in Time*: heavy, scuffed work boots with striped knee socks, a full skirt over a pair of shorts—"in case I do some cartwheels, I don't want all of Independence seeing my skivvies"—a blouse, a sweater, a lacy shawl, and, today, a gauzy purple scarf wrapped around her head. She had a closet full of scarves, and usually Alice could tell her mood by which one she chose. Alice hadn't seen this purple one before, which made her nervous.

Henrietta held out a plate with a piece of cinnamon toast on it. The cinnamon and sugar were perfectly melted into the butter.

"How was school today?" Henrietta asked as she snapped off the television that was blaring campaign ads for the governor's race.

"Great!" Alice said, while chewing.

"You're a terrible liar," Henrietta told her.

"Guess I didn't get the family trait," Alice mumbled.

Henrietta narrowed her eyes. "Storytelling and lying are two entirely different things." She paused. "Well, mostly entirely different."

Alice kept eating her snack.

Henrietta looked ready to press her, but then a whooshing sound filled the space between them. The sky outside grew dark. Heavy rain fell against the glass windows, and wind whipped the remaining leaves from the small maple tree outside.

Almost as soon as the storm began, it was over. Henrietta rushed to the door and pushed it open, letting a cool wind blow in.

"Strange," was all Henrietta said before returning to the counter where she was examining her latest acquisitions.

Every object in the Museum was for sale, which made it like a shop. But every object also had a small notecard beside it that listed what it was, how old it was, and who had owned it. On the counter, next to a chipped teacup, was a brass candlestick shaped like a narwhal—you spiked the candle onto the horn. In Henrietta's handwriting were the words:

Narwhal Candlestick
ca. 1912
Brass
Owned by:
    Martha Cuthright
    Emerson Downing
    Unknown

Alice always liked the "Unknown" ones. They'd usually been left on the back staircase by people cleaning out their attics, but Alice liked to imagine more wonderful stories. Her father, of course, would make up terrifically preposterous ones. She wondered what he would make of the narwhal candlestick.

"Your mother says I'm supposed to go over your vocabulary words with you."

"I know all my vocabulary words." Another benefit of invisibility: plenty of time to learn vocab words and math facts.

"I know you do. Your precocity, nay your perspicacity for language astounds me. So, I've got a task for you."

Alice swallowed the last of her toast.

Henrietta held a small box. Alice read the name on it. Shiloh Marble.

She shook her head.

"You're going to the rink anyway. Remember, it's my canasta night, so you're having dinner with Donny. Don't let him give you hot dogs and baked beans again. You know what's in hot dogs?"

"I really don't want to hear about how there's like fingernails and mice droppings and whatnot," Alice told her.

"Preservatives!" Henrietta explained. "I heard about it on *Mary Lawrence* yesterday."

Mary Lawrence was a local semi-celebrity who had her own television show to talk about the issues of the day. Henrietta loved her and took every word she said as the one-hundred-percent honest-to-God truth, which was funny because Henrietta Watanabe did not believe anyone told the truth, the whole truth, and nothing but the truth. "She said they are full of nitrites that turn into nitrates in your body. Or maybe it's nitrates that turn into nitrites. Either way: tumors. Plus, there's enough sodium in there to make a salt lick. That's what we should do with them all. Gather up all the hot dogs and put them out for the deer."

"Won't the deer get tumors?" Alice asked.

Henrietta narrowed her eyes and held out the box. "Go to the rink. Give it to Lewis. Tell him to give it to his mom."

Alice didn't answer.

Henrietta stepped close. Swirled into her clothes was the smell of sweet lavender and honey. Alice breathed deep. "He's not mad at you, you know. The two of you have more between you than most brothers and sisters do. He understands. Or he will understand if you'd just talk to him. None of this is your fault. Your father—"

Alice snatched the box out of Henrietta's hands.

She wasn't going to talk to Henrietta about her dad. Because it was Alice's fault. All of it. It was her fault that Izzy was mad at her. Worst of all, it was her fault that her father had to leave Independence. Nothing anyone said, not all the understanding in the world, could change that fact.

Chapter Three

LEWIS

Lewis Marble watched Alice's uncle, Donny, drive the Zamboni. The giant overhead bulbs shone spotlights on him. The machine melted the ice, then smoothed it out like shiny taffy being pulled. It used to be Alice's dad who ran the Zamboni. Alice would ride with him. She'd sit on his lap and adjust the dials. Her dad would do swirls, curling out shiny S-waves behind them. Lewis had always been terrifically jealous watching her ride that Zamboni. Now Alice was nowhere to be seen.

Lewis hit the ice as soon as Donny finished. He skated the length of the rink back and forth six times, as fast as he could. His body leaned forward. His skates kicked up ice shavings and left thin tracks across the perfectly smooth glass.

Lewis liked the sharp noise of the hockey stop. He liked the way flakes of ice drifted up like snow in a snow globe.

More than that, he liked the sound his stick made when it hit the puck. It was solid and full and sure of itself. He hit puck after puck. When he finished his bucket, he scooped them all back up again before doing sprints one more time. His breath came in heavy puffs, and he sweat through his jersey.

Alice's dad, Buzz, had told him that the legs were the most important part of the game. He said the 1980 U.S. Olympic hockey team—the Miracle on Ice team—skated for hours each day. So Lewis did, too. He wanted to make the Olympic team when he was eighteen. Then college. His dad said UMaine, that's where all the Marble men had gone, but Lewis wanted one of the Boston schools. It used to be Harvard. He and Alice were going to go together. But he and Alice weren't making plans together anymore. He had his own plan: Olympics, college, another Olympics, then the NHL. He'd be as big of a star as Buzz himself. Bigger, maybe. People would talk about him like they had talked about Buzz before. *"I remember when Lewis Marble was just a kid and scored those three goals against the Orono team. Sent them to states."* Or *"I watched Marble's gold medal goal over and over again. Never seen such a perfect shot in all my days."* Lewis liked to imagine what the town would name after him. A new school, maybe. Or better yet, Buzz and Donny could decide to rename the ice rink the Lewis Marble Ice Arena. That would be awesome. But none of it would happen if he wasn't at the top of his game.

So he practiced.

Slap! He started on the bucket of pucks again. Right into the net.

But it wasn't enough. As good as he got, as accurate as he made his shot, it wouldn't matter without Alice. Without Alice in goal, the team had no room for error. Without Alice, they could not win the state championship. So, without Alice, he was not a champion. He was just a kid who played hockey well. Very well. But not well enough.

"Twist your wrist a little more." The voice came from behind him: Coach Donny. He sounded enough like Buzz for it to be confusing, as if Alice's dad had suddenly reappeared from wherever he had been and was back on the ice where he belonged.

"You think?" Lewis asked. He thought his stick handling was pretty good as it was.

"If you want to hit the corners, yeah. And slide your hand about an inch down."

Lewis did what Coach Donny told him to do. Then he lifted his stick and fired a shot that clanged against the corner of the goal before dropping onto the ice at the back of the net.

"Jim Craig himself couldn't have stopped that one."

Lewis smiled back. "What about Alice Dingwell?"

Donny's smile faltered. "She hasn't been on the ice in over a month, so—"

Lewis tapped his stick on the ice. "Well, she's got a lot on her mind what with everything—" He stopped himself. He didn't really know what was going on with Alice's family. She wouldn't tell him. He'd heard rumors, but his mom always said that rumors were lies that had grown legs. He didn't know what was going on with Alice and the other girls. Or Alice and him. He just knew that *things* were going on. Things that somehow, someway meant that she didn't want to play hockey anymore, and he'd lost the opportunity to practice against the best goaltender the state of Maine had seen in decades. Maybe the best ever.

Plus, he was losing Alice's friendship, which felt a lot worse. They hadn't had a real conversation since the night her dad went away. Without her, he felt lopsided.

Donny blew on his hands and clapped them together. He never wore gloves. His hands were red and chapped. "You keep hitting them like that, and no one's gonna stop you."

Lewis couldn't help but smile.

Donny blew on his hands again. "Figure skaters will be on the ice any minute."

"One more bucket's worth?"

"Make it quick. And keep your hand down."

"Sure thing, Coach."

He repositioned his hands. *Slap! Slap!*

The Animal Council

The call began in the center of the forest where the larger animals lived. Moose and Bear and even Bobcat pounded at the earth and raised their voices.

The birds picked it up and took it to the sky. The crows proclaimed it loudly. The chickadees not quite so loud, but twice as beautiful. Finches, nuthatches, gulls. The pigeons took the task very seriously.

As the word spread, the animals came together in the center of the forest. Eager squirrels and chipmunks arrived first, chittering away. Then the deer, who lingered at the edge of the group, keeping their distance from Fox and Bobcat. The snakes sent representatives rather than slither there themselves, while the newts were all too happy to attend.

The nocturnal animals came last. Skunk, possums, the

weasels. Raccoon paced back and forth. She'd been sleeping and woke to find her kits missing, all but one, who admitted the other five had gone exploring. She paced and paced even as Moose called the meeting to order.

It took several minutes for all the animals to settle, and the quiet lasted only for a moment before their cacophony of calls filled the air once more. Each of them had an idea. The mammals proposed the animals work together to solve the problem themselves, leaving the people out of it. The rodents favored including the humans, and the birds took the side of the rodents, a strange coalition to be sure. Gull claimed to represent the sea creatures, though no one was sure if he was telling the truth or not. The insects, who were most abused by the humans, sided with the mammals.

None of the animals trusted the humans, it was true, but many felt that the point of the web was connection. The two worlds touched in so many places, relied on each other so heavily. Wise Owl pointed out that there weren't two worlds at all. Just one, and it was in danger.

They decided there was one child who they could trust, a child born to a father who knew the power of story and the danger that awaited. If they could reach her, they decided, then she could reach the other humans, starting with the children. Children, animals knew, were more capable of understanding problems such as these, despite their sometimes sudden and random acts of cruelty.

Once that decision was made, another followed. A strange one, to be sure. They chose their messenger, and the bird they chose was one no one had expected.

Chapter Four

MELANIE

Melanie Finch watches from her attic as the storm clouds form, stacking up one on top of another like someone gathering bubbles in a bath. Around her neck she wears a pendant, and she clutches it in her hand, warming the glass ball. It is her most treasured possession. Inside is preserved a beautiful peacock jumping spider. *Maratus volans.* The red, blue, and black of its abdomen shine vibrantly. She keeps it hidden beneath her clothes during the day, knowing other children will find it strange that she wears a spider around her neck. But in the attic, she unveils it.

Warm, dry, dusty. It is where she goes when she needs to think thoughts too big for the downstairs rooms that are crowded with oversize furniture, glittering chandeliers, and portraits of people no one remembers.

It is her aunt's house, but the attic is hers.

The attic has a circular window, like a bubble made of glass. That is where Melanie sits thinking her big thoughts and watching the cumulonimbus clouds loom bigger and darker.

Behind those clouds, what?

If she wills it hard enough, would they part and let the sun stream through?

If she wills it hard enough, would she be pulled into them, into a wormhole back to once upon a time?

She squeezes her eyes shut. Nothing happens except the rain starts to fall hard against her bubble.

Thunk. Thunk. Thunkthunkthunk.

She wishes she had brought her lantern. Not a real lantern. Her aunt thinks she will burn the whole place down. No. A battery-powered lantern that she hangs from a hook, since there are no lights in the attic.

The sky turns purple gray.

The birds hide themselves on the wind-free sides of the trees. It's easy to feel bad for them, looking so frail in the wind and knowing the rain is coming, but birds do better in storms than people. They are small enough to take shelter by pressing against a tree trunk. Before the storm, they can trap warm air with their feathers and use it like a heated blanket so long as the storm doesn't last too long.

People, Melanie thinks, should evolve more. They should find better ways of protecting themselves. Before she can think on that too long, something happens that Melanie has never seen. The sky swirls into a tube and shoots straight down. Like something—or someone—is being delivered from the sky.

Melanie has a wish for who.

The wind rips leaves from the trees and flings them against her bubble.

Oak. Maple. Elm. Beech. Locust. One after another layering up. The rain washes them away almost as quickly.

Then, like someone snaps their fingers, it's over.

From up in the attic, way up high, Melanie sees the animals come out. They creep from the forest and the fields, from underground and above, looking around, all heading in the same direction. There are foxes alongside snakes, and neither seems afraid. Nocturnal skunks and raccoons step into the day.

This is the moment that Melanie knows. The wrongness she feels, it isn't just her. It's something bigger. More than that, it's time for Melanie to act.

Chapter Five
ALICE

Across from the Museum was the dry-cleaning shop. Mr. Cleary stood inside sweeping. He was a tremendous sweeper. According to her father, he was also a boxer. He'd once pointed to the shop and said to her, "Someday, when it's not too busy, we'll ask to see his belts. He was the featherweight champion of the world, Alice," he told her. "Folks said he was as fast and smooth as Muhammad Ali."

Alice had a hard time believing this story. Mr. Cleary had to send the mechanical belt around at least three times before he could find the dress or suit her parents had dropped off. Luckily their family didn't have much cause to get clothes dry-cleaned.

Alice figured her dad had a story for everyone in town. Maybe because they all had stories about him. Or maybe because her father was as good of a listener as he was a teller.

He'd sit with people, hear their stories, and hold on to them the way Alice's mother collected rocks from the beach.

One day, Alice had tugged at his sleeve. "I've got one for you," she said. They were passing the crooked mailbox of the Bird House. "Up there lives a horrible witch. She has three moles on her nose, each with a horribly long whisker. Her birds snatch people's pets and bring them to her, and she cooks them into her stew. And—"

But her father stopped her. "No, Alice. That's not the type of story we tell."

"What do you mean?" Her cheeks grew hot. Her father's voice wasn't angry, but she knew she had disappointed him. Everyone told the story of the witch in the woods. Kids sang about her while they skipped rope at school:

> *There's a witch in the woods, woods, woods,*
> *She'll get you good, good, good.*
> *Her birds fly high, high, high.*
> *They'll get your eye, eye, eye.*

He stopped walking and looked her square in the face with those warm gray eyes of his. "Alice, listen to me," he said. She leaned in closer. "You can tell a lot about a person by the stories they tell," he said. He took her hand in his. "What type of stories are they? Are they full of wonder? Are they hopeful?"

Alice watched her feet as they clomped along the sidewalk.

Her father had told so many stories. Now that she was older, she was certain that most of them were untrue—like that Mr. Cleary was a boxer or that Henrietta had been a spy. The ones about Alice herself seemed the most embellished: *You were born on a night full of darkness, but when you arrived, you brought the moon-light with you. You came into the world bathed in silver, and I knew you were meant for something special.* They were tales to make the world seem more beautiful, less awful. Even a simple story, like how he met her mom, he dressed up in magic. He claimed she had appeared in the mist of a city fountain like a goddess revealing her true form. Alice knew her mom was pretty and all, but she'd grown up in Maine and hadn't sprung fully grown from a fountain in the middle of a Boston park.

He always made Alice the hero. Or her mom. Or him. Heroes were important to her dad, probably because he was the biggest hero the town had ever seen. He always told her, "Most of all, you need to watch and see who the heroes are and who are the villains."

She'd thought about those words for years and years. She should have asked him what he meant. Heroes were heroes, and villains were villains. You didn't get to choose. She would ask him now, if he were there. But he was not. He was far from her and far from home, and Alice was certain it was all her fault. Maybe that made her one of the villains.

Just like that, her little town of Independence, Maine, turned gray again.

She walked past the boarded-up library, turned onto Park Street, her usual route. As she did so, a whole aviary worth of birds took to the sky. Between their calls and the beats of their wings, the noises of birds drowned out all others. Then the birds, together as one, fanned out and headed for the forests on the edge of town. Alice covered her head as a pigeon flew in low, cooing all the time.

She watched them for a moment, scarcely believing what she had seen. She wondered what had spooked them.

She set back on her way. She'd cut through the new park they were building. It was going to be named in honor of her dad, a decision made before he'd gone away, and walking through it always made her feel closer to him, like they were inspecting it together, making sure everything was up to snuff. But there was a police car blocking the entrance. Its red and blue lights alternated lazily, and no siren rang out.

Alice stopped.

For a second, she thought, *Maybe he's back*. Though her father's reappearance coinciding with police lights should have made her frightened, her heart soared. Until it crashed. Stevie Tibble, the town's only police officer, raised his hand in a wave. "Hey there, Alice. How's things?"

She walked toward the police car and Officer Tibble. "What's going on?"

"Microburst is our best guess."

Microburst. It sounded like something out of one of her dad's comic books: a superhero, maybe. Or a super villain.

"Weather event," Officer Tibble clarified, as if he could sense her confusion. He ran his fingers over his mustache. "It hit here and bounced along thataway."

"Like a tornado?"

"Not that severe." He looked over his shoulder, then back at her. "Listen, Alice, I—"

"Can I walk through?" she interrupted him, shifting the box from one arm to the other.

He pushed his hat back on his head, revealing bushy eyebrows. "Sure. Damage is pretty well contained. Just be careful of the sea serpent."

Alice couldn't help but roll her eyes. The sea serpent was a bench. That had been her dad's only request for the design of the park. He'd once told her that sea serpents were the most misunderstood animal on the planet, even more so than snakes.

"Are sea serpents even real?" she had asked.

"Of course they're real."

They were down at the beach early in the morning before anyone else was there. They poked in the tide pools looking for crabs. Some kids like Brady Sykes picked up the crabs and snails and threw them, but Alice and her dad just looked.

"I saw one once. Right out there." He'd pointed out beyond where the waves formed. "I've never told anyone before because people don't treat misunderstood creatures like sea serpents very well. It's better that folks think they're imaginary or the next thing you know there will be hunting parties and harpoons."

"Dad," Alice had said. "Be serious."

"I am," he'd replied. "It's the same thing with dragons, but at least dragons have some respect in this world."

Alice thanked Officer Tibble and stepped into the park. As she made her way over the soccer field and into the playground, she stopped short. A tree limb had smashed through the front windshield of one of the construction vehicles. Glass shards littered the ground around it. Farther along was the trailer that was construction central. It, too, had been the victim of a fallen tree branch: the whole roof was bent like a V.

Then she saw what Officer Tibble meant. She ran across the field toward the bench. It had been tipped over, and the serpent itself was cracked in half. She ran her hand over its bumpy head and tried to fight back the hot tears in her eyes.

She stood, gripping the box from Henrietta close to her chest. She wanted to run the rest of the way to the rink, to forget she had ever seen her father's serpent broken to bits.

※

Slap!

Alice's body stiffened, and her left hand shot out. Instinct. She was like those dogs in experiments, the ones who started drooling when they heard a bell.

Clang!

She squeezed her eyes shut. She had to talk to Donny before the figure skaters got there. She took the bleacher stairs two at a time to the edge of the rink. Her body leaned against the wall. It wasn't often that she was on the bench during games, but when she was, she was never actually sitting. She leaned against the boards and cheered on her team. Now, she leaned out and called, "Uncle Donny?"

He skated over in the easy, casual way of his. "What's up, Allie?"

"Did you hear about the park?" she asked him. Lewis skated behind Donny, slowly, but she tried to ignore him.

Donny shook his head. His eyebrows knit together. He had brown eyes, like Alice herself, with flecks of gold that seemed to flash when he was angry or excited. They flashed now.

"There was a microburst," she said. The word felt funny and wrong in her mouth. "Something happened. The bench was broken and the backhoe and, I mean, I think it was the backhoe, and—"

"Your dad's bench?" Donny asked. Flashes of red appeared on his cheeks, and she shrank back. Donny tugged his fingers through his hair. "Hey, okay—sorry. It's just—"

The cold air off the ice was familiar, like coming home, but it also pushed her away.

Lewis skated up and asked if everything was okay. His

pale white cheeks were slashed with red, and his breath came in quick puffs. He'd been working hard. Without her. She hadn't expected it would be so easy for him.

Alice looked at the box for his mom still clutched in her mittens.

"There's been some damage. In the park," Uncle Donny said. He looked at Alice. "I've gotta get out of my skates."

He skated off, leaving Alice and Lewis alone. Lewis scuffed his blades on the ice. Alice thought for sure he was going to say something. Her body tensed. He hadn't asked her why she'd quit the hockey team.

Maybe he just knew.

Maybe he knew that the ice belonged to her father. He was the ice king. She, much to her chagrin, had always been the ice princess. But what does a princess do when the king leaves the kingdom?

Lewis didn't ask her. He didn't say anything, only followed Donny toward the locker room, and Alice was left alone.

There was not an inch of that rink she did not know. She knew where the Plexiglas above the board had a wrinkle. She knew which planks of wooden siding had knots that looked like faces. She knew where her dad always had to go over twice with the Zamboni because something about that spot made the ice form with bubbles that cracked during games.

The cold rose off the ice, filling her nose and eyes, making her weep.

"Come on, kiddo!"

Alice turned, and there was Donny by the door. With Lewis. They all walked out together, back the way Alice had come.

Officer Tibble had moved into the playground and was standing above a person who was crouched by the broken backhoe. Uncle Donny and Officer Tibble nodded at each other in that way grown men did. Alice found it so strange. Sometimes she saw the boys at school try to mimic it: just a little lift of the chin.

"Figured you'd be back," Officer Tibble said to her. Then, to Lewis, "Hey there, Lew. How's the stick work going?"

"All right."

"Has to keep his hand down," Alice murmured.

The crouching person stood, and a smile spread across Uncle Donny's face. "Piper!" he said.

Piper Hammersmith, the animal control officer, smiled back. "I'm awful sorry about all this," she said.

That was something else Alice didn't understand: when people said they were sorry about things they had no control over. There were so many things to truly be sorry about that no one ever apologized for, but then they went and said "sorry" about the weather.

Uncle Donny, though, ran his hand over his head and said, "Yeah. I'm glad Buzz isn't here to see it."

Alice and Lewis both tensed.

"I could certainly use his help with this. Although maybe you'd do. You've got raccoon experience, too."

She pointed below the broken branch. The group bent over; three small faces peered back at them, each with eyes surrounded by black.

"Baby raccoons!" Lewis exclaimed.

"Did the microburst drop them there?" Uncle Donny asked.

"I'm not sure, but they are giving me the darndest time getting them out." She looked at Alice and Lewis. "Apologies for the language."

Alice squatted in front of the opening, still holding Henrietta's box under one arm. She saw the raccoons' shining eyes and little else.

"Hey there," she whispered. She reached out one hand.

The raccoons stirred, and one reached its paw out to her. She smiled wider.

"Come on then," she said.

The raccoon twisted and contorted itself so it came out of the slide. It landed on the ground with a soft *plop*. Immediately, it started clicking and cooing. A second raccoon crawled out. Then a third and a fourth. Alice thought they were all free, but then a fifth, smaller than all the rest, squeezed out as well. When they had all landed, they started walking toward Alice on wobbly feet. She scooted back to give them room.

"Hand me that," Piper said.

Uncle Donny passed her a plastic crate.

The raccoons, though, had other plans. They stopped in front of Alice, chattered for a moment, but as soon as Piper stepped near, they went running and tumbling away from the park and into the woods.

"Huh," was all Piper could think to say.

"Huh, indeed," Uncle Donny agreed. He reached over and put his hand on Alice's shoulder. "You go on home, okay? I want to make some calls about getting this cleaned up."

"Construction's going to need to stop for a stretch, Donny," Officer Tibble said. "This backhoe is toast. Plus, with all the talk—" He stopped himself and glanced at Alice. He took off his hat and held it against his chest. "You know some people are going to take this opportunity to raise questions—"

"I know," Uncle Donny interrupted. The harshness of his voice made Alice jump. He sighed. "Tiny and his crew owe me some favors. I'll give him a call and get this going again fast as I can." He turned to Alice. "Straight home," he said.

"I could give you a ride," Lewis said. "I mean, my mom could."

"I'll walk," Alice said.

"Call me as soon as you get there. Fix yourself some dinner." Uncle Donny checked his watch. "Your mom should be home in less than two hours."

"I know." She was already backing away. She didn't want to stay there another minute looking at her dad's park ravaged by the storm. The leaves stuck to the plastic structures and the mud splattered over everything made her feel hollow inside.

Then she remembered the box she was still carrying. She shoved it toward Lewis. "It's for your mom. From Henrietta."

Before anyone could stop her, she turned and dashed out of the park.

Chapter Six
ALICE

The easiest way back home would be to cut through the woods, but that would take her past the Bird House, and there was no way she was doing that, not on a day like this. Her dad told her not to spread cruel stories, but the tales about the Bird House weren't rumors or legends. They were true.

Everyone in town called it the Bird House because birds of all types flocked to it. Goldfinches, sparrows, crows, hawks, gulls—all these and more made their home at the old house. The birds flew together—swooping above the house, above the tree line, and into the sky—a mass that twisted and shifted as if it had a single brain. Sometimes the flock was so large that it would block the sun and cast a momentary shadow.

Alice had been to the Bird House only once, with Lewis. Some of the older boys at the rink told them if you brought milk anywhere near the house it would spoil instantly. That's what happened when witches were around. She'd told the boys that was ridiculous. They shrugged as if to say she was free to disbelieve them—but at her own peril.

They were eight years old and treated it like a science experiment. "It's a simple matter of proving or disproving," she'd said to Lewis as they sat in his clubhouse, a hollow he had scooped out beneath the roots of an old pine tree. "We get a milk at lunch, and after school we bring it up. We don't even have to stay that long. They said it happens instantly."

The next day he'd purchased a milk at lunch and snuck it out of the cafeteria. It was chocolate, and Alice wasn't sure if that mattered. She also had not taken into account the effect of the milk sitting in Lewis's cubby all afternoon. After school, they walked toward home together, pausing by the crooked post that marked the end of the Bird House's long, twisty driveway. "Okay," Alice said.

"Okay," Lewis agreed.

They walked up, up, up the steep drive until the house loomed into view. It was a faded blue color, with red shingles and trim. The front steps sagged in lazy smiles. The windows shone black as night though the sun was high.

The milk did not curdle.

Instead, a huge flock of birds—seagulls and starlings and crows and petrels and doves and pigeons and even a snowy owl—lifted from the trees, the roof, and the lawn. The noise was so loud that Lewis and Alice could not hear their own ragged breaths or the pounding of their footsteps as they raced back to Minnow Lane.

Alice thought of that adventure almost every time she walked by the end of the driveway, but this time, she didn't. Her head was spinning so much thinking about the micro-burst and how, of all the places in the town, it had chosen to land on her father's park, to destroy his bench.

The mailbox at her house was off-kilter. It had been all fall. Alice tried to right it like she did every time, but it just tilted again. The sand around the base of the post was loose. She had tried filling it in, even mounding the dirt around the post, but nothing worked. So, now she tried to ignore it. She opened the door, pulled out the mail, and slapped the door closed again.

It looked like a stack of bills and fliers for stores they would never go to, but then Alice noticed, peeking out, the telltale blue envelope that meant a letter from her dad. She held the mail closer to her chest. For once it wasn't raining, but everything still felt damp, and she didn't want the letter to get damaged. She could feel her heart beating against her hands. Only her dad's letters unnerved her this way.

Her dad started writing her letters when he first deployed. He told her wild tales of his adventures on the battlefield. *Today we encountered the most astounding beast! Twice the size of a normal man, but only one eye.* He told her these myths, she knew, because he didn't want to scare her with the truth. But now that he was no longer at war, the stories scared her even more. Why couldn't he be back in their house? What was so frightening that he couldn't tell her the truth?

She opened the front door and Jewel, her cat, darted out, brushing against Alice's leg. Jewel was gone into the bushes before Alice could even say hello.

In the house, Alice sorted the mail at the counter: bills in one pile, fliers another, then catalogs, until all she was left with was that envelope the color of a springtime sky: cool and pale and full of the promise of warmer days not yet arrived.

Her dad's handwriting was neat and blocky. He wrote in all capital letters. She could see where he had dragged his pen across the paper of the envelope when he wrote her name. The "E" in Dingwell was smudged.

She slipped her index finger under the flap of the envelope. It gave way easily, like the letter was aching to get out. She pulled the piece of lined paper out and felt the frills on the edge from where he had torn it out of a notebook. She took a deep breath before she carefully unfolded it.

Dear Alice,

Greetings from distant shores. I have been working on leaving this island and getting back to you, but Calypso insists I am not yet ready. She gives me her ointments and potions, a soft bed to sleep in, and food good enough

FOR THE GODS. I WILL GLADLY GIVE THIS ALL UP WHEN THE TIME COMES.

WINTER IS ON ITS WAY HERE. PERHAPS IT HAS ALREADY REACHED YOUR SHORES. SO OF COURSE I THINK OF THE ICE, ALICE. ARE YOUR SKATES SHARPENED? DID YOU GET NEW PADS? I REALLY THINK YOU'VE GROWN TOO MUCH FOR YOUR OLD SET. IT'S IMPORTANT THAT YOU GO INTO BATTLE FULLY PREPARED. YOUR TEAM IS COUNTING ON YOU, NOT ONLY AS THE LITERAL LAST LINE OF DEFENSE, BUT AS A LEADER. I'VE SPOKEN TO YOUR UNCLE ABOUT YOUR PADS, BUT HE SEEMS CONFUSED ON THIS MATTER.

A scratching sound came from the kitchen window. *Scritch-scratch, scritch-scratch.* Alice snapped her head up, but she couldn't see anything. She told herself it was just a stick banging against the window in the wind and went back to her letter.

THERE IS A POND ON THE ISLAND HERE. DO YOU REMEMBER THAT OLD BOOK I USED TO READ YOU? REMEMBER THE STORY OF THE FROG PRINCE AND THE ILLUSTRATION THAT WENT WITH IT? WELL, OUR POND HERE LOOKS JUST LIKE THAT, AND WHEN IT FREEZES, CALYPSO SAYS I WILL BE ABLE TO SKATE ON IT. THAT WILL SURELY MAKE ME STRONGER, DAY BY DAY, AND SOON I WILL BE ABLE TO ESCAPE THIS PLACE AND RETURN TO OUR ICE. UNTIL THEN, STAY STRONG, STAY SMART, AND LISTEN TO YOUR MOTHER. SHE IS SMARTER THAN ALL OF US.

Don't forget to look at the stars each night.

Be bold, be brave, be fierce.

Yours truly,

Dad

Alice read the letter three times. She was always left with the same question: If he wanted to come home, why didn't he?

She tried to imagine the grounds of the island, to see the pond that her dad could skate on. He was a graceful skater. She loved to watch the way he'd glide and swirl and turn away from defenders and toward the goal, always ending up right where he was supposed to be: wide open and ready to score. Fast, too. She'd never seen anyone even half as fast as her dad—though maybe someday Lewis would be.

Scritch-scratch. The sound came again. Alice still saw nothing in the window. She folded the paper carefully, put it back in its envelope.

Scritch-scratch.

She lifted her head. Something moved by the window.

Slowly, she crossed the room until she stood by the sink. She leaned forward and squinted, but to no avail. Whatever was at the window was hidden in the shadows.

Chapter Seven
LEWIS

Tuesday morning. Seven thirty-seven on the clock. Lewis pulled his Bruins hat down over his ears before he stepped out into the cold morning air. He didn't like to be late for school. It was unprofessional to be late. Pro players were never late.

The real reason he always left his house at exactly 7:37 was because that's when he needed to leave to get to where his street intersected with Minnow Lane just in time to meet Alice. Or so it had been every day from the first day of kindergarten to the third week of September. He still left at the same time: he wasn't going to let whatever funk she was in mess up his routine. Maybe also so he could catch her someday and they could walk together again. They wouldn't have to say anything. He wouldn't expect her to explain why she'd stopped playing hockey and stopped being his friend. Sometimes he thought these things had been a long time coming. Sometimes he thought it was whatever had made Buzz leave home. He knew he should ask her, but she was a goalie with her game face on whenever he even thought about it. She didn't let anyone get by her defenses. So instead he let himself imagine that someday they'd just start walking and it would be like it had always been between them.

For about thirty seconds that day, he thought that might happen. Right as he came around the curve of Hemlock Street, Alice walked up Minnow Lane. He quickened his pace, but then he came to a dead stop. So did Alice.

Walking down the middle of the road was a bird. A large bird with thick legs, a long neck, and a body shaped like a boulder. It looked like the missing link between birds and dinosaurs.

Lewis's feet carried him so he was right next to Alice, who stood with her mouth hanging open, her breath coming out in puffs. Both watched the bird's progress, frozen. A row of cars was backed up on each side. As it came to the sidewalk, the bird stopped and stretched out its neck. Lewis couldn't see its face, only a tuft of feathers that sat atop its head. Then the most unusual sound came out of it, like a grunt that was stuck in its long neck. It spoke, it seemed, right to Alice.

Alice jumped back, and the creature made the sound again. The bird jerked its head back across the street. Alice didn't move. Frustrated, the creature moved even closer to Alice, who backed away. The creature kept going toward her.

Lewis, suddenly unfrozen, started waving his arms. "Hey!" he yelled.

The bird turned and looked at him. It made that same strange grunting noise over and over.

"We can't understand you," Lewis said.

That, at last, clicked with the creature. Or maybe it was the driver who laid on his horn. Either way the bird sauntered off. When Lewis turned to ask Alice about it, she was already gone, hurrying down the road.

"It's an emu," a voice said.

Lewis blinked as Melanie Finch emerged from the bushes at the end of the driveway to the Bird House. Melanie's hair was thin and nearly white. It blew around her face and stuck to her lips. She brushed it off with her slender fingers.

"A what?" he asked

"An emu. A large flightless bird."

They turned onto Main Street, right by the dry cleaners. Mr. Cleary was out front sweeping the sidewalk. He would make his way up and down the whole length of the sidewalk before opening for the day. He looked up and gave a wave to the kids. Alice and Lewis waved back.

"Emus can't fly at all?" Lewis asked. "Like a turkey?"

"Nope," Melanie said. "Not even a little."

They turned onto School Street. It almost felt familiar, Lewis thought. Almost normal.

As they approached the school, Melanie took a deep breath

in, and then let it out in a slow sigh. She looked right at him with those watery eyes.

"Are you okay?" he asked her. It was hard to tell, but it looked like she was about to cry.

The question seemed to startle her. "Do you like stories?" she asked.

"Sure," he said. "I guess."

She nodded. "There is something I could use some help with." She took a deep breath. "Do you know about the Story Web?" He shook his head.

Lewis pulled open the door and walked next to Melanie through the crowded hall. Some of the older boys looked at him with confusion. Lewis ignored them.

At the row of fifth-grade lockers, Melanie's was at the far end from Lewis's. He slipped off his coat and hung it on a hook inside. Brady checked him with his shoulder. "Melanie Finch, huh?" he asked. "What's your play?"

"What?" Lewis asked. Since the start of the year, Brady had been talking so strangely, like he was trying on a costume that didn't quite fit.

"I know you don't like her, so what's up?"

Lewis reddened. "It's nothing," he said. "Her house—"

"The Bird House," Brady interrupted.

"It's on my way to school. She just came out at the same time as I was walking by." He left out the part about the emu. "It's not like I could run away from her." His stomach felt unsettled as he said this last part, but Brady could sniff out a weakness like a bloodhound. The last thing Lewis needed was Brady pick, pick, picking about Melanie. It's not like he and Melanie were friends. They'd just walked to school together that morning. No big deal.

"Whatever," Brady said, which was pretty much Brady's favorite word. He didn't use to be that way. He and Lewis had been friends once, talking hockey and superheroes and daring each other to eat disgusting food combinations. Lewis figured that things just changed sometimes. People changed. Maybe that's all that was happening with Alice.

She was at her own locker, two down from Lewis's, moving in that timid way she had ever since her dad went away.

"I'll show you the Story Web," Melanie said. He hadn't even seen her coming, but she was right beside him.

"The Story Web? Okay."

She nodded. "Soon. The thing is, we have to save it."

Then Weird Melanie, the witch's niece, went into the classroom. Lewis turned to Alice. She stared at him, eyes wide with surprise.

Crow

The decision to send the little bird had been a contentious one. There were those who said that such a big task should not be entrusted to such a small bird. A messenger, they said, should be swift. Its shadow should be impressive.

Crow, in particular, was unhappy with the choice. The Web was too precious a thing to leave to just any old bird. Crow insisted that the messenger needed to be loud. Crow was the loudest of the birds. Crow also cast a fine shadow. His feathers were a beautiful oily black, if he did say so himself.

Why would they send a tiny little bird when they could send him?

Why should he stay behind while the little bird went on to glory?

He should not. He *would* not.

Crow lacked patience and had little use for conversations. He preferred action. So, while Moose and the others worked to prepare the little bird, Crow flew away.

Chapter Eight

ALICE

The Story Web.

Alice heard Melanie say those words, and it all came rushing back into her head. Getting lost in the woods, the willow tree, the huge web. Alice remembered walking through the forest with her father and what he'd told her about the Story Web and the spiders who made it. He had held her small hand tightly in his big warm palm. "You're very lucky to be able to see a Story Web. Not everyone can."

They walked across the top of a boulder. Her father jumped down, then reached up to lower her to the soft ground of the forest. "You know the story of Arachne, of course." Her father had a book of stories that he read to her from: *The Story Web.* One of her favorite stories in the book had been about Arachne, a girl in an ancient Greek village who was very proud of her weaving and claimed to be a better weaver than the goddess Athena. It was never a good idea to insult a goddess, and Arachne paid the price. Athena came to her village disguised as an old woman and gave her one last chance to say that Athena really was the better weaver. But Arachne was full of pride and said she stood by her words. So Athena revealed herself and challenged Arachne to a weaving contest. This was why Alice liked the story so much. In so many stories, the winner was simple. Either the mighty won because they were mighty, or the weaker won because of some internal quality like patience or kindness. But in this story, it was more complicated. Athena wove a scene showing the glory of the gods and goddesses. Arachne wove a scene showing all their mistakes and misdeeds. It was beautiful—Athena couldn't deny that. But she also couldn't stand for the insults to her fellow gods and goddesses, especially about her father, Zeus. She struck Arachne's weaving, destroying it. There never really was a winner. It ended with Athena touching Arachne's forehead and turning her into a spider, dooming her to weave for the rest of her days.

That evening years before in the woods, they had walked down the hill toward the stream. As her dad helped her hop from rock to rock across the water, he said, "There's more to the story. Ancient Greek tapestries, they told stories. When Arachne became a spider, her webs held stories, too. Some people still have the blood of Arachne in them. Some spiders, too."

"That's who made this Story Web?"

"Yes."

"The spiders or the people?" Alice asked.

"Both. The people tell the stories out loud or on paper, and the spiders weave them into the web. We're always making it and remaking it. It's a very fragile thing. It needs constant monitoring. If you ever see another strand like that, you let me know. We'll follow it together and check on the web."

"Can everyone see the web?" she asked.

"No, only special people."

"Can Mom see the web?"

"Oh, most definitely."

"Can Uncle Donny?"

"When he's not being a reprobate," her dad replied.

"What's a reprobate?"

"A punk up to no good."

Alice considered this. "So you have to be good to see it?"

"You have to be quiet and pay attention. Uncle Donny can have a hard time being quiet."

"I see," Alice said, although she was not sure she did. Years later, she still wasn't sure. She liked listening to her dad tell stories, though, so she said, "I see," so that he would keep telling them. His book started off with a scary message about what would happen if stories weren't shared—the Freezing. She had never liked that part and always flipped right past it. But she had liked the other stories, liked sitting in her father's lap or curled up with her mother while he read them aloud.

They were all just stories, though. The Story Web was no more real than the gingerbread man or Red Riding Hood and the wolf.

But how had Melanie known about any of this?

All morning she wondered. It was nice to have something to think about other than her own invisibility. Maybe that's why Izzy bumped into her on the way into the cafeteria. As a reminder. "Whoops," Izzy said. "Didn't see you there."

Alice thought that would be the end of it, but then Izzy said, "So Lewis ditched you for the witch's daughter?"

Alice realized then that Melanie was walking right in front of them.

Sadie, who was behind Izzy, started singing, *"There's a witch in the woods, woods, woods. She'll get you good, good, good."*

Melanie's back stiffened. Alice felt her palms itch, and she started to sweat. She remembered what her dad had said about the Bird House and the story of the witch living there. *"You can tell a lot about a person by the stories they tell."*

Brady Sykes, who was walking by, joined in, louder than Sadie: *"Her birds fly high, high, high. They'll get your eye, eye, eye."*

Melanie hurried ahead.

"You don't have to be so awful," Alice muttered.

"Excuse me?" Izzy asked. She stopped just inside the cafeteria and glared her icy stare at Alice. It wasn't so long ago that things were different.

It used to be that when Alice walked with Sadie and Izzy down the hall, people parted to get out of their way. Even kids in sixth and seventh grade would slide to the side to let them through. Alice liked the feeling. She missed it. She wasn't sure why they weren't her friends anymore. There were so many possible reasons. She hadn't worn braids to the fifth-grade social the way they had agreed. When Brady asked her to dance that night, she said yes, even though Izzy had wanted to dance with him. But then she'd started crying right there on the dance floor. Was that it? Maybe there was no reason at all. Whatever the cause, now she was on the other side with no one behind her.

"Nothing," Alice said.

She scurried over to the cafeteria line. Once she had her lunch, she planned to head to the library. All of a sudden, though, it was like something grabbed her by the shoulders and gave her a good shake. She felt her jaw tighten the way it did when a player was racing down the ice toward her, puck dancing on his stick. She heard her dad's words in her ear: *Be Bold, Be Brave, Be Fierce.* Maybe she couldn't be bold or brave or fierce enough to stand up to Izzy, but she wasn't going to run away. Not this time.

She sat at a table in the corner and started eating a fruit cup, invisible again, telling herself that the fruit didn't feel like mush in her mouth.

Caw, caw, caw-caw!

Alice looked up just in time to see a crow swooping around the beams on the ceiling of the cafeteria. She ducked as it swooped. It shot back up and landed on one of the thick wooden crossbeams. *Caw! Caw!* It called out again, turning its head from side to side.

"What the—" Alice heard Sadie say.

"Is that a crow?" Emma Roberge asked. "A crow in the cafeteria?"

Ms. Bly, the lunchroom monitor, rushed forward. She stopped short beneath the crow. "Hey!" she yelled.

Caw! the crow called back.

That made everyone giggle, but the laughter was cut short as the crow, spotting something, took off from the crossbeam and dove.

The crow landed without a sound at the center of Alice's table. Alice waved her hands at it frantically.

The crow lifted its beak and cocked its head to the side. It narrowed its red-rimmed eyes at her. *Caw! Caw!*

Alice clamped her mouth shut. The bird hopped around the table. It shook out its feathers.

Caw?

It sounded like a question. Before Alice could respond, a small trash can slammed down on top of the crow. The janitor, Mr. Charlie, said, "There we are. Safe and sound."

Alice wasn't sure if he meant the bird was safe or the kids.

"Go on along, Alice."

Alice stood up but wasn't sure where to go. She guessed it was the library after all. She felt eyes on her and turned. Izzy stared back at Alice, her lips twisted into a smile.

Waxwing

Waxwing knew that most of the other animals had little faith in her. She was small. Her call was not as loud as other birds. But Moose, who always loved a good story, pointed out that a small but mighty character was what this tale needed. Moose's faith in her was what propelled her. She would not let him down.

She flew out of the woods and through the mist, dodging the dastardly cars and the cats who, as usual, had stayed away from the animal council. They were far too aloof for group gatherings.

Waxwing arrived right on time, flapping her small wings as the building came into view.

Closer.

Closer.

Smack!

Her whole body shook.

An invisible wall!

She flapped her wings and lifted into the air to try again.

Smash!

The same result? What enchantment surrounded this building?

She would remain undaunted. She had a mission to complete. A final time she tried. She circled above, round and round, and encountered no obstacles. Surely there was some way to defeat the spell that held the castle so protected.

Faster, she decided.

So she dove down.

Fast, fast, fast.

Crash!

She landed on the ground, her wing crumpled beneath her.

Her eyes filled with tears. She was glad none of the other birds were here to see that. Birds so rarely cry. But she was absolutely devastated. How could she be the messenger with a broken wing?

Chapter Nine
ALICE

Alice watched a small bird with a yellow crown throw itself against the glass front door of the ice rink. It smashed into the glass, fell back, then flew up and tried again with the same result.

She stepped closer. The bird flew into the sky, a whir of gold and gray. Alice thought that was that, but then it rocketed back down and slammed into the door again. This time it fell backward and landed with a soft crash in the juniper bush that crept along the front of the ice rink.

Alice dropped her backpack and hurried toward the bush. The bird's body trembled. It was too far into the bush for her to reach, so she crouched and reached out with her damp pink palm.

She waited. Cold mist settled on her hand in tiny droplets.

A rustle came from the bush. She leaned forward, her

hand curled in an invitation. Her breath came in white puffs above her blue and red scarf. She held still, stiller, stillest. The bird in the shrub held even more still. She thought if she could just stop moving long enough, the bird would forget she was a person, forget she was alive. It would hop right over to her hand, dainty as you please.

It's hard to keep still, though. Hard to keep quiet, even when you're an invisible girl.

It was no use. She was not going to be the type of girl who birds and forest animals flocked to. She was no Snow White.

"What are you doing?"

Startled, Alice rocked back and landed on her bum on the damp ground. "Oh," she said. "It's you." She couldn't hide the disappointment in her voice. Lewis stood behind her with his hockey bag hooked over his shoulder. His Bruins hat with the stupidly large pom-pom rested toward the back of his head.

"Why are you beckoning that bush?" he asked.

"I'm not beckoning the bush."

Lewis, a careful listener, asked, "What *are* you beckoning?"

There was a time when she would not have thought twice about telling Lewis that she was trying to help an injured bird. She would have told him because she told Lewis everything. Now, though, she hesitated.

The rustle came again. Lewis stepped closer. Alice pushed

herself back up to her crouching position. Her butt was wet, but she didn't care.

Bzeep. Zeeep.

It was the saddest bird call: small and fragile and lonely.

"It's a bird!" Lewis exclaimed. He leaned closer. "It's a cedar waxwing. At least, I think so. See the yellow on the tail and the red on the tips of the wings?"

"It was pounding itself against the door again and again," she told him. Her voice came out hoarse like a creaking old door that had not been opened in a long while.

"Sometimes birds see their reflection in a window and attack it because they think it's another bird moving in on their territory."

The bird hadn't seemed angry as it ran into the window. More like confused. It had been hitting the glass right next to the door handle.

"At my grandmother's house," Lewis went on, "she put a picture of an owl in the window to scare away this robin that kept crashing into her upstairs window. Maybe Coach should put a picture of a hawk or something in the door."

"No," Alice said. "It wasn't like that. It was like it was trying to get inside, and now it's hurt. If it would come out, I could help it."

"You should probably let it be."

The bird, though, did not seem to like this suggestion. It

hopped toward Alice, flapping one wing while the other hung limp at its side.

"Look," she said. "I think its wing is broken."

The bird stopped.

Alice took a breath in and held it. She extended her hand again. The bird hopped right onto her palm. Alice lifted it so it was level with her face. It had a tuft of golden-brown feathers on top of its head, shooting back like a punk rock hairstyle. Its black eyes were surrounded by black feathers, making it look fierce, but when she looked more closely at the shiny black eyes, there was something familiar and kind about them. They reminded her of her father's eyes, the way he could look right at you and seem to know what you were feeling.

"Whoa," Lewis whispered.

Alice blinked, and the bird blinked back.

"This is getting really strange," Lewis said. "First, the emu this morning, then the crow at lunch, and now this. It's like the day of the birds."

"I should get it a box," Alice said.

"Then what?"

"I guess I'll look after it until it's well enough to fly again." Alice knew her mother would never let her bring a wild bird into the house. Maybe she could find a way to sneak it in. She couldn't let it go now that she had felt its soft feathers against her palm, felt its tiny heart beating.

"You could bring it to the Bird House," Lewis joked.

"Very funny," she said.

Before he could say anything else, she asked him to open the door for her. He did, holding it open as she walked through, cupping the bird in both hands.

"I'll bring it up to the office," she said, more to herself than to Lewis.

Lewis nodded toward the locker rooms. "I've got practice."

"I know," Alice said.

"I know you know," Lewis replied. "I was just saying goodbye is all."

"Goodbye." She was already walking away from him, toward the stairs that led to the office. She didn't see him watching her go, didn't even feel his eyes on her, and she certainly didn't feel the wish rising off him like steam.

✺

In the rink office, Alice placed the bird onto her father's desk. It hopped along the perimeter of it, stopping to look at the cup of pens, the small golden clock, and the Wayne Gretzky bobblehead. Alice sat in the old swivel office chair. She had carved her initials into the armrest when she was six or seven, and they were still there. The bird hopped onto the armrest and landed right on the letters.

"Spry," she said, spinning herself back and forth. "Even with a broken wing. My dad would say you had good legs on you."

At these words, the bird lowered its head.

"Anyway, I can't keep you. I'm not allowed to have another pet. Just Jewel. That's our cat, and we can only have her because she's been around so long. Dad found her in his truck one morning. We're not supposed to be pet people. Also, you're a wild bird. Mrs. Zee said you should let wild animals be. I never should have helped you in the first place." That didn't sound right, though.

The bird hopped nearer to her.

"Aren't you afraid of me?"

The bird hopped nearer still.

Alice propped her head on her hand so she could see the bird better. "Maybe I should take you to the Bird House," she told it. "I mean, sure, it's a little spooky, but you are a bird."

The bird shook its head.

"Oh, so you're not a bird? Let me guess, you're a prince and if I kiss you, you'll turn back into your human form. You're tweeting up the wrong tree. Not interested."

The bird scratched at the chair, then settled as if it were sitting in a nest.

Alice tried not to think about how she had said more words to this bird than she had to any human for as long as she could remember. Even if she still had friends, what would she say to them? She could not tell them the things she worried about—her father, mostly, but also her mother who worked so much. And Uncle Donny who was lonely without his brother and struggling to keep the rink going. He never said that to her, but she had a good sense that there was more money going out than coming in. Things she had never worried about before because her dad and Donny worried about them and kept that worry hidden between them. Now it was as clear as the first scratch on smooth ice.

"Wait here," she said. Alice opened the small closet. She found a shoebox with a couple of old receipts in it. She put those in the file cabinet, then brought the box over and placed it in the seat of the chair. Without prompting, the bird hopped into the box and then looked at Alice with those silver-black eyes. "Like gray-eyed Athena," Alice whispered, and decided that with eyes like Athena, the bird must be a girl.

The bird looked so small and the box too cold. Alice knew that some birds wove yarn into their nests. She and her parents had even once found a nest with an old snake skin twisted among the twigs. On top of the file cabinet was a mini teddy bear in a Bruins jersey. She pressed it into the side of the box, careful not to touch the bird. "Do you have a name, little bird?" she asked. "Everything has a name, I suppose." The bird blinked her silver-black eyes slowly. "I could give you a name. But that would be like a step toward making you a pet. And I already explained how I can't make you a pet." Even as she said this, she watched her finger reach out. The bird didn't move. Alice held her breath. Then gently, ever so gently, she ran her finger over the top of the bird's head.

The bird let out a sound like a sigh.

"Oh!" Alice gasped.

She ran her finger over her head again. Her feathers were as soft as kitten fur.

"My friend—well, my sort of friend—Lewis, he likes this book called *My Side of the Mountain*. The boy in that has a bird that isn't really his pet but more like a friend, I'd say. He calls the bird Frightful, which I always thought was a strange name. Maybe for a hawk—that's the kind of bird it is—maybe Frightful is a good name for a hawk because it scares the smaller creatures. But for you? You're more like hope. Or brave. It was pretty daring of you to come to me. What were you even after trying to get into the rink?" Her finger passed over the bird's head again. "How about Dare? How about I call you that?"

The bird nodded.

"Here's the thing, bird. If I take you home, you're going to have to be very careful. My cat will gobble you up. Plus, my mom is generally anti-pets." She bit her lip. She didn't need to be explaining all this to the bird. "I have homework." She watched the bird a moment longer. "You're probably hungry," she said. Uncle Donny kept trail mix in his desk, and Alice sprinkled some into the box. She expected Dare to eat the sunflower seeds, but she went straight for the raisins.

While Dare sat in her box, Alice did her homework, solving math problems and writing out sentences for her vocabulary words. Dare settled down next to the teddy bear.

As Alice finished her homework, the figure skaters started pouring out onto the ice in their slim-fitting pants and shirts emblazoned with glitter. Izzy skated slowly and did a lazy-looking spin before joining her team at center ice. Alice took that moment to slip away, holding the box down low and hoping no one noticed.

She made it downstairs just as the boys started tumbling out of the locker room.

"Hey, Allie Cat," Trevor said. "You missed practice again."

"What you got there?" Silas asked. She'd always liked Silas. He was smart and said he was going to work for Google someday.

"A box," she replied.

"A secret box?" Trevor asked.

She smiled. "A shoebox. With shoes in it."

Another bunch of boys came out of the locker room, seventh graders who pushed Trevor and Silas along and out the door. "'Bye, Allie! 'Bye, Dingaling!" they called as they went out the door. Alice knew that Lewis would be last. He was the youngest and so he got stuck with the final cleanup—tossing stray tape into the trash can, gathering loose pucks. It didn't matter that he was probably the best player on the team.

She checked the clock that hung above the door: 4:57. It was late. She needed to get home quickly if she wanted to avoid questions from her mom, and the only way to do that was to cut through the woods.

※

Alice held the box close to her chest as she followed the path. The wind blew through the trees, turning the leaves over— a sign of rain according to Henrietta. The path sloped up a little, but thankfully it didn't go all the way up to the Bird House.

Still, Dare seemed to sense the other birds were near. When a crowd of starlings murmured up and out of a tree darkening the sky for a moment, Dare scratched hard against the box. "It's okay," Alice whispered to Dare. "It's fine."

Alice and Lewis used to spend hours and hours in the woods playing games. They were pioneers; they were explorers. They were astronauts on winter days when the icy snow looked like moonscapes. They were Amelia Earhart and Fred Noonan crash-landed in the South Pacific but finding a way off the island. They were bears, raccoons, birds.

Now they were nothing.

If someone had asked her why they weren't friends anymore—though no one had—she could've given lots of reasons. Because she didn't play hockey anymore. Because she didn't play make-believe games anymore.

But the truth was, Lewis knew her better than anyone, and that scared her. Lewis would know what question to ask, what words to say, to unlock all the fear and worry and anguish that she had hidden away on the day her father had gone. She did not want those feelings to get out. It seemed the whole town wanted to keep that story hidden.

"No one talks about where he went," she said to the box. Dare bzeeped back. "It's like he's on vacation or something. No one talks about it." Rain began to drizzle on them.

Alice felt tremendous guilt for causing her father to leave. The fact that no one talked about where he had gone made Alice feel even worse. She had done this to him. She had sent him away, and because of that, people saw him differently. Rather than look at that new version of him, they looked away.

The starlings landed in a tree above her and made their worried sound over and over again, as if they were trying to warn her of something. She looked up the hill toward the Bird House. Only its black roof was visible, with dark clouds above it.

"We should hurry," she said.

She tucked her head to keep the mist that was turning into rain from getting into her eyes. As she did, she saw the strand of a spiderweb waving in the breeze. "Oh!" she exclaimed. Should she follow it? "Just a story," she muttered, and hurried on. The wind was kicking up, slashing her hair damp across her face.

The starlings followed, calling louder and louder. Dare, too, chirped frantically in the box.

Alice pressed on. She gave a wide berth to Lewis's

clubhouse even though she knew he wouldn't be there. She came to the river where she found the fallen side-by-side trees that served as a bridge. The trees were slick, but she made it over.

She rubbed her nose, which was starting to run. The edge of the forest wasn't too much farther now. As she reached it, the starlings swooped in one large cloud, up and over her until they were in front of her. They beat their wings at the damp air. They seemed to nod at her, the whole crowd of them, like they were one body. Then they made a triangle pointing back toward the woods.

"No," she said.

They pointed again.

"No!" she called again, louder this time. They held still, so she yelled. "Go away!"

With that, they dove right in front of her, then went back into the woods. She felt the wind off their wings on her face.

The path came out in Mr. Cleary's yard. He pushed open his back door and stuck his head out.

"Alice Dingwell, is that you?"

"Yes, Mr. Cleary," she said.

"You okay?"

"Yes," she said. "Just heading home and I thought I saw—I thought I saw one of those mean dogs that Mr. Lambert keeps."

"Well, you head along home. Storm's coming."

She nodded and ran behind his house, through the Piedmonts' lawn, past Mrs. Winslow's raised garden beds, and on and on until she came to her own backyard.

Jewel twined around her legs as she went into the house, meowing the whole time.

Alice peeked into the living room. Mary Lawrence was on the television talking about the best way to make apple pie, and her mom was sleeping on the couch in her pink scrubs.

"Shh," Alice whispered to Jewel.

Her mom lifted her head. "Alice?"

"Sorry, Mom. Jewel's being pushy."

"I was only dozing." She sat up. "Good day at school?"

Alice nodded. "Just let me put my bag down and grab a snack." She was already rushing away as she spoke, almost tripping over the cat who was not going to let the box out of her sight. When Alice got to her room, she used her foot to hold Jewel away and quickly shut the door.

She carefully lifted Dare out of the box. Chewing on her lip, Alice surveyed the room. There, tucked into a corner and nearly forgotten, was an old wooden dollhouse. Alice and Lewis used to play with it, pretending it was the hockey house where all the hockey players lived together. Alice pushed Dare through the front door.

"Wait here," she said.

Dare hopped around and poked her head out one of the windows, which made Alice smile.

"Seriously. Wait here. I need to go talk to my mom."

Ze-zeep?

It sounded like a question, so Alice said, "My mom. The adult person who owns this house—this big house—and is not interested in pet birds."

Zeep.

Now her call sounded sad, but Alice didn't have time to worry about it. She slipped back down the hall and went to sit next to her mother on the couch.

She glanced out the front window. There, in the big maple tree, rested all the starlings, their eyes trained on her.

Waxwing

Waxwing had seen large houses from the outside but never from the inside. She had always stayed far away from people. Her cousin once flew into a house and never returned. Waxwing had not known that bird-size houses existed. But what strange objects there were inside! Hard boxes with odd designs on them. Tiny things that looked like humans but did not speak or breathe.

She hopped over to a ledge that let her look out. The world outside the small house was not unlike the world inside. Both had a round piece of fabric on the floor. Both had a shining orb—each now dark—above. The biggest object in each room was the large, soft rectangle. Waxwing's was empty, but the girl slept in hers. It was her nest, Waxwing thought.

Waxwing watched the girl sleep. Her chest went up and down. She rolled from side to side, and little moans escaped her.

How sad this little girl was! If she were a bird, her call would be all panicked warning.

Dare plucked at a feather in her chest. Here she was, the chosen messenger, and what could she do? The girl didn't understand her. Waxwing hadn't been able to tell her about the Story Web and how she needed to save it. Instead the girl had talked and talked, and Waxwing hadn't understood a word. Even if she could get the girl to understand, how would she lead Alice to the web when she had the broken wing?

She turned toward the window, opened a crack so a small breeze blew in, bringing with it the smell of the forest. The other birds were up there. All the creatures. Moose. They'd believed in her. What was she going to do now?

Chapter Ten

LEWIS

The day after the day of the birds, Lewis slid into the chair at the family desk just before Lenora, the meaner of the twins. "I have homework!" she cried, dropping her heavy purple backpack. It fell with a *thud* next to her basketball sneakers. Lenora, at fourteen, was nearly six feet tall.

"You have a tablet from the school you can use. I've got nothing."

"That's right. A whole lot of nothing going on," Lenora said, but she mustn't have felt much like fighting. She only gave him one long glower before she turned away from him and clomped up the stairs toward the girls' bedroom.

Once he was alone with the computer, he didn't know what to search for. He'd spent the whole day at school thinking about the emu, the crow, and the little bird Alice had found the day before. He looked around the desk. On top of the pile of mail was a postcard that read: "TotalMart = TotalJobs." There was a map of town with an arrow pointing next to the rink. It said: "Potential Future Sight of TotalMart." That didn't make any sense. That was where Buzz Dingwell Park was going in, although the construction hadn't started up again. Anyway, whoever had made the postcard had spelled "site" wrong. He tossed the card aside. Then he typed the word "emu."

Melanie was right—the emu was a large, flightless bird like an ostrich. Tall and fast, they were native to Australia but now were endangered. What was one doing in Independence? Could an emu even survive in Maine? Then again, it was the Bird House. All kinds of birds could live there with the—

Witch.

The word bounced into his brain. He thought of the day they'd brought the milk to the Bird House. Back then he'd believed in witches, but now?

He typed in "Story Web." He scanned through the results: it was all sites for teachers.

"What are you looking at, Lulu?" Laurel asked him. She was the oldest of his sisters, already in high school, and the one who could be the most reasonable. *Could* be. But not today.

He tried to remain calm. His sisters could sense fear.

Laurel squinted at the screen. "Story web?"

"No," he said, which was stupid, because there was nothing wrong with his search. His sisters would think it was for school.

"Boring snoring," Laurel said. Then she cocked an eyebrow. "Is that a fake search?"

"What do you mean?" This time there was no keeping the anxiety from creeping into his voice.

She put a hand on his shoulder. "You're hiding something."

"Lew's hiding something?" Leila asked. She was Lenora's twin, the nicer one. She was equally tall but didn't play sports. She was in the drama club and had once confessed to him that she thought she could be a model because she was so very tall.

"One hundred percent," Laurel said. "When he heard me coming, he put in some bogus search, but I'm onto him."

"Is this about you hanging out with the witch's daughter?" Linda asked. His sisters always appeared like that, stepping through doors at the worst possible moments. Linda was the youngest, only a year and a half older than him but two years ahead in school. She was not tall like the twins or graceful like Laurel. She had dishwater-blond hair, washed-out blue eyes, and, frankly, was frequently forgotten.

"No," Lewis said.

"You were hanging out with the witch's daughter? Is she a witch, too?" Laurel asked.

"No."

"Sure you were," Linda said. "All the boys in my class saw you walking down the hall. It's embarrassing, actually. I mean, if you're going to get interested in girls other than Alice, could it at least be someone who isn't a witch?"

"She isn't a witch, and I'm not interested in Alice."

A smile spread across Laurel's lips. "But you are interested in the witch's daughter?" Laurel sat on the desk chair with him, squishing him over so he practically fell off.

"Niece," he said. Immediately, he realized his mistake. This was tantamount to saying yes.

"Wait, which girl?" Leila asked. "Not Alice."

"No, the witch girl," Laurel said. "Alice isn't a witch at all."

"Melanie Finch," Linda said. "That's the witch girl."

"Tell us about her," Laurel instructed him. Her brown eyes flashed, and her lips twitched.

He shook his head. No way, no how.

"Is she pretty?" Lenora asked.

"Is she nice?" Leila asked.

"Does she like you back?" Laurel asked.

He jumped to his feet with a sound between a groan and a grunt. "I'm going!" he called. He stormed out of the house and into the rain while his sisters singsonged, "Lulu's in lo-ove. Lulu's in lo-ove." There was only one place he'd be safe, and he headed straight for it.

❋

Lewis's clubhouse was a hovel, but to him it was perfect. His four sisters were always running over the house, over him, over his voice, and over his thoughts. He needed a place of his own. At age eight, he'd gone in search of a clubhouse. First, he and his parents built a tree house in the yard, but his sisters had quickly taken it over. So he'd gone deeper into the forest. He'd found an old, dying apple tree and began digging out around its dried roots. That had served for a while. He could bring his books out there and just sit and read. Eventually, he'd brought Alice out, too, and they'd play adventure games. They were pirates escaping with treasure through tunnels on an old island, or they were aviators lost in the woods after their plane crashed. It was Alice who had the idea to cut away at the roots so the space was more open and you were less likely to get poked in the eye as you crawled in. Once the roots were cut, the dirt started to fall and fill the hole, so Lewis decided to add walls. His mom helped him to haul plywood out to the club-house, and he had pounded it in, securing it with cement at its base. "I might move out here myself," his mom said.

"No girls allowed," he'd told her. "Except for Alice."

His dad called it Lewis's "man cave," an expression Lewis hated. Also, it was much quieter and calmer than the man caves his friends' dads had. Brady's dad had one that had the biggest TV Lewis had ever seen and a pinball machine and posters of women in bikinis sitting on cars. His clubhouse was nothing like that.

Eventually, it got a door that swung upward and could be hitched to the tree above, sticking out like the awning at a store entrance. He had an old camp chair, a plastic tote with books and comics, and even a little transistor radio that only got the AM stations.

Lewis ran straight to the clubhouse—or, perhaps more accurately, straight away from his sisters. He lifted the door, latched it open, then slid inside. He let out his breath and shook the raindrops from his hair.

"Hello?"

He rocketed back toward the door. "Who's there?"

Melanie sat up from behind the sleeping bag. "Oh, hello, Lewis. Is this your little hideaway? I found it last week. I didn't know it belonged to anyone."

"Of course it belongs to someone," he replied, then wished he hadn't when he saw her face fall. "I made it myself."

"It's a very nice hideaway."

"It's a clubhouse."

"Who's in your club?"

"Excuse me?"

"Is Alice in your club?"

"Not anymore," he muttered.

She raised an eyebrow, but he didn't give her any more details.

"Why were you wandering in the woods?" he asked. "Were you looking for something?" Maybe her aunt sent her out to look for herbs for her spells. Or newts to get their eyes and frogs for their legs.

"I like to walk in the woods. Is that okay?" She didn't ask it like a challenge, the way Brady seemed to ask every question. She really seemed to want to make sure she wasn't doing anything wrong or bothering anyone.

"It's fine. You should wear orange, though. It's posted 'no hunting,' but people still come through." He had forgotten his own orange vest as he'd torn out of the house.

"What do you do in your club?" she asked.

"We read," he said. "Or sometimes we play adventure games."

"Well, that sounds fun. What type of adventure?" Before he could answer, she said, "I like reading, too. Old books, mostly. What books do you have?"

Lewis opened the latches on his plastic tote. He kept some of his favorites in it, the ones that gave him comfort to go back to again and again. It felt strange to be showing someone else these special books, like opening his underwear drawer. She carefully pulled out one called *Undefeated*, a book about American Indian football player Jim Thorpe, and another one called *The Boys Who Challenged Hitler*. He liked to read biographies of people who changed history. Sometimes, in his head, he wrote his own biography, imagining all the heroic things he would one day do.

"This one is really good," he said, handing her *My Side of the Mountain*. That one was fiction, but it was still one of his favorites. It was about a boy who ran away and lived in the woods just because. He loved his family and all, but he wanted to be on his own. Lewis certainly could relate to that. Plus, the boy had a hawk that he'd trained to hunt for him.

Melanie took the book from him and opened it gingerly, like it was a treasure wrapped in silks. "Can I borrow it?" she asked.

"Of course," he replied. How had he gone to school with her all these years and not realized that she, too, was a lover of books?

There was a scratching at the doorway. Lewis took his eyes off Melanie and saw a porcupine under the door. He froze. The porcupine was so close, it could shoot its quills right at them and there'd be nowhere for them to hide from the attack.

"Shoo," Melanie said.

"Aren't porcupines nocturnal?" he asked.

"Yes," she said.

The porcupine sniffed the air, turned, and waddled away back into the woods.

She sighed. "He's right of course," she said. "It's time to go."

Lewis peered at the sky. There was no sign of night falling. There was something weird about that porcupine. "Go where?" he asked.

"To the Story Web, of course."

Porcupine

There are many misconceptions about porcupines. They cannot shoot their quills, for example. On the other hand, they are excellent tree climbers. Yes, the porcupine is a very misunderstood animal. For that reason, Porcupine was quite pleased with the information she had gathered, even if it wasn't good news. She waddled deep into the forest and up the hill to where the animals were gathered and speaking in heated voices.

"There are children going to the web," Porcupine announced.

The animals argued on.

Porcupine tried again. She cleared her throat. "Children! Going to the web!"

Moose alone heard, raising his head to look at her. The others, though, continued their cacophony. Loud Crow and shrill Weasel, barking Coyote and howling Bobcat.

Porcupine climbed onto the stump of a tree that had broken during the last storm. Its jagged top stood nearly three feet tall, and when Porcupine reached the top she could see out over most of the animals. "The girl!" she yelled. She was nearly out of breath. "She is not in the woods. Not at the web."

Finally, the crowd of animals looked at her.

"But there are others?" Moose asked.

"There are. Two of them." She worked to catch her breath.

"Well then," Crow said. "The problem was we had the wrong child."

"We didn't have the wrong child."

Crow cawed back, "She is not at the web, and these other children are." Crow was still smarting from the inglorious way he had been captured in the garbage can. The idea that the council had been mistaken, that they had the wrong girl, did much to soothe his wounded soul. "They'll save the web," Crow said with great assurance. Crow said all things with great assurance.

"When are they going?" Moose asked.

"Now. They are on their way now. At this very moment." She huffed out each word. It was the most important information she had ever possessed.

"If they are going to the web, then they are the right children," Crow said. "It's simple logic."

"She is not the wrong girl," Moose reiterated. "She is frightened. Confused. We need another messenger."

The council then fell into heated discussion about who that messenger should be. Moose, though, knew it was only a matter of time before he would have to visit the town himself.

Chapter Eleven
ALICE

As the rain poured down outside, Alice was warm and dry in the Museum. She'd wanted to go home and check on Dare after school, but Henrietta had seen her walking by and dragged her into the Museum. Wednesday was polishing day, so after their snack of cinnamon toast, Alice set to work cleaning the old glass bottles with a vinegar-soaked rag. The scent of vinegar filled her nose and covered her hands. The glass was different colors: blue, green, purple, clear. People liked to put them on their windowsills and let the light stream in or use them as vases. The bottles were a top seller in the Museum. "Why would someone want an old bottle they didn't even find themselves?" Alice asked Henrietta. "It's just a bottle."

"No story, you mean," Henrietta replied. She glanced at the television. Mary Lawrence was doing a cooking segment with Izzy's mom, Becky Clancy, who ran a food blog and always sent Izzy to school with a perfectly packed bento box for lunch.

"I guess." Alice carefully picked up a long, thin bottle.

"You've got more of your father in you than you think."

Alice knew she had plenty of her father in her. She just didn't know what that meant anymore.

"He ever tell you how we met?" Henrietta asked.

Alice shook her head. "All he told me was that you were a spy," Alice replied with a laugh.

"Why are you laughing?" Henrietta asked. Her scarf that day was bright red. Alice should've known better than to trifle with her.

"Nothing. I just— I didn't think it was true."

"Your father is prone to exaggeration," Henrietta said. "But that is not the same as lying." She clicked off the television, silencing Mary Lawrence midsentence.

"He says my mom appeared in a fountain. He made a wish, and there she was."

"Maybe she did," Henrietta replied.

"He said you were air-dropped behind enemy lines in Nazi Germany."

"I was a translator and interpreter," Henrietta told her. "I went to Japan—not Germany—and it was after the war." She picked up a bottle and a rag and started polishing alongside Alice. "I was in the camps and—"

"What camps?" Alice asked.

Henrietta smirked. "Still not teaching that? Okay, then." She put her bottle down. "During the war, there were some who thought that Japanese Americans wouldn't be loyal to the United States. That we'd be helping the enemy. So, they rounded us up and put us in camps. My family was living in San Francisco at the time. They came and got us. We had to leave our homes behind, our pets—all of it."

"How could they do that?"

"People do any number of awful things when they're frightened." She twisted her pearls around her fingers.

"But—"

"You want to know about what I did or not?"

"I do!"

"A recruiter came. He offered us a chance to join up."

"Why would you join the military of a country that was holding you prisoner?" Alice asked.

Henrietta was silent for a while. Rain hit against the window. "This is my country," she said. "It makes mistakes. People make mistakes. Grave errors. But it's still my country." She sighed. "I signed up. Went to basic."

"Basic training?" Alice asked. She had a hard time picturing Henrietta Watanabe scaling walls or climbing under barbed wire.

"Yes, indeed. In Iowa. Iowa was a foreign land to a California girl. They gave us uniforms made for the women of Themyscira—"

"You read *Wonder Woman*?" Alice interrupted.

"Of course I do. Why do you ask?"

Alice shrugged. "I just didn't figure you for a comics person."

"A story is a story is a story. Anyway, we had to hem those skirts practically in half to fit us. And I'll never forget this—the underwear they gave us was brown. Anyway, I got through basic, and then I was sent to the Military Intelligence Language School. The recruiters assumed we all spoke and read Japanese already. I spoke a little with my parents at home but certainly wasn't fluent. They got us up to speed real quick. I spent most of the war translating documents. Most were nothing much. Some were important. After the war I was part of a team that went to Japan with General MacArthur. That was . . . something."

Alice could tell by the sound of Henrietta's voice that she didn't want to say anything else about it. Her dad's voice would get that way whenever the subject of his war came up—anything that wasn't about his friends and him playing tricks or swapping stories. "No one in Independence knows about this," Alice told her. "They think you're just the lady with the antique shop."

"Your dad knows."

"How?"

"Same as you. He asked." She shrugged. "He liked to collect stories, and there are loads of them in this town. Buckets full of untold stories. Hidden stories."

"Some stories are meant to be hidden," Alice said.

Henrietta folded her hands. "You don't believe that."

Alice looked at the bottle in her hand, a green one. She'd been polishing it over and over while Henrietta spoke.

"I can see it in your eyes. You have stories you want to tell. You want them out of the dark. Stories fester there. They grow mean. People fill in details with lies. Like with Anastasia up in the Bird House."

Alice snapped her head up.

"Could've been me up there in the woods. All alone not wanting to talk to folks. Or maybe not ready. Not easy. I came here after my war because I wanted some place quiet where people wouldn't bother me. It's a real fine line between wanting some peace and quiet and being all alone. If I didn't live in town where I could walk for the newspaper and a cup of coffee. If I didn't have this shop with people coming in and out all day. Who knows?"

"What are you saying?"

"I'm saying folks don't know her story, and they made one up. And it wasn't a kind one, was it?"

Alice shook her head.

"Pay attention to the stories people tell, Alice—"

"They tell you a lot about a person."

"So your father did listen," Mrs. Watanabe said with a smile. "I figured he learned that lesson the hard way at the Bird House that day."

Before Alice could ask what Henrietta was talking about, the chimes above the front door rang, and Alice's mom rushed in, pushing her damp hair out of her face. "What's with this crazy weather?" she asked. "Raining like the Flood's coming. I'm going to need to build an ark." She smiled, but her eyes were tired.

While Alice got her things, Henrietta and her mom chatted about work and the hospital. Alice's mom told a story of a man who broke his thumb hammering in election signs. Then she said, "But the best was we had a guy come in swearing he had rabies," Alice's mom said. "Said he got it from a raccoon, but we couldn't find a bite on him. Turns out the raccoon *didn't* bite him, just walked right in the front door of his house."

"That old business again," Henrietta said, shaking her head. "Animals like Independence. Twenty, twenty-five years ago, back when Buzz was a boy, we were practically overrun."

Alice wanted to hear more, but her mom said, "You ready?"

Alice nodded.

"Thanks, Henrietta," Alice's mom said. "I don't know what I'd do without you."

"It takes a village," Henrietta replied.

Alice's mom paused. "I guess you're right. I don't have the biggest village, but it's a good one. Good night, Henrietta."

"One last thing, JoEllen. Can you tell me again about how you and Buzz met?" Henrietta glanced over at Alice and gave her a wink.

Alice's mom's body tensed. Little pinched creases appeared at the corners of her eyes.

"Come on, Mom," Alice said. "I've only ever heard Dad's version."

"Okay." She unwound her scarf from around her neck. "It was down in Boston, my first year of college. Here I was, this girl from the country, down in the big city. I wanted to fit in, so I got these ridiculous shoes. They were strappy sandals with a wedge heel. I could barely walk in them. My friends and I went out dancing at this club. That was an eye-opener! The music was great, but there were just so many people, and they were all so fancy. Anyway, we were walking back to the T, through Copley Square. My feet were just killing me. I could barely keep up with my friends."

That was hard for Alice to picture. Her mom was a fast walker, and Alice had to jog to keep up with her when they walked down the street.

"My friends kept yelling at me to hurry up. But then we passed by this enormous fountain. The pool was so big, and the moon was reflecting off it. It almost looked like the rivers back home. I thought about how we'd go swimming in the river, how good that felt, and I just chucked off my shoes and walked right in. My friends thought I was crazy. I can't even tell you how good that felt. It was like all the pressure, all the pain came right off my feet."

As she spoke, her face relaxed and her cheeks turned a warm pink. Alice hadn't seen her like that in ages.

"No way I was coming out of there. I just walked right on the edge of that fountain, splashing the water up around me, kicking it at my friends, but none of them would come in with me. I got to the edge, and then, there was your dad. Just standing there with that goofy smile."

Alice's mom had her own goofy smile.

"He said, 'I made a wish, but I never thought a mermaid would really appear.' And that was that. I probably fell in love with him that very night."

"What about your shoes?" Alice asked.

Her mom laughed. "That's what you want to know? After the most romantic story of my life?"

Alice nodded. What she really wanted to say was, *So it was true? More or less true?*

"I honestly can't remember. Your dad had this kind of scooter bike back then. Not really a motorcycle, but more like a souped-up BMX. He gave me a ride home, right up to my door. I guess I ran in barefoot."

"You left the shoes in the park?"

"Hopefully, someone found them who could wear them without agony."

Alice tried to take this all in: her mom abandoning her shoes, her dad having a scooter. But of course the detail she kept coming back to was that her father had told the truth. He made a wish, she appeared in the fountain, and they fell in love. Alice wondered why she had never heard her mom's side of the story before. She supposed because her father was the storyteller of the family. But her mother was good at it, too. Maybe that's why her dad had been so certain she could see the Story Web, too—Alice stopped herself. The Story Web wasn't real.

Henrietta raised her eyebrows at Alice, as if to say, *See?*

So maybe some of her dad's stories had a bit of truth in them. That didn't mean they were all true. Alice was certain that the Story Web was pure fiction.

Outside, the rain had stopped. She stared up into the murky gray. She wasn't sure what she was looking for, but she saw nothing.

It was only when she lowered her eyes that she saw something: a tiny web tucked into the corner of Henrietta's stairs. Raindrops clung to the strands, and one thread stretched out over Henrietta's storefront walk, waving in the gentle wind.

Chapter Twelve

MELANIE

Snap, snap, snap.

Each step they take breaks a twig, a leaf, an acorn. Birds flutter their wings and chitter their noises down. Humans are apex predators, so the animals are right to be afraid, but Melanie wishes it weren't that way.

The rain drips, falling with gentle *splat*s between her and Lewis.

She is used to silence between people. She is not used to it being uncomfortable.

"Um," Lewis says. "So, what is it that we're going to see?"

"The Story Web."

Birds chirrup to one another in the trees. A chickadee, a robin, a grackle.

"What? Like a spiderweb?" he asks. There is so much he does not know, but Melanie feels certain he can help.

"Yes. It's my responsibility."

Lewis rubs the top of his head. His hair is somewhere between brown and blond, like a fennec fox. Lewis has big ears like a fennec, too. Melanie wonders what else the two have in common.

"It's always there? This web? In the same place?"

"Yes." She isn't used to so many questions.

They are careful as they skid down the slope into the gully.

The sun begins to sink below the horizon line. The sky softens. The air grows colder. Finally, she says, "I'm sorry. The thread—"

But Lewis points to the old willow tree. "There," he says.

Melanie drops to her knees on the still-warm earth and crawls under the branches of the tree, with Lewis right behind. When they stand, the giant web is in front of them. It is nothing like it had once been. Instead of shimmering silver and luminescent pearls, the web is a dull gray. Stray threads brush against the ground. The top right corner droops, untethered.

"It's worse than I thought!" Melanie says.

"What is this?" Lewis asks.

"This is it," she cries. "The Story Web. What's left of it."

Lewis is quiet. Quieter than still water. Quieter than white clouds. Then he says, "But how do you know? How do you know it's not just some big spider's web?"

She sees the web through his eyes: like a cobweb in the

dark corner of a basement. He can't see the magic there. Not yet.

She thinks of her parents, of the book they read. She can still feel her mother's sweater against her cheek.

"I have a book about it," she replies. She takes a deep breath. How can she explain it to him? He must believe if he is going to help her. "The web has always been here," she says. "It's not always the same shape or the same number of threads. It changes a little. But it's always here because it's us. Or, it's part of us. I mean, it's how we're all connected. It's all our lives—" Her words are all jumbled, like broken shards of glass. She takes a deep breath. "It's a Story Web. Each strand is a tale."

He steps closer to the web. She's afraid he might touch it, so she puts her hand on his sleeve.

"Each strand is its own story?"

"More or less," she says. "Sometimes stories overlap, I think."

"But that's a real web," he says. "And a story is . . . a story."

She isn't sure how to explain it to him. A Story Web isn't so much a thing you understand. It's something you believe.

"The spiders gather the stories and weave them into the web. The strands lace together, crisscrossing one another to make the fabric that ties the whole world together. It *keeps* the world together."

Lewis takes another step. "It doesn't look so good."

"If we don't fix it—" Melanie begins. "It's why the animals are coming. This web, all the webs—they hold our world together. If they break, then we break. It's called the Freezing. The whole world will splinter."

"Literally?"

She can see it happening: the world freezing and shattering into a million pieces.

A story pricks at her mind. She needs to tell him so maybe he will start to see. Maybe he will help.

"My mom left me this book of stories. It's called *The Story Web*—it's all these classic stories, like fables and myths and fairy tales from all over the world. It's funny because it was every story you could imagine, but I liked the prologue best. That's the part of the book that comes first, like an introduction—"

"I know what a prologue is," Lewis tells her.

"Okay. A lot of people skip them, but I like them. I even have it memorized." Melanie clears her throat. She feels strange sharing this thing that belonged to her and her parents with a stranger. But it is necessary, so she begins retelling the story.

In the beginning, the worlds of animals and humans lived in harmony. They conversed freely, one neighbor to the next. Hardly ever did they quarrel. Strands of stories connected all the creatures of the earth. These strands were woven together into an intricate lace pattern. This web stretched through and around the earth and held it together.

The spiders were the most honored in this world, for it was they who built the web of stories that held all the creatures together. When a section frayed, they could count on the creatures to come with new stories, new threads the spiders could use to fix the web.

But time passed on and tensions arose. Was it a human who threw the first stone? A dog? A bear? A tiny fly? We shall never know. We know only that the creatures grew apart. Each animal found their own realm. The fish and whales and mermaids stayed in the sea and never sang up to the mammals on the land. The birds took to the trees and skies and rarely came to gossip with the rodents who lived underground. Those were dark days indeed!

The spiders worked as hard as they could to maintain the web. Tensions grew faster than they could spin, and shared stories were scarce. The web grew more and more fragile.

Then came Arachne. A weaver quite proud of her own work—too proud they say—and a bit of magic turned her into a spider, where she would be doomed to weave webs for the rest of eternity. But Arachne knew the tales of the Story Web and the once honored spiders. Perhaps she could not be the greatest human weaver, wrapping tales into tapestries, but she could bring honor back to the spiders by rebuilding the Story Web.

And so, slowly, slowly she began to repair the web. Her magic made the strands stronger, the knots tighter. But here is the rub! It is not the spider who tells the story, it is the people. So *she was dependent on the humans, gathering their tales. When the humans grow apart from one another and from the animals, when they stop listening to one another's stories, the web frays and tears.*

Remember, it is the Story Web that holds the earth together. Without it, we shall splinter apart.

So, dear reader, you must not only read these stories, you must share them. You must tell the stories, and you must listen. It is how we all survive.

"Look!" Lewis whispers.

An orb weaver is on the web. *Argiope aurantia*. Fat black body and bright yellow markings. As Melanie spoke, the spider began to weave in the corner of the web. It hasn't gotten far. Two strands connecting three of the radius threads, but it is something.

"The book says the spiders need our stories, right? So maybe we just tell stories?" Lewis asks.

"Do you have a story?"

Lewis shakes his head. "I don't think so. Not yet." He looks away from her. Ashamed? She isn't sure why. "Do you still have that book?" he asks. "Maybe there're more details in there. Or maybe we should just read the stories from the book to the web?"

"Sure, I have it," Melanie says. "It's at my house."

"The Bird House?" Lewis asks.

She sees the fear in his eyes.

Melanie nods. "You want to come over?"

It is a simple question, one kids have asked each other thousands of times. Millions probably. Lewis swallows hard. "Yes," he says. And he means it, she thinks. Or, at least, he's trying to.

Chapter Thirteen

LEWIS

Lewis had been to the Bird House only one time before, with Alice. He still got a sick feeling when he thought about going up there with the chocolate milk. When it came to witch hunts, the hunters were never the good guys. They should have left Melanie's aunt alone. He couldn't deny, though, that the sick feeling also came from remembering what had happened that day, the way all the birds had lifted at once and blackened the sky.

Now, years later, Lewis stepped back onto the lawn, this time with Melanie by his side. Cold air whipped over the hill and down toward them. He thought he heard coyote calls on that air, but it was too early in the evening for that. The roof ridge was lined with crows. Seventeen of them. On the second floor, in a window with a deep ledge, a starling nested. Little baby birds poked their heads up. A flock of turkeys walked around the edge of the house. If they noticed the two kids, they didn't seem to care. They kept pecking at bugs on the ground. "We're really high up," Lewis said. It was a ridiculous thing to say, he knew that, but he had to say something.

"Yep," Melanie said. "We have the best view of the town."

"So you can spy on everyone?" Lewis asked.

Melanie looked back over her shoulder. "Not usually, no. Is that what you would do?"

Lewis shook his head.

"We mostly watch the birds coming and going. We look out toward the ocean."

As if on cue, a large bird emerged from the woods and bobbed its way toward them.

"Is that the emu?" Lewis asked with surprise.

"Her name is Elspeth."

"The emu's name is Elspeth?"

"Yes. I named her when I was younger. On one of our visits."

"The emu lives with you?"

"It's a rescue emu," Melanie explained. "My aunt takes in rare birds that can't survive on their own."

Lewis glanced at Melanie. She was tall, probably the tallest girl in fifth grade, and she moved more slowly, carefully, like the world had bumped up against her a few too many times.

Lewis took a deep breath and continued his walk across

the patchy grass. Melanie led him around to the front of the house onto a large circular driveway dotted with white splotches, like someone had splattered paint all over the blacktop.

A flock of seagulls sat along a fence at the top of the driveway and regarded them with some confusion. A large oak tree by the house was full of small, twittering birds. Pigeons strutted across the edge of the driveway and chickens pecked at the grass.

"Wait," Lewis said. "Is this white stuff— Is it bird poop?"

"Of course it is," Melanie said. "Birds have to poop somewhere."

Lewis blushed. He shouldn't have said anything, even though the old Victorian was drizzled in white the same as the driveway. "Sorry."

"It's okay," Melanie said. "I suppose it is a little odd if you aren't used to it. But the birds don't come inside. Except for Nocturne, that is. And the rare birds in the solarium. But really, our house is perfectly clean." She stepped onto a walkway flanked by two birdbaths and led them to the front door. "I'm sure the book is in the library. We'll just hurry in and find it. No one will even know we're here." She took a key from around her neck and unlocked the massive bolt. No one in Independence locked their doors. Lewis felt his heart rev up. What if Melanie's aunt truly was a witch, and he was being led to her lair?

The door swung in, and standing in the doorway, as if she had been expecting them, was Anastasia Seersie, the witch of Independence, Maine.

The first thing Lewis noticed about Melanie's aunt was her startling gray eyes. They were almost green gray, like a paler version of the ocean in winter. She was also the tallest woman Lewis had ever met. She stood in the doorway of the Bird House, and the top of her head nearly reached the doorframe.

"Having a friend over?" she asked.

"I just wanted to show him one of my books," Melanie began to explain.

Melanie's aunt held up a hand. Her fingers were as long and slim as she was. "Let's invite our guest inside first, please."

"Of course, Anastasia," Melanie replied.

Melanie's aunt stepped back and, to his never-ending surprise, Lewis found himself stepping into the Bird House. A sleepy-eyed owl watched as they entered an enormous foyer with a black-and-white checkerboard floor, and an iron chandelier hung by an impossibly thin chain above their heads. A sweeping staircase curved away from them to the upstairs rooms, bracketed by pillars of pure white marble. The house had the buzzing quiet of a museum.

Melanie fidgeted with her hands. Lewis wanted to put a hand on her shoulder, but her aunt ushered them into a huge living room filled with pink brocade furniture. There were two small couches with backs curved like violins and six armchairs—the seats of which were so high Lewis wasn't sure he would be able to get into one.

Melanie's aunt lowered herself into one of the chairs. The owl from the front room swooped in and perched itself on the back. Scant light came in from cracks between the blinds. "Sit, sit," Melanie's aunt ordered. "Go get the cookies, Melanie!"

Lewis sat on one of the couches so at least his feet would touch the floor, and so Melanie could sit beside him. Melanie's aunt regarded Lewis without speaking until Melanie came back carrying a silver tray full of butter cookies in all sorts of fantastic animal shapes. She placed the tray on a table in front of Lewis and was about to sit down herself when her aunt said, "The curtains!"

With effort, Melanie pulled back the heavy drapes and let in what was left of the daylight.

Melanie's aunt sat with her hands folded on her lap and did not make a move toward the cookies. Lewis knew it was polite to wait for your host to eat, but the cookies were so tempting, with their swirls for tails and shining sugar eyes. He shifted back and forth on the couch, jostling Melanie.

"Please, help yourself. I'm not much for sweets."

Lewis lurched forward and chose a cookie shaped like a squirrel. Melanie chose a bird whose wings were made of opaque candy. They tasted like butter and sugar melting in his mouth, and Lewis was afraid he wouldn't be able to stop eating them. "These are delicious, Mrs.—" he mumbled through the crumbs.

"Call me Anastasia. Now," Anastasia said, "it's time to get to know you better. I understand, Lewis, that you excel at the game called hockey?"

Lewis swallowed the sweet buttery cookie in his mouth. "Yes," he said. "I'm on the bantam team this year. I started last year with them. Usually you need to be a year older, but the coach—"

"Alice Dingwell's father," Melanie's aunt interjected.

"Yeah, last year. But now it's her uncle. Donny. Anyway, they put me up onto bantams. I'm going to go to the Olympics someday. Hopefully twice. And also play in the Frozen Four and the NHL."

"The Olympics?" she asked. "Now there's a worthy goal."

"Hockey was in the summer Olympics at first. Isn't that weird? That was in 1920. Canada won, of course."

"Of course," Anastasia agreed.

"It is Canada's game," Lewis said. "Then in 1924 they switched it to the winter games. Canada won the first four, then they got silver in 1936. There weren't any Olympics for a while because of wars and stuff. But in 1948 they had them again, and Canada won." Lewis could recite the winners of every Olympic matchup since that first one in 1920. He cleared his throat. "The United States women's team won the first time they could play. That was 1998. The American men won their first gold in 1960. And then twenty years later—" Lewis clapped his hands and made whooping crowd noises. "Do you believe in miracles?"

"Yes. Why?" Anastasia replied.

"No, it was from the game—what the announcer said?" He took a deep breath. "The US wasn't supposed to win. The Russians—the USSR, technically—they were a much better team. Way better. But the US had heart, you know, and they worked hard. And that one game against the Russians, that one special time, they won." Lewis didn't know why he was babbling on about this, but he couldn't seem to stop himself.

"It was a miracle?" Anastasia asked. "A true miracle?"

"I don't know about that," Lewis said. "But Al Michaels— he was calling the game on TV, and just as time was running out he was like, 'Do you believe in miracles?' Because that's what it felt like. Coach Buzz—"

"Alice's father?"

"Yeah. He always had us watch the movie before big games."

"It doesn't sound like a true miracle to me," Anastasia said.

"What makes a true miracle?" Lewis asked.

"It's when the supernatural world comes into the human world and helps out," Melanie told him.

"Well, I guess it wasn't a true miracle, then," Lewis said.

"But it was still amazing. That's why it lives on from generation to generation."

"The best stories do," Anastasia said. Then she closed her eyes and stretched her arms above her head. "It's time for my evening walk." She looked at Melanie. "You may get your book. Stay downstairs. Have him on his way quickly."

With that, she strode across the room, her sandals making a slapping noise with each step that echoed off the walls.

☀

The door to the library was under the stairs that twisted upward. As Melanie pulled it open, Lewis said, "Like Harry Potter at the Dursleys'." But as soon as he stepped into the room, he realized how wrong he was. It was no cramped cupboard. Instead, the bookshelves spiraled along the inside of the staircase, book after book after book going up, up, up. A window at the far side of the room let in faint light. There were two purple velvet chairs with high backs and fluffy footrests. It looked about a million times more comfortable than Lewis's clubhouse!

The books on the shelves were all big and thick with spines in dusty red or deep green. Some were leather and had gold lettering and filigree. Lewis could read and read and read for the rest of his life and still never get through them all.

"This is the most amazing place I have ever been in my entire life."

"It's a waste," Melanie said. She crouched next to the door where the spiral of shelving began. "All these books and only two of us to read them."

Melanie pointed to a small triangular cabinet. With a sharp yank, she pulled open the door and began removing books. They were all old and dusty looking, with yellowing pages and worn covers. *Anne of Green Gables, In the Year of the Boar and Jackie Robinson, A Wrinkle in Time, Bridge to Terabithia, M.C. Higgins, the Great.* "Most of these were my mom's," she said. She pulled out a beat-up copy of *Harry Potter and the Philosopher's Stone*, the British version of the book, and a stack of *Tintin*s in French. She kept pulling out books until the cupboard was empty.

"Maybe it got mixed in with the other books," he said.

They both looked at the spiraled shelves of books.

"I'll start at that end," he said.

The books were beautiful. Leather-bound with their titles printed on the spines in gold letters, fluttery ribbon bookmarks that spilled over the top. He recognized some titles. *Grimms' Fairy Tales* and *Works of Hans Christian Andersen*. Other books were unfamiliar. He pulled out one by Huang Zhing that had a golden tiger on the front. He slid it back in next to a book with a title in French, *Histoires ou contes du temps passé*. Lewis's grandmother was French-Canadian, and now he wished he'd heeded her attempts to teach him some of the language. There was lots of nonfiction, too, mostly about animals. Many of the books he longed to pick up and page through, but they were on a mission. They had to find that book and fix the web or—or what? He wasn't really sure.

"So what exactly happens if we don't fix the web? What do you mean by 'the Freezing'?" he asked, using the word she had said out by the web.

"The earth freezes and breaks apart," Melanie replied from the opposite side of the room. "At least I think so. I'm not entirely sure. It was my parents who told me about it. It was their book. I'm sure I packed it up when I moved here."

"Wait, it might not even be in this house?" He spun so he was looking at her.

She shrugged. "It can't be anywhere else."

Her cheeks were pink, and her shiny eyes looked even shinier, like she might cry.

"Okay," he said. "Frozen, fractured earth. Sometimes it feels like that already."

"What do you mean?" Melanie asked.

"Oh, you know," he said. "Like when you turn on the television news and people are just arguing, arguing, arguing. Or at school, how cold people can be." He shrugged.

"Like the boys who climbed the wall here. Or like the man who doesn't want the park," Melanie said.

"What man?" Lewis asked.

"I don't know. Anastasia said that there were some people who don't want the park. They think it isn't good for the town. She disagrees. She thinks it's going to get heated."

Lewis thought of the postcard that had come to his house. So that arrow hadn't been a mistake? Someone wanted to build a store instead of a park. "That's just stupid," he said.

"If it's already beginning," she said, "then it's even more urgent that we find the book."

"It will tell us what to do?" he asked.

"I hope so."

They each turned back to the shelves and kept searching. Another thirty minutes and they were side by side. They had checked all the books. *The Story Web* was nowhere to be found.

Melanie sunk onto one of the purple chairs. Her eyes were definitely crying now.

"It's okay, Melanie. We'll find it. We can ask Ms. Engle if she has a copy at school."

Melanie shook her head. "I don't think— It's just such an old book. My parents got theirs at a flea market. I remember it had the price written in pencil on the inside cover. Three dollars and forty-seven cents. Such a strange number, right?"

Lewis wasn't thinking about the price, though. He was thinking about the flea market. "I think I know someone who can help us," he said.

Chapter Fourteen
ALICE

"Taco Tuesday!" Alice's mom sang with her head inside the refrigerator. It was Wednesday. She wore her scrubs, even though it was her day off. Alice's mom pretty much only wore scrubs. She emerged from the refrigerator with sour cream, a jar of salsa, a bag of shredded cheese, and a package of guacamole balanced in a precarious fashion. While Alice went to the pantry to get the taco shells, her mom pulled a bag of ground turkey out of the freezer.

Taco Tuesday was Alice's favorite dinner because it was the closest to cooking that they did. She took the shells out of the package and put them into the toaster oven so they'd get good and crispy.

"Can you clear off the table?" her mom asked.

More than half the table was covered in papers. Old mail, newspapers, magazines her mom intended to read someday, and all of Alice's school papers. Alice straightened the stacks of magazines, recycled the old newspapers. Then she took her pile of old schoolwork. None of it was important—math tests from September and worksheets she had completed ages ago. She was about to recycle that, too, when something slipped out of the pile. It was a project they had done during the first week of school. There was a smiling photograph of her at the top. Her eyes were bright, and every tooth seemed to show in her grin. You could still see her summer freckles across her pink cheeks. Her hair was smooth and pretty; her shirt was a bright orange.

My name is Alice Dingwell. I am ten years old. This year in fifth grade I want to learn how to do double-digit multiplication. I want to read at least thirty books, and I am going to try to read more nonfiction, since I mostly read fiction. My goal for outside school is that our team will win the state hockey tournament again and I will be named as one of the top players. My favorite color is green. My favorite food is quesadillas. My favorite sports team is the Bruins. My best friends are Izzy and Sadie and Lewis. I hope that fifth grade will be my best year ever!!

She remembered creating this poster. Mrs. Zee had given them a form to fill out. Then they'd typed their paragraphs on the school laptops. Mrs. Zee had printed out their paragraphs and taken their pictures, and they'd glued them onto construction paper. Mrs. Zee hung them in the room, and they'd stayed up all September. The memory of creating the poster was clear, but she could not remember that girl.

Her mom walked by and brushed Alice's hair over her shoulder. "I love that picture of you," she said, and put a tub of sour cream onto the table.

Alice nodded. She left the poster on the table and brought the rest to the bin by the kitchen door.

"How was school?" her mom asked.

Alice didn't answer. Her gaze landed on the mail and a single pale blue envelope in the pile. "I'll be right back," she said. She grabbed the envelope. Her mom saw it in Alice's hand, and she pressed a smile onto her lips and said, "Go on and read your letter. I'll get dinner put together."

Alice opened the door just enough to slide in without Jewel following her.

In her room, Alice sat on her bed. It was better to read the letters sitting down. Dare scratched and tweeted from her dollhouse, so Alice moved the bird onto the bed beside her. She fed her dried blueberries.

The envelope was bent in the lower corner. She tried to straighten it out but realized she was only putting off the inevitable. She opened the letter.

DEAR ALICE,

I HAVE COME TO THE LAND OF THE LOTUS EATERS. THE
FOOD HERE IS SO DELICIOUS, I CANNOT STOP EATING. IT MAKES ME
HAPPY AND FULL. DAZED, EVEN, BY THE WONDER OF IT ALL. THIS
MORNING I HAD FRENCH TOAST WITH FRESH BERRIES. FOR LUNCH,
IT WAS CLAM CHOWDER AND AN ARUGULA SALAD. BUT DINNER—
DINNER!—THAT WAS THE MOST MAGICAL. IT WAS CHICKEN.
CHICKEN? YOU MIGHT ASK. CHICKEN IS JUST CHICKEN. BUT NOT
HERE. HERE CHICKEN IS A MELODY, A SYMPHONY, A WHOLE
OPERA. IT IS ANOTHER REASON I FIND IT HARD TO LEAVE THIS
PLACE. IF YOU WERE TO COME TO VISIT AND TASTE THE FOOD,
THEN YOU MIGHT UNDERSTAND.

Alice wondered if that was an invitation. It was worded so
strangely: *If you were to come to visit.* She wasn't sure if she wanted
to visit.

AFTER, THERE WAS PUMPKIN PIE, WHICH I KNOW IS NOT YOUR
FAVORITE, BUT MAYBE EVEN THIS YOU WOULD HAVE LOVED.

THE ICE IS STILL NOT READY FOR SKATING, WHICH IS
PROBABLY GOOD. AFTER THE FOOD I'VE EATEN, I FEEL LETHARGIC.
THAT MEANS SLOW AND LAZY, LIKE MOLASSES. NO WHIPPING
DOWN THE LINE FOR ME. PLUS I HAVE NOT YET FOUND A TEAM
TO SKATE WITH. ONE MAN SKATING IS LONELINESS DEFINED, I
SHOULD THINK, AND COMPLETELY LACKING IN POWER.

In truth, I still have some trials to complete before I come home. I am working on it, though, as fast as I can.

Please give your mother a hug from me and another one from you.

Check the stars. When the clouds clear, we may be able to see Cassiopeia.

Be bold, be brave, be fierce. It is what I am trying to do.

Much love,

Dad

The letter felt heavy in her hands, like it had much more weight than a simple piece of notebook paper.

She rubbed at her eyes. *Crying.* She was crying. Alice Dingwell never cried. Her whole face grew hot, although the only one watching her was the little bird. Dare hopped into the crook of her elbow. When Alice looked down at her, a big fat tear fell and landed on the bird's head. Dare didn't even flinch.

"It's just—" Alice began. But there were no words.

She tossed the letter aside. "He should just be here!" she cried.

She flopped back on the bed and held the envelope to her chest. Dare, startled by the sudden movement, fell onto the bed beside her. After a moment, Alice reached under her bed and pulled out her letter box. The old shoebox had thirty-seven letters in it. This new one made thirty-eight. Thirty-one were from his deployments. Three were from different week-long trainings he'd gone to over his years in the Army Reserves. Three more—now four—were from his days at the hospital. She didn't like to read those.

She took the thirty-one letters and spread them out over her bed, closed her eyes, and picked one. This was her little ritual. To reread all of them in one go was too much. To ignore them, too difficult.

The one she pulled out was in a stained blue envelope. She knew this letter before she even removed it from its envelope, practically had it memorized. The frills from the notebook were still intact but ragged from the paper being removed over and over again. The creases where the letter had been folded were beginning to tear.

MARCH 19

DEAR ALICE,

HAPPY BIRTHDAY! NINE YEARS OLD TODAY! NINE IS A VERY GOOD AGE TO BE. TO MARK THE OCCASION, PLEASE BE SURE TO DO THE FOLLOWING:

1. HAVE MOM MARK YOUR HEIGHT ON THE WALL. REPORT
    BACK TO ME HOW MUCH YOU HAVE GROWN IN INCHES AND
    CENTIMETERS. A DIAGRAM MIGHT BE USEFUL.

2. Race Uncle Donny, goal line to goal line and back. I think this might be your year. Remember, he's slow off the whistle, but man, that glide . . .

3. Smash your cake into your face. You really enjoyed that when you were a baby, and there's only so many days in your life you can get away with smashing cake into your face. Bonus points if you can also smash a bit into Mom's. Pictures please.

As for me, my journey continues apace. You ask when I will be home, and I must report that is still unclear. The winds never seem to blow with steady speed or direction. I've considered traveling to Delphi to consult with the Oracles, but access is severely limited, I hear, and well above my rank. There is a Cassandra here, but she seems disinclined to prognostication. This may be for the best. Did Cassandra ever predict any good fortunes?

I wanted to give you an update on the wild dog Cerberus. He has continued to terrorize the camp for weeks, coming around and barking with all three of his heads. But today my friend H went out with some leftovers from the mess hall—something like a sloppy joe. He brought out three bowls and placed them in front of the beast. It was like the creature was completely transformed. He ate the food, then curled up right at H's feet and fell asleep. When our sergeant

SAW IT, HE SAID H DESERVED A MEDAL OF VALOR. NOT SURE
THAT WILL REALLY HAPPEN, BUT THAT'S ONE CREATURE TAMED
AND ONE MORE TRIAL COMPLETED BY OUR UNIT.

DON'T FORGET TO CHECK THE STARS EACH NIGHT, ALICE.
SOON YOU'LL SEE ME UP THERE, RACING BACK TO YOU. UNTIL
THEN, BE BOLD, BE BRAVE, BE FIERCE. AS ALWAYS.

LOVE,
DAD

When she finished reading, Alice refolded the letter and, with care, placed it back in the envelope. She restacked the old letters and placed them in the box, then curled up, hugging her pillow to her face. Alice felt her tears sink into the pillowcase. She wished it would just suck them all out of her, and then she'd be done with it. But tears don't work that way.

"Alice!" her mom called. "You okay?"

Alice sat up. She swiped hard at her face. "I'm fine!" she yelled back, trying to make her voice sound normal.

Be-zeep.

Even the bird could see she was lying.

"Dinner's ready!"

Alice looked at herself in the mirror. Her cheeks were pink and her eyes a little red, but she looked more or less okay, she thought. She untucked her dark hair from behind her ears and shook out her bangs so that they fell into her eyes a little more, hiding the traces.

She folded the letter and put it back into its envelope.

"Alice!" her mom called again.

Alice stood straight, breathed in. "Do I look okay?" she asked Dare. The bird nodded. Alice lifted her carefully and placed her back into the dollhouse. "I'll be back after dinner." She left her more berries.

Alice trotted down the hall. Her mom watched her carefully and kept her eyes trained on Alice as she made herself two tacos, then sat at the dining room table.

"So," her mom said. "How's your dad?"

"Fine," Alice replied. Her stomach flip-flopped. She racked her brain for something else—anything else—that she could talk to her mother about. The Story Web? She could ask about that. But no, that was foolish. Just a story. Just Melanie being weird. She cleared her throat. "There was a crow at school yesterday."

"What do you mean? In the school?"

"Yes. Inside the cafeteria. It landed right on my table." Alice smiled. The story felt a lot funnier now that she was telling it to her mother. "It was marching around crowing at everyone. Then the janitor put a trash can on top of it. I wonder what he did with it."

"Probably set it free to terrorize some other cafeteria."

Alice pictured the crow flying away from their school, maybe down toward Portland or to the mountains. "Like a carrier pigeon," she said. "It's bringing messages from school to school."

"What kind of messages?" her mom asked, leaning closer. "Secret messages?"

"It wasn't a very good secret keeper. It brought a lot of attention to itself."

"Maybe the crow was a distraction. While you were all paying attention to it, the carrier pigeon went in and delivered the message."

"To Mr. Gringles." Alice laughed. Mr. Gringles was the old music teacher who hummed "Twinkle, Twinkle, Little Star" while he tap-danced down the hallway. No matter how awfully they played, he'd say, "Good, good."

"It's a love letter from the music teacher at another school."

"Or a plan to pied-piper all you kids to some foreign land," Mom added.

That sounded a lot more plausible to Alice.

They ate in silence for a few minutes. "And your dad's letter? He says he's doing well?"

"Yes," Alice replied.

"Okay. It's just that— I mean, I imagine you may have some questions for me."

"No," Alice replied.

"Because it's okay. It's normal. It's okay." Alice could feel her mother trying to think of the right thing to say to her. Ever since her dad had gone, this strange tension was building between them, like storm clouds stacking up. Sometimes Alice wished her mother would explode thunder and lightning all over her. She deserved it. It was Alice's fault that her dad was in the hospital, and her mom should be angry with her. More than angry. Livid. Outraged.

But Alice's mom was not, or, at least, did not let the anger out. She was quiet. So, before the silence grew into a wall, Alice cleared her plate and started on the dishes. She glanced out the window as she washed, back toward the woods. The trees sloped up a gentle hill away from their house—back toward Lewis's home and, beyond that, the Bird House. She thought of Melanie living up in that house. It must be strange and scary there. She'd never really considered what it must be like to be Melanie, sharing the house with crows and ravens and vultures. Was she sad up there? Alice wondered. Did she feel very much alone?

Mother Bear

Mother Bear watched from a knoll in the forest while Baby Bear cavorted across the field, still wet with morning dew. Her heart lodged itself in her throat. Children, bears or otherwise, may never know what it is like for their parents to watch them set out on Very Important Business. She sat back on her haunches and chewed on a twig.

When the animal council had suggested Baby Bear go, of course Mother Bear's chest had swelled with pride. But now her paws fairly quaked. She was nervous for his safety, nervous for his success, nervous for the whole world.

He got tangled in his own feet, rolled over, then popped back up.

It seemed a lot to ask of such a young cub. The others thought he would be able to reach the girl. He would be more unusual than a bird but not frightening, or so they hoped.

Mother Bear would have preferred to go herself, but this is something that parents, bears or otherwise, must do: sit back and chew nervously while their children venture out into the wide world.

Chapter Fifteen
ALICE

Mrs. Zee's handwriting was neat and straight. Sometimes Alice wondered if teachers took special classes in how to write so neatly. Today on the board she had written the words "THE HERO'S JOURNEY."

Underneath she had drawn a circle. There were different points along the circle, almost like a clock face, where Mrs. Zee had written more details. The journey started in the Ordinary World, whatever that meant. Alice had thought her life was ordinary before. She had her friends, Izzy and Sadie. She had her hockey team. She had her dad. Now the absence of those things had become ordinary.

Next came the Magical Birth. Then Call to Adventure. Her dad had talked about that, especially when he talked about going into the military. "You can't refuse the call," he'd always said, which was funny because one of the next things on the circle was the refusal of the call. She was tilting her head to read more when the intercom beeped. The principal's voice crackled: "Attention, friends, we are instituting a safe-in-place action. Please go to your safe-in-place stations. I repeat, we are instituting a safe-in-place action."

Action. Not drill. Action.

Lewis took Melanie by the hand. It was a bold gesture, and a brave one, too. He just grabbed her hand and tugged her over to the back corner of the room next to the sink. The whole class sat and tilted their heads up to look at the star map that Mrs. Zee had hung there. They murmured constellations as they waited for the lockdown to end.

Lewis hated the drills. He had always hated them. Maybe that's why he had grabbed Melanie's hand, Alice thought. Maybe he was still just looking for a hand to hold until it was over. In first grade, they all had to crowd into the bathroom. Mrs. Snell, who was about a million years old they had been sure, would put down the lid on the toilet seat, and she would sit there and read them stories as though she were sitting on her rocking chair in the story corner. Story after story until the drill was complete. Lewis would cling onto Alice's arm and sniffle and try to keep the tears inside his eyes.

Alice watched him now. No tears. He had learned to hold them in, she supposed. She wondered what it meant that she remembered those moments with such fondness. Did that make her a good friend or a bad friend?

Alice thought of her father. How fire alarms made him jump and shake and usually led to a night alone in her parents' bedroom or out in his truck. Her mom had taken the batteries out of the smoke detector in the kitchen because it went off so many times. Alice had put them back in, and then— She clenched her hands into fists and peered at the star map. This was something else her father had taught her. The constellations were set in the sky by the Greek gods whose stories he loved to tell. There was Orion, the hunter, placed in the sky by Zeus. Ursa Major and Ursa Minor, the bears, they were sent to the stars by Zeus, too, to protect them from the jealousy of his wife, Hera. How many nights had they sat outside in the quiet and stared at the sky together? She could practically feel the warmth of his body, the smell of him and of the pine trees around their yard. "Look up at the stars every night. If you know your stars, Alice, you'll always know your home." He used to tell her this, and she thought he'd meant that she could use the stars to navigate home, like ancient mariners used to do. But now she wondered if he meant that the stars were a true way to know your place. The world changes—houses and people and towns—but the stars never do.

The loudspeakers whistled, and the principal spoke again: "Friends, it seems we have a visitor in our playground. A baby bear has found its way down from the woods. Animal control has been called, but . . ."

Her words were lost as all the students rushed to the

windows. Even Mrs. Zee came to see. A small bear, not much bigger than a good-size dog, danced and rolled around their playground. It batted at a swing and jumped back when the seat nearly hit it in the nose. "Ohhhh!" the kids cooed.

"I don't get it. Why can't we go outside and see it? It's just a cute little baby," Sofie Green said.

"Where there is a baby bear, there's a mama bear," Mrs. Zee said, and all her students nodded.

"My dad was out hunting once, and they saw a bear," Brady announced. "One of his friends decided to go right up to it."

"What kind of idiot would do that?" Liam asked.

"I'm pretty sure it was *your* dad's cousin," Brady said. "Anyway, this bear swiped right at my uncle's friend, knocked him flat on his back. There was blood and guts everywhere."

"Gross!" Emma replied.

"The bear was probably just startled," Melanie said, but her voice was quiet, and Alice wasn't sure if anyone else had heard.

"Yeah," Lewis said. "It was probably just trying to get away. It didn't mean to hurt anyone or anything."

"All right, softy," Brady said.

"Lewis is right," Mrs. Zee said. "Most animals don't want to hurt people, but if they get scared, they may attack. That's why we need to stay inside."

The bear started bounding toward the school, right toward

their first-floor classroom. It fell forward into a somersault and slid along the wet grass. The class giggled. When it popped up, it looked right at Alice. A smile spread across its face.

No, Alice thought. That was impossible.

Then Sophie whispered, "Alice, I think that it's looking at you."

Alice felt the gaze of her classmates—hot and intense. Where was her invisibility when she needed it?

"Once we were camping and this bear came into our campsite at night," Liam said. "We could see it through the tent, bashing around in our stuff. It ate all our bacon, so in the morning my dad went out and found a doughnut shop so we could have breakfast."

"It ate your raw bacon?" Brady asked.

Liam shrugged. "A bear's gotta eat."

"I thought they ate blueberries," Izzy said. "Like in *Blueberries for Sal*."

That was a book Alice's mom had read to her over and over and over again. *Kuplink, kuplank, kuplunk* she would sing as Sal dropped her berries into a pail. When they would go out picking on the blueberry plains, Alice would sometimes linger behind her parents hoping she, too, would run into a bear. She would not back away as Sal had. She would hold very still and watch the bear, and maybe she and the baby could be friends.

She still felt that ache, she had to admit. Alice leaned so far forward that her forehead touched the cold glass of the window. As much as she wanted the bear to ignore her, she also wanted to be out there with the cub. Wanted to hold out her hand and feel the bear's heavy paw in her own. How different it would be from the light weight of Dare when she hopped into her hand.

For a moment it almost seemed like the bear heard her longing. It stopped and pointed its nose into the air. Then it trotted toward the window. It was a goofy, bounding gate, and Alice was sure it was coming to her.

But it didn't.

It stopped by the window at the other side of the room as if something had caught its attention. It turned its head and went straight at the window. Straight to Melanie.

"Oh!" Mrs. Zee exclaimed. "Get back from the windows, kiddos. Back, back, back."

None of them moved.

The bear lifted its front paws and put them on the window. Then it let out a sad sound somewhere between a moan and a cry.

"What the?" Brady asked.

"Kids, please, step back."

Melanie lifted one hand and placed it flat on the window, right up against the bear's paw. Alice burned with jealousy. Melanie whispered something. Her lips barely moved. The bear trotted off across the playground and into the woods.

Chapter Sixteen
LEWIS

After hockey practice, Lewis hooked his bag on his shoulder and raced toward the door of the rink. He found himself pausing in front of the trophy case. Their runner-up trophy from the year before was on display in the center. Lewis's favorite thing in the case was an old picture of Alice's dad. In the photograph, Buzz was seventeen, but he looked younger to Lewis. He held a pen up in the air, and he had a crooked, goofy smile. Behind him, Donny held a Boston University jersey. Signing day. Alice's father had played four years there, won the Hobey Baker award and two national championships, and then he'd gone on to the Oilers where he played two seasons. He was as fast as anyone in the NHL but not as big, and he moved down to the American Hockey League, and then a year in Germany before he came back home. He and Donny bought the ice rink from Willy Laughton, who had owned it for years. Times were tough, and even though the town still loved its hockey, there were fewer folks who could afford all the gear. Buzz joined the Army Reserves. No one thought he'd be deployed. He did his monthly drills, his yearly trainings. And then, when Lewis and Alice were finishing up second grade, they sent him overseas. It was supposed to be a six-month deployment, but he was gone for a little more than a year. That was the life story of Buzz Dingwell—a story that Lewis had studied carefully—up to the point where things started to go south.

"Back before he went crazy," Brady said from behind Lewis.

Lewis hooked his gear back up on his shoulder. The strap dug in, but he didn't mind.

"Of course, from what I hear, he was never the great guy everyone always says he was." Brady smirked. "In fact, I heard a story about him and the witch in the woods. I wonder what your new girlfriend would think about that."

Lewis didn't want to, but he blushed.

"Where'd he even go?" Brady asked.

"None of your business," Lewis shot back.

That made Brady smile. He could see he'd gotten under Lewis's skin. "What I can't figure out is why Alice can't play anymore. It's her dad who's nutty, not her. I mean, she's a little bit nutty—"

"Shut up," Lewis said.

As they argued, some of the other boys from Lewis's grade

came in: Liam, Taylor, and a few of the fourth graders. Lewis played up an age group. So had Alice. Brady and the others were still in peewees.

Their eyes lit up at the obvious tension in the air.

"You guys were shoo-ins for the championship this year."

Lewis squared his chest. "We still are."

"Not without Alice you aren't."

Lewis didn't want to get into it with Brady. He had to go meet Melanie at the Museum to find the book so they could figure out—well, he wasn't sure what, exactly, but he was sure it was important. "I have to go," Lewis said. "Have fun at your little-kid practice."

As Lewis went to leave, Brady stepped in his way, and they bumped shoulders. "Hey!" Brady said.

"Watch yourself," Lewis shot back.

"You bumped into me!"

"You did!" Liam agreed. "You totally checked Brady."

Brady dropped his hockey bag. "Are you going to punch me? Go on, do it! I can't believe wimpy Lewis Marble is actually going to punch someone!"

"Fight!" Liam cried out gleefully.

Some of the older boys from Lewis's bantam team were starting to come out of the locker room.

"You okay, Lew?" Silas asked.

"Go ahead, Lulu, punch me! You'll get kicked off bantam, and then you guys will have no chance of winning!"

"Watch yourself," Trevor said.

Lewis felt his fists clamp. He hated fighting. He hated hitting. It was the one thing about the sport that bugged him, the way the players would throw their gloves to the ice and start pounding each other. Prove it by putting pucks in the net, that's what he always thought. But right at that moment he wanted to punch something, and Brady was inviting him. He stuck out his chin.

"Whoa, whoa, whoa—what's going on here?" Coach Donny strode out of the locker room. He towered over all the boys and made them realize just how small they were. "Did I hear something about a fight?"

"No, Coach," Brady said. His voice dripped syrupy sweet and only made Lewis want to punch him more.

"I wanted to punch him, but I didn't," Lewis said.

Donny raised his eyebrows. "Wasn't quite expecting that level of honesty, but I'll take it." He clapped his hands together. "Peewees, change up. Bantams, get lost. Lewis, a word."

When the other boys were gone from the waiting area, Donny asked, "You angry about something?"

"Yes," Lewis replied.

"You want to talk about it?" Donny asked.

"No," Lewis said.

"I figured. You and Alice. She doesn't want to talk to me, either. Hey—maybe you two should talk to each other!"

Lewis scowled.

"It was worth a shot. You wanna skate it off?"

Lewis wanted to. Even after the sprints they'd done, he wanted to do more. He wanted to skate until his legs exploded. "I have somewhere I have to be," he said. "I'll run."

He turned to go, but Donny had something else to say. "I'm proud of you, Lew. Buzz would be as well. Nothing harder than not punching someone who's asking for it."

Lewis figured there were a lot of things that were harder than that, but he said, "Thanks, Coach," and pushed his way out the door.

The rain had settled into a cold mist that pricked his face. His bag thumped against his back. He wiped water out of his eyes as he ran across the street right to the Museum. Melanie appeared out of nowhere, like a ghost.

"Hi," Lewis huffed.

"Hi," she replied.

They stared at each other. Lewis was glad his cheeks were already pink from running.

"Should we go in?" she asked.

"What? Oh, sure."

He hesitated at the door. There was one potential problem: Alice.

When the bells rang, Alice looked up from her perch behind the counter. She was using a price-tag gun to label the bottoms of army figurines. She narrowed her eyes at them. The mannequin next to her seemed to glare, too.

"Hi, Alice!" Melanie called cheerfully.

Alice kept putting price tags on soldiers, lining them up in neat, even rows.

Lewis tugged Melanie by the sleeve over to the bookshelf.

The books were carefully organized by Henrietta. Lewis started in the children's area and found nothing. He pointed to a small shelf. "That's folklore and mythology," he told Melanie. "You check there, and I'll look in short stories."

While he looked, he stole glances at Alice. She had her eyes trained on the television, but he couldn't believe she was watching Mary Lawrence talk to local politicians about the candidates for governor. Anyway, the sound was turned down so she couldn't hear their yelling even if she were watching.

"It's not here," Melanie said. "Maybe it's out back. We should ask."

"We're not ask—"

But Melanie was already back across the store. "We are looking for a book. A special book," she said to Alice.

"The books are over there," Alice replied.

"We thought maybe it was held in back."

"I doubt it," Alice said.

"Come on, Alice," Lewis said.

She turned to look at him, eyebrows raised. He didn't know why she was so mad. She was the one who had stopped talking to him.

On the television, Mary Lawrence launched into the local

news roundup, leading off with a story about the park. Alice grabbed the remote and turned up the volume.

"A storm damaged much of the equipment at this work-site," intoned Mary Lawrence. "Now some locals are wondering if building should continue."

Alice gritted her teeth. Lewis, too, felt his body tense. Locals like who?

Mr. Sykes's face filled the screen. Of course.

"Independence is fortunate to have a number of places for outdoor recreation," Mr. Sykes said. His face was stiff, and his eyes shifted from side to side. "What we don't have are jobs."

"Turn that off!" Henrietta yelled from the back room.

Alice didn't move, so Lewis picked up the remote and clicked off the TV.

"It's called *The Story Web*," Melanie said, as if she'd missed the whole news story. She didn't notice Alice's face go pale. "It's a thick book. Blue cover, I think—"

"Who told you about that?" Alice asked.

"About the book? My parents did. They used to read it to me—"

"Stop it," Alice said. "Just stop it."

"Alice," Lewis interrupted. He leaned in. "I don't know what this is about, but—"

She glared at him. Hard. "Don't lie to me, Lewis Marble. You know I can always tell when you're lying."

"I'm not—"

"Did my dad tell you about it once? Is that what this is?" Alice shook her head. "I mean, I know I—I know I haven't—and your—" She sounded like she was choking on the words. "Find some other way, okay?" Her voice cracked.

"Alice, I have no idea what you are talking about."

Alice squeezed a soldier in her hand.

Then it occurred to Lewis why Alice was getting so upset. The Story Web meant something to her. "Do you know about the web?" he asked.

She crossed her arms across her chest. "Lewis, I swear to you—"

"Guys," Melanie interrupted.

"I'm not messing with you, Alice. Something's wrong. Something's wrong in Independence, and there's this giant web in the woods, and—"

"Guys, look."

"What?" Alice exclaimed.

"Look!" Melanie pointed out the window.

There, in the middle of Main Street, stood a moose.

It tossed its head from side to side, its antlers coming dangerously close to a banner for the Harvest Fest that crossed the street.

"A moose," Alice whispered.

As if it heard her, it turned. It took a step.

"Oh my g—" he began. Before he could finish, he felt someone brush past him. Alice. Followed almost immediately by Melanie. They pushed through the door one right after the other, the bells chiming to mark their exit. After a moment's hesitation, he went after them.

Alice stood in the middle of the street, practically nose to nose with the moose. Melanie was right behind her.

Lewis walked as slowly as he could toward Alice's stiff back. He told himself that there was not a moose standing directly above Alice and Melanie. Moose were herbivores, he was pretty sure, but they could stomp on a person. Or it could ram the girls and flip them into the air with the impressive set of antlers that swept off the top of his head like dragon wings.

The moose, though, just stood there. Its nostrils flared, open and shut, open and shut, emitting puffs of white air. As Lewis drew near, it tapped one front hoof against the street, but that was it.

Alice's breath came in fast puffs, too, audible and shallow. But Melanie was still. Then she reached out her hand as if she were going to pet the moose right on top of his nose, like it was a horse.

"Melanie," Lewis whispered. "I don't think you should do that."

The moose took a single step back.

Alice still had not moved.

The moose nudged its muzzle against her shoulder, and she gasped.

There was a squealing of brakes. The moose stiffened.

"Get back, kids! Get back from that animal!"

Chapter Seventeen
MELANIE

The moose's fur shines like coffee fresh from a pot. She feels her hand going up. What would it be like to touch that fur? Would it be soft like a fox or rougher and matted, like a beaver? The bellow beneath his chin quivers.

Melanie grasps her pendant. She whispers the spider's name. *Maratus volans.*

The moose focuses on Alice. So curious, moose are, and this one has trained all his curiosity on Alice. He snorts out a puff of air, like clearing his throat. Then he presses his nose into Alice's shoulder.

Be brave. The words are clear as whip-poor-will calls in her mind.

"He's telling you to be brave," Melanie whispers to Alice.

"I know." Then, softer, to the moose, "I will."

"Get back, kids! Get back from that animal!"

White truck. Not one scratch. Not one dot of mud, not even on the silver platter hubcaps.

The door swings open. A work boot steps out. A man follows the boot, then hitches his belt up over his waist. His keys jangle together. "I'll take care of it."

His words are solid, sure, final, and wrong.

He reaches into the back of his truck. There is a clicking sound, latches being undone. Then the grating sound of metal against metal.

The man emerges, raindrops on the brim of his ball cap, holding a rifle across his body.

No! Melanie thinks, but the voice that calls out isn't hers.

Chapter Eighteen
ALICE

"No!" Alice screamed.

She held up both hands, putting herself between the moose and Brady's dad.

"Out of the way, Alice," he said to her.

"It's a moose," Alice replied, as if that were a reasonable response.

"Exactly. What's a moose doing in the middle of the road?"

"There must be something wrong with it." Alice recognized that voice: Becky Clancy, Izzy's mom.

"Sure is," Brady's dad said. "Best thing to do is put it down."

"Last I checked, that's not your job, Alan." Henrietta walked out from under the awning of her store. Her layers of clothes seemed brighter and heavier out here. "Anyone call Officer Hammersmith?"

Brady's dad scoffed at that. "Why call for backup when I can take care of it myself?"

"No," Alice said, more firmly this time. She wasn't looking at him, though, she was looking at Izzy, who had appeared in the crowd with her mom.

"Officer Hammersmith won't shoot him," Lewis said. "She'll sedate him, maybe, but she won't kill him." His voice was calm, with none of the jittery edge of Mr. Sykes's voice.

"Right," Alice agreed, though she wasn't positive Lewis was correct. He was right beside her, though, and she was reminded how sure he always made her feel. When an opponent had the puck and she'd see him zipping in on defense, or when Izzy was mad at her, or when she messed up on her spelling test. He was always there. Always Lewis. Even in the early days with her dad, when the cracks were first starting to show, she'd go and find Lewis, and the world would feel more right.

"Kids," Mr. Sykes said. "This isn't some 'save the world, all animals are precious' mumbo jumbo. This moose is dangerous."

"You're the one who looks dangerous," Alice said.

"You ever even shoot that before?" Lewis asked.

"Why don't you kids just come out of the way," Becky

Clancy said. She had her phone in one hand, ready to dial. "You come with me. I'll drive you all home and—"

"He's not dangerous," Alice said, and then, to prove it, she held out her hand toward the moose. She moved too fast, though, and the moose backed up, his back leg pressing against a small car. The driver crawled out of it, hands over his head.

Alice lowered her hands. "It's okay," she said to the moose. It was the way she sometimes had to approach her dad, if he'd just woken up and wasn't quite in their world yet. *It's okay, Dad. It's me, Dad.*

"It's okay," she said again. "We're all safe here."

Why hadn't she said that to her dad that afternoon? Then maybe everything would be different. Maybe—

The moose interrupted her thoughts by lowering his head. She moved carefully toward him. "It's okay. I'm here."

The moose pawed the ground with his hoof.

"Alice Dingwell," Becky Clancy said.

Alice looked past her, at Izzy, who wrinkled her nose. Alice gave a tiny shrug as if to say, *I have no choice.* That's the thing with friends—even former friends. You can talk to them with just the smallest of gestures and they understand. So Alice understood, too, when Izzy replied with a simple shake of her head. *You must not do this.* It was too weird, too Melanie-like.

But Alice kept walking. She held up her hands. "It's okay. I'm here."

Which meant things weren't just temporarily over with Izzy. This wasn't just another go-round on the carousel, up and down and up and down. Their friendship, if you could call it that, was well and truly over.

In the moment, Alice didn't care. She only cared about the moose.

"Shh," Alice told him. She was only a few inches away from him now. She held out her hand, palm-side down, the way you did when you met a new dog, to let him smell you. The moose snuffled at her hand. "Okay," she said.

On the street, no one moved.

"We need to go, moose," Alice told him.

She reached into her pocket and pulled out a piece of hard candy that Ms. Barton had given her that morning in the school office. "One second," she whispered as she unwrapped the candy. Sour apple flavor. A moose ought to like that. He sniffed it and curled his lips, ready to bite. Alice walked around him while pressing one hand against his neck to get him to move with her. He followed her hand with the candy. Walking backward, she led him through the cars. He stayed right with her, never trying to take the candy from her hand, as docile as a pony at a fair.

They went down the alleyway alongside the Museum, and Becky Clancy again called Alice's name, but neither Alice nor the moose paid any mind. They walked across the blacktop, and across a narrow field, and into the woods. Together they disappeared.

They stood still among the trees. The moose's breath came in heavy snorts that made white puffs in the air. Alice exhaled herself, adding a thin trail of white to his clouds. He held his head high, looking deeper into the woods. It reminded Alice of when Lewis got a penalty called against him. When the ref explained the call, Lewis would just stare high into the stands, like it didn't bother him. But Alice knew it did, and she was pretty sure the moose was feeling the same way: embarrassed, indignant, and maybe a little mad.

"You can't come into town," she told him. "People get scared, and when people get scared, they do foolish things."

The moose punched his hoof into the dirt and pointed to the woods with his antlers.

With a trembling hand, Alice stroked his neck. The fur on his neck was matted at the top, like he had rolled in mud—and perhaps he had—but below it was soft, like an old teddy bear.

The moose breathed out between his lips, making them quiver back and forth. Alice smiled. "You're a good moose," she said. "I know you're a good moose. But other people don't understand you. They aren't used to animals just coming into town. They aren't used to wild animals at all anymore really. They think you're the other kind of wild—the dangerous kind of wild, like mean and violent and unpredict-able." She stroked him again. "People will get all worked up." Her voice hitched. "You don't understand what happens when people think you're dangerous. They send you away. They send you—" She stopped talking and rubbed at her runny nose.

Overhead, grackles and crows flew back and forth. There was even a brave little chipmunk that hopped toward them. Alice wanted so much to make the moose understand the dan-ger he was in.

"They say it's for your own good when they send you away. That you need to get better. But you're just being you. You're just being a wonderful, curious moose."

Alice leaned her head against the moose's neck. He let out a gentle sound, like a cow sighing. He rubbed his chin against the top of her head. She could practically hear her father's voice in him. *Be bold, be brave, be fierce.*

"I'm trying," she whispered.

She was crying now, freely. The tears slipped down her face. The moose sniffed them, and for a moment Alice thought he was going to lick the salt right off her cheeks. Instead he backed away, still staring right at her.

"Go," she whispered.

He didn't move.

"Go," she whispered again.

He closed his eyes, slowly, then opened them again. He

stared right at her with his chocolate brown eyes, so deep and soulful. She wondered if she could jump on his back. If they could ride off to someplace new, someplace wonderful and safe for both of them. The moose, though, turned and ran off into the woods without her.

Moose

When Moose left the forest, the other animals took notice. Moose left so rarely, and almost always in the twilight hours. Moose, you see, was rather shy.

Shy but curious.

And the people always did seem to react well when he did appear.

There was the time he got stuck with green pine and shining lights around his neck. The time he played with the children on the ice and brought them back their strange black food—what humans counted as food he could not understand. Each time he had been met with delight.

So, he lumbered out of the woods, to the road.

The cars stopped.

The birds stopped.

The boy stopped.

The girl did not stop until they stood nose to nose.

She smelled like salt licks and honey. He felt her heart aching or perhaps saw it in her eyes. Whatever the reason, he leaned forward and snuffed his snout against her shoulder.

Then there had been the shouting, the man with the loud killing stick, more shouting.

She held out her hand to him. Together they went into the woods. Her pain had nearly knocked him over. It was in her eyes and pulsed off her body. He had wished she could come with him, deep into the forest where the other humans couldn't harm her.

But they needed her to act first. He knew she understood him. He had told her about the problem, how urgent it was.

It hadn't been enough. The girl went back into town, and he went back into the woods, the state of the web just as precarious as it had been before.

Chapter Nineteen
LEWIS

Lewis's bedroom was tucked at the top of the stairs. In summer it was hot, even with a fan running in the window. In the winter it was cold, and he stacked four blankets on top of himself. But it was his. His sisters had to share, two to a room a floor below him.

He had a small bedside table with a hockey-stick lamp. There was a shelf over his bed with trophies and Bruins bobblehead toys. His bureau was pressed right up against his bed, and sometimes he made blanket forts and hid under them and pretended he was an astronaut or an undersea explorer or an archaeologist in a mine. Even now at eleven years old he sometimes played the games, although he didn't tell anyone.

That night he was waiting in his bed for his mother. It was a three-blanket night, and he was rubbing his fingers against the fleece of a University of Maine stadium blanket while he waited for her. She had promised to tell him a story.

He had asked for a story for the first time in months. Maybe it had even been a year. But that day had been . . . different. He still hadn't found just the right word for it. Frightening and exhilarating and, in a weird way, beautiful. Watching Alice go off with that moose, he'd been proud of her but also a little jealous that it had been her to star in the story, not him. All this had swirled around his head, and he wanted some time with his mom, one-on-one. He couldn't just ask her to come sit with him. What would his dad make of that? An eleven-year-old boy who still wanted his mommy? So he had said, "Hey, Mom, you think you could tell me a story tonight?" He had tried to sound casual. His dad raised his eyebrows, but his mom had said, "Sure, hon."

He heard her feet before he saw her appear in the doorway. She wore an old sweatshirt of his father's. Her long hair was pulled back in a ponytail, and her cheeks were red. "I'm here," she announced. "What story do you want me to read to you?"

"Can you tell me a story?"

"Like make one up? I'm not very good at that. You really should ask your father if that's what you want. Do you remember the stories he used to tell you all? You were so young, but—"

"I remember." His father used to make up long and

twisting tales to tell them all before bedtime. But the girls had outgrown it, and Lewis supposed his father didn't have the time or energy to make up such stories for an audience of one now that he was commuting back and forth to Portland every day. And also, it seemed his father wasn't interested in stories anymore. If it wasn't about the governor's race or college hockey, he didn't seem to care.

"How about I tell you my moose story again? That's a good one considering the events of the day."

"I don't know your moose story."

"I never told you about the moose?"

Lewis shook his head. "No, I don't think so."

"Well, this is a great story!" she promised. She scooted her body over next to his. Both their legs stretched out side by side, and they were the exact same length. By the end of the school year, he'd be taller than her, and he wondered if that would change anything, if she would still come up to his bed to tell him a story when he asked.

Lewis's mom cleared her throat. "It was a dark and stormy night," she began.

"Are you kidding me?" he asked. "I thought this was a true story."

"What? It was. Thunder. Lightning, all of it. Anyway, you asked me to tell a story, so I'm telling you a story."

"Okay, go on," he said.

"It was a dark and stormy night. It had been a ridiculously

stormy fall and winter. Your aunt April and I were sleeping over at our nana and pop's house. This was just a couple of weeks after our dad had died. It started snowing earlier that day and hadn't stopped. Then there was the thunder. The windows in our room rattled with each boom. We were in the same bed, under an old quilt that smelled like mothballs. Aunt April said, 'I think the world is ending, Shiloh. I think the monsters are here.' You know there's no such thing as monsters, right?"

"Yes, Mom, I know."

"Good. I told April it was just the thunder and an old house during a bad winter, but she wouldn't listen. She liked to spend time with Buzz Dingwell, and he was always telling tall tales, stuff he read in old books and comics. Anyway, she got out of bed and went right to the window, her nose pressed against the glass, and told me the earth was cracking. I didn't believe her, but I still went up and stood next to her. We stood there shivering in our nightgowns. I didn't see what she saw and was about to tell her to stop being so dramatic when a bolt of lightning flashed and there it was: a black crack stretching out from Nana and Pop's front lawn all the way into the nothingness. It was darker than a cave at night and shimmery like oil."

Lewis could picture the crack in his head. But what did it mean?

"We ran straight back into bed and had that quilt over us

all night. We didn't care how much it stank. In the morning, we got all bundled up in our snowsuits and went to investigate that crack in the earth. It was full of stuff: a sled, an old wheelbarrow, Lucy Price's bicycle, a string of Christmas lights, a bunch of posters from the election just passed. And stuck deep in the crevasse was a moose. He had the most soulful brown eyes I'd ever seen. I hadn't seen anything like them until you were born, Lew. That's why we call you Moose sometimes."

She tugged him a little closer to her, and he didn't mind.

"Anyway, April about flipped her lid. She saw those antlers and started screaming, 'A monster, a monster!' That got that moose terrified. He backed up, but his antlers were too wide, and they got stuck along the edge of the ditch. April was screaming, and the moose was bellowing. Then Pop came out. He looked at us, and he looked at that moose, and he said, 'Well, I guess I'm going to have to get my gun.'"

"What? Why?" Lewis asked

"I don't think he thought the moose could be saved. He was going to put him out of his misery."

Lewis could understand that. He would never want to see an animal suffer. "The moose in town wasn't stuck, and Mr. Sykes wanted to shoot him anyway. He had a rifle and—"

"Right out there on Main Street? Swinging it around?"

Lewis nodded. "Alice got between him and the moose."

"Oh, Alice," Lewis's mom said. "Of course she did that."

Lewis wasn't sure what she meant by that. "The moose

wasn't bothering anyone, Mom. He wasn't dangerous. Why would Mr. Sykes want to shoot him?"

His mom thought on that for a moment. "People get scared, Lew. When people get scared, they think the best way to deal with the problem is to go on the attack."

"I guess that makes sense," he said. He thought of hockey games, where the other team was bigger, maybe got a few goals in. His team never retreated. They attacked, attacked, attacked.

"Well, unless the threat isn't actually a threat," she said.

"Like the moose," Lewis said.

"Like the moose," his mom agreed. "And other things. Mr. Sykes believed the moose was dangerous. Who knows why. Because he's big, I suppose. Big and not usually on Main Street. So Mr. Sykes's brain said, *Danger, danger, danger!*"

"I wasn't scared of the moose," Lewis said. "I was scared of Mr. Sykes." He tucked his head closer to her and spoke into her shoulder. "It's the most scared I've been in ages."

She squeezed him tight. "Oh, Lew."

"So what happened to your moose?" he asked.

"Oh, right! Nana called the police, and they sent Buck Hammersmith the animal resource officer—Piper Hammersmith's dad. Bet she's been busy this week. Anyway, he came out and gave one look at the moose and was like, 'Um, this is something I've never seen before. We need to call the wardens.' We just sat out there and waited. April calmed down, and we sat on the edge of the ditch and talked to the moose in soothing voices until the wardens showed up. They gave him a tranquilizer, and he fell asleep, but he couldn't lie down, because of the antlers being stuck in the ditch. Then the wardens went into the ditch and wrapped a sling around the moose. They brought in a little crane, and backhoes, and trailers. It took most of the day. April and I watched the whole thing while we ate sandwiches. Nana made coffee, and we brought it out to the men. Finally, they hauled him out of the ditch. They took the sling off him, and they gave him a shot to undo the effect of the tranquilizer. But here's the strangest thing: he didn't run off. He walked right up to us and stared at me and nuzzled the top of my head with his nose. It was the softest thing I had ever felt. It reminded me of my dad. He used to tousle my hair and call me sweet pea. Then he snatched an apple right out of April's hand and ran off into the woods."

"I think maybe that's the same moose we saw."

"Honey, that was ages ago."

"How long do moose live? Because I swear Melanie and Alice and I saw him today. He came right up to Alice and nuzzled her, just like you said. Remember how her dad would always touch her shoulder before she went out on the ice? It was like that."

Lewis's mom pulled him closer to her. "I guess it's possible. We could look it up."

There was something else familiar about his mom's story: that crack in the ground was just like in Melanie's story: the earth cracking apart with ice and snow all around. Was that the Freezing? Had it almost come before?

They sat together for a while, him pressed up against her. Her shirt was soft and smelled familiar. Her hair tickled his cheek.

"What were you even doing on Main Street?" she asked him. "You were with Alice?"

"I was with Melanie," he said.

"Who is this Melanie person anyway?"

"She's just a girl." Lewis looked at his lap.

"The one your sisters were teasing you about?" She rubbed her hand through his hair. "When you were a kid, a little kid, girls used to make you swoon. You couldn't even look at a girl if you thought she was cute." She let the statement hang in the air. When Lewis didn't say anything, she kept going. "It's perfectly normal; I mean, you're just the right age to start having an interest in girls. Maybe a little earlier than your friends. I know I certainly had crushes when I was your age."

"She's just— She's always been so quiet, and I've never really talked to her, but now I am and it turns out she's really nice. She lives with her aunt up in—up in that old house off Minnow Lane."

"The Bird House?" his mom asked.

"Yeah. She lives there with her aunt."

"And she's been hanging out with you? And Alice? You and Alice together?"

"Sort of."

"It's just that you and Alice, I mean, since her dad went away, you haven't spent much time together."

They still weren't spending much time together, not as far as she could help it anyway, but it was all too complicated to explain to his mom.

"You can ask me about him," she told him. "About Buzz. I'll tell you what I can."

He thought about it. But what could he ask her? He knew where Buzz was. At the psychiatric hospital down near Boston getting help. Maybe the rest of it wasn't his business.

"I'm good," he said.

His mom leaned over and kissed the top of his head. "Sleep well, my friend."

She stood up and walked around the end of his bed to the door. She paused for a moment as if she wanted to say something else, but if she did, she kept it to herself and left Lewis alone to think about moose and missing parents and missing friends.

Chapter Twenty
ALICE

Uncle Donny burst through the door waving the local newspaper. "You're famous, Alice!" he exclaimed and dropped the newspaper on the table in front of her. Her mom peered over her shoulder, and they both read the headline:

MOOSE ON THE LOOSE!!!—in giant, bold letters. Underneath, also in bold letters but not quite as large: *Bear, moose, and more terrorize local young people.*

"It's your night off, Donny," Alice's mom said as Alice began to read the article. Most of the story was wrong. It talked about the bear and the lockdown. They interviewed Brady Sykes, of all people, who said he was glad to get out of ELA classwork. Alice hoped Mrs. Zee read that and really gave it to him.

Uncle Donny pulled off his hat and held it in front of him, like he was trying to be a gentleman. "Tonight I am here to be the hero, rescuing you from the doldrums of your day-to-day existence."

Alice looked up from the paper. "Gee, thanks," her mom said.

"Also, I am here to celebrate my fellow hero, Alice, the saver of the moose." He took the paper from her and read out loud, *"The moose was led away by one child, reportedly Alice Dingwell, daughter of local legend Buzz Dingwell."* He shook the paper. "I see they left out the part about your being the niece of local super-legend Donny Dingwell."

Alice's mom rolled her eyes, but she was smiling.

Alice took the paper back. Becky Clancy was quoted. She was all in a tizzy, saying the streets weren't safe and demanding to know what animal control was going to do about the "scourge of wild creatures overrunning our streets." That was hardly accurate. Alice skimmed some more until she got to the part about Brady's dad: *Alan Sykes was on hand and was ready to shoot the moose if necessary. "My priority is protecting this community,"* he said. *"No matter the threat, I know what my responsibility is."*

Alice frowned. They had not been in any danger. Not even for one minute.

"Why are you really here?" Alice's mom asked Donny.

"It's Family-Style Spaghetti Night at the Spaghetti Shed. Last time I went by myself and tried to get the family portion, Ashley gave me a hard time. She said I had to bring a family."

Alice's mom smirked. "Any family?"

"Well, sure, I suppose any family would do. But I'd prefer it to be my family."

Alice's mom stood up and wiped her hands on her jeans. "I could be convinced," she said.

Alice's heart soared. She loved the Spaghetti Shed. She dropped the paper on the table. The second story on the front page was about the park. *Park Construction Halted ... Forever?* The storm had damaged the equipment, and there wasn't money in the town budget to replace it, which made some people question if they had enough money for a new park. There was a picture of Brady's dad and his quote: *"Do we really need a Buzz Dingwell Park?"*

Alice pushed the newspaper away in disgust. Her mom handed Alice her raincoat. "So, a moose, huh? You never mentioned that to me."

"We were totally safe."

Her mom arched her eyebrows but didn't push Alice. "It's been quite the week, huh? Crazy stuff going on at the hospital. I swear we've had more fistfights in the past two weeks than in my whole time working there."

"What are they fighting about?" Alice asked.

"What does anyone fight about?" her mom replied as she shrugged on her own coat. "Money, politics, romance, cars."

"Sports," Donny added.

"You know what I think most of it is, though? It's just people wanting to be angry about something."

"Why would people want to be angry?" Alice asked.

"Sometimes it feels good to be angry." Her mom sighed and pushed her bangs out of her face.

"You know what makes me angry?" Donny asked. "Being hungry. Let's go!"

He hustled them into the car, and they drove through town to the old barn that had been turned into Alice's favorite restaurant. "You aren't the first Dingwell to have a run-in with a moose, you know," Donny said as he eased his truck into a parking spot.

It was warm and buzzing with most of the tables already taken. The smell of garlic overwhelmed Alice. Oversize televisions showed football and basketball. The Bruins game hadn't started yet.

Everyone smiled and waved as they came in, and Donny stopped at several of the tables to chat. Alice's stomach grumbled. Her mom looked around the room as if checking for someone. Alice figured she was remembering who wasn't there.

"How's the team looking this year, Alice?" Jed Brighton asked her. His kids had played hockey and had grown up and moved out of state like so many kids did, but Jed still came to all their games. He sat in the top row of the bleachers and cheered in his low, loud voice.

"Um," Alice began.

"We're looking strong," Donny said. "That Lewis Marble

can really skate, and the older boys are stepping it up, too. Got a real nice line we're looking forward to testing."

Alice peeked over at the booth where they always sat. It was empty, and she said, "Donny, I'm really hungry."

He put his hand on her shoulder, and they walked over to the booth. Before they even sat down, Ashley Spriggs arrived. She was maybe five years younger than Donny. She had lots of blond hair that she wore in a gravity-defying bun on the top of her head. She put a bowl of popcorn on the shiny wooden table and said, "Your regular pitcher, Donny?"

"Yes, ma'am," he said. "If by regular, you mean root beer."

Alice glanced at her mom.

"Fine," she said.

Donny held out his fist for a bump. Alice tapped it, and Donny grinned.

"So a pitcher of root beer and the spaghetti and meatball family special," he said.

"Back in a minute," Ashley said.

Uncle Donny took a handful of popcorn and started throwing pieces into his mouth.

"So, what's the story about the moose?" Alice asked.

Uncle Donny threw a piece at her mouth. She batted it away. He raised an eyebrow but didn't say anything about her reflexes and how they hadn't dulled at all.

Before he could start the story, though, Frank Lakim slid into the booth next to him.

"JoEllen," he said.

Alice's mom nodded and took a piece of popcorn from the bowl.

"I'm glad you're here," Frank said. "Both of you."

Alice thought she saw her mom roll her eyes.

Alice knew she was the one being left out. She scooped up a handful of popcorn and tried throwing them into her own mouth. She got three in a row before one bounced off her cheek.

"I heard about construction on the park," Frank said. "How it stalled."

"Temporarily," Donny said.

Alice chewed the popcorn in her mouth slowly. The buttery pieces were suddenly too salty and too rich.

"Maybe," Frank said. He nodded toward the bar. Alan Sykes sat there, a golden-hued beer and a plate of cheese fries in front of him. Alice loved cheese fries.

"What do you mean?" Donny asked. Alice knew exactly what Frank meant.

"Alan is thinking that maybe the town should use the space for something different."

"Like what?" Alice's mom asked.

"There's some interest from TotalMart."

Donny shook his head and leaned back. "No way one of those is moving into Independence."

"Folks could use the jobs, Donny," Frank said. "That's how Alan's selling it. You know it's true. Since the mill closed—"

"The mill closed almost thirty years ago," Donny said.

"And what a mess that was," Frank replied. "Thought the town was going to rip itself apart."

Alice stopped tossing popcorn. "What do you mean?" she asked.

"It's complicated, kiddo," Frank said. "Boring grown-up stuff."

"Boring grown-up stuff like what?" Alice asked.

Frank sighed. "Back in the seventies, the mill was sold to some big conglomerate in Iowa—"

"Indiana," Donny corrected.

"One of those I-states," Frank said. "It doesn't really matter. What matters is the mill stopped being profitable in the nineties. Paper was being made more cheaply in other places. They were going to sell it. Some folks wanted to give 'em big tax breaks to stay. Others wanted to try to talk to some of the international firms. There was one from South Africa that was buying up Maine mills. Other people wanted the town to buy the mill itself."

"What happened?" Alice asked.

"Nothing. The town couldn't decide. Too much fighting. The mill failed. People lost their jobs."

Alice thought of the empty mills and the empty storefronts. Donny shook his head.

"The answer isn't some big-box store," Alice's mom said.

"We'll bounce back," Donny agreed. "I've been reading;

towns in the southern part of the state, they're fixing up their mills, bringing in new businesses."

"That takes time. And money. TotalMart is here now."

"Whose side are you on?" Alice's mom asked.

"What do you mean?" Frank asked. "Why do you think I sat down? Alan's going to make a move."

Alice swallowed her popcorn and wished Ashley would hurry with the root beer.

"Let him try," Donny said.

"Buzz wouldn't have just sat here eating popcorn," Frank said.

"Don't," Alice's mom said. Just one word. Frank shut his mouth.

Donny drummed his fingers on the table. "Not now, okay?" Frank looked at his meaty hands.

"It's family night," Donny said. "Let me think on it." Then he grinned, like he was shaking off the bad mood. "The moose got into the mill once it closed. Remember that?" he asked Frank.

"It got stuck in some of the old equipment."

"Right," Donny said. "I was just about to tell Alice about the time we played hockey with a moose. You ever hear about that?"

"I've heard all Buzz's stories," Frank said. "And I think my supper's ready." He slid back out of the booth and gave Donny a little salute.

"'Night, JoEllen. G'night, Alice. Keep that glove down."

Alice looked at the table, but her mom said goodbye.

"Okay," Donny said. "Now we can get down to business. Here is the incredible true story of the world's worst hockey team and the most amazing game ever played."

Waxwing and Cat

Thunk!

Waxwing startled from her sleep, falling out of the tiny bed in the home that the girl gave her.

She blinked open her eyes and saw—

Meow!

Waxwing hopped back from the evil cat whose face filled one of the small openings of the house.

Escape! It was her only hope. She must go into the woods. There she could find Moose and confess her failure.

Waxwing moved slowly. The cat struck! It pressed its paw through the gap. Its front leg was not long enough, thankfully, and Waxwing darted away.

The house had stairs, and Waxwing took them, hopping carefully down one to the next.

Oh, how she wished her wing worked! She would fly

above this dreadful cat. Instead she slipped out an opening on the lower level. She dropped to the floor, and almost instantly the cat was upon her. She tucked under something warm and shiny—a little overhang that protected her. Slowly, slowly, trying not to draw its attention, she hopped. She could see her exit route: a small hole in the floor that led who knew where. She just knew the cat couldn't follow her.

The cat feigned indifference, but Waxwing was wise enough to know that trick. She never took her eyes off the cat. Closer, closer, closer, and then, squeeze! She dropped through the hole, landing on a pile of soft leaves. Outdoors? Yes! She was outdoors. There were the woods! Her home! She moved slowly toward them. There were many dangers for a bird with a broken wing.

Chapter Twenty-One
ALICE

"You know the pond out behind that development on the other side of town? Benson's Pond?" Donny asked. "That used to be the site of mammoth, mega hockey games. It was the Frozen Four and the Stanley Cup and the Olympics all rolled into one. Boys would show up and we'd split into teams and just play our hearts out. Your dad and I would always be on the same team. *Here come the Dingwell boys!* We were undefeatable. It was great. Maybe a little too easy, though, so your dad and I started coming up with ways to challenge ourselves. Like, if I was in goal, I'd keep my eyes shut until I heard the skates practically on top of me. You should try that, actually, for practice."

Alice squirmed. Everyone talked like she'd be back on the ice any minute. Even Donny. Especially Donny.

"Anyway, your dad, he would grab a left-hand stick and try that. Or he'd make himself count to three when he got the puck before going on a breakaway. But we'd still always win."

"Donny!"

Alice looked at the sound of the booming voice. It was Jimmy Roberge, whose daughter Emma was in Alice's class. Alice looked but didn't see her.

Donny reached up, and the men shook hands.

Mr. Roberge asked how she and her mom were doing, which was such a strange thing to ask them, Alice thought. Everyone knew they were awful. Alice's mom told him they were doing well.

He sat down in the booth next to Donny.

"I'm just telling them about the old pond hockey games," Donny said.

Mr. Roberge helped himself to some of their popcorn. "Those were pretty legendary," he said.

"Remember how mad Alan Sykes would get?" Donny asked.

"Oh, he hated to lose." Mr. Roberge turned to Alice. "He made up a rule that no brothers could be on the same team just so Donny and your dad couldn't play together. I mean, he certainly wasn't worried about the Taylor brothers." He leaned in toward Alice. "Never met a smarter pair of brothers, but hockey was not their sport. You know Jason Taylor is working for NASA now?"

Donny nodded. "And Shane is a professor down at Boston University. Smart guys. I mean, maybe not quite as smart as Buzz and me—"

"Don't recall the Taylor brothers falling off any buildings."

"You fell off a building?" Alice asked.

"Now see, you're starting rumors about me. *I* didn't fall off any buildings. Anyway, we aren't talking about that—"

"Yeah, we don't want to summon the witch," Mr. Roberge said with a laugh.

"Anyway," Donny said. "Your dad was not happy about that rule. No one but no one splits up the Dingwell brothers."

"Are you talking about the World's Worst Hockey Team?" asked Bobby Bixby, a tall, lanky man. He was leaning over from the booth behind theirs.

"Classic game," Mr. Roberge said.

Bobby Bixby came around the end of their table. He had a little spaghetti sauce on the front of his white T-shirt. "I am a proud member of that team. Pip-squeak they called me. They put me in goal! And who was that kid who Buzz grabbed? Someone's little brother?"

"Dale Zelonis!" Uncle Donny said. "He was nine years old and spent every game chasing our loose pucks when they went off the ice and into the snow. That was Buzz's team.

The saddest team in the history of hockey. Everyone thought he was doing it to say that even with the worst players behind him, he could still win the game. But— Well, here's what happened." Donny leaned back, basking in the attention.

Ashley returned with the pitcher of root beer. She stayed and listened as Uncle Donny picked up the story.

"It's a Saturday in February. It's maybe ten degrees out, and the sun is high in the sky. One of those days where the sun is so bright on the snow you think you're going to go blind."

"Your dad and his team come marching in like soldiers. Their faces are dead serious, not even a hint of a smile. They skate out on the ice and do two laps around the pond," Mr. Roberge continued.

"Then he brings them together. He talks to them in a low, quiet voice. None of the rest of us can hear it. What did he say to you?" Uncle Donny asked Bobby Bixby.

"I'll never tell," Bobby replied.

"Well, they start banging their sticks against the ice, louder and louder, and they're whooping up at the sky. Alan Sykes looks a little scared, but we all take the ice, and the game starts. Your dad gets the puck first, of course, scoops it right away from Alan, and he's breaking down the ice right toward me. He's smiling. You know that smile, right? Lopsided and wild? He's got that look and he's coming so fast and no one is on him. I'm bracing myself, keeping my eye on the puck.

There's only one person who can stop your dad's slap shot, and that's me."

"But he doesn't shoot!" Bobby Bixby exclaimed. "He flicks it over to little Dale Zelonis, who smacks it right past Donny."

"I mean, it was no great shot, but I was not expecting it at all. Nice trick, right?"

"Dale was talking about that for weeks," Ashley said. She picked up the empty popcorn bowl and walked back toward the kitchen.

"Now we're on to them. Your dad gets the puck again, another breakaway. But I've got my eye on Dale and Jason. They aren't going to fool me again. Your dad skates the puck around the net. Dale and Jason wait in front of me. Both of them are concentrating so hard you can actually see the gears moving. Next thing I know, your dad's in front of me, Jason has the puck, and then *slam!* Bounces right off the pipes and into the net.

"The next play, Alan gets the puck. He's going down the ice with his wingmen beside him. Your dad is skating like he's doing a little twirl around the park. No urgency at all. Bobby, you were standing stock-still, and let me tell you, I wanted to yell out, 'Hand up! Hand up!' But you're just standing there, and Alan is ready to take his shot when out of nowhere comes Dale, and he checks Alan."

"He checks him!" Bobby exclaimed.

"Alan barely moves, but it's long enough for your dad to get the puck. He and Jason come streaking down the ice, passing the puck back and forth. Jason shoots. I dive. And it dribbles under my armpit. Under my armpit! How does that even happen? Well, Alan is now convinced that I'm a traitor, and he pulls me from goal and has me sitting on the bench. But it doesn't matter. Your dad's team beat us four to two. You know how many goals your dad scored? None. Absolutely none." Donny took a big swig of root beer. "You see, that's the thing about your dad. He doesn't like to lose, but he's no show-off." As Donny spoke about her dad, the other men started to look away. Alice could feel them getting nervous, like they weren't sure where this conversation was going or if they were going to talk about where Buzz was now. "He was the best hockey player I ever saw, and of course he knew he was good, just like you and Lewis know you're good, but he also knew that hockey is a team sport. Most of life is a team sport. I don't know what he said to those guys, but he convinced them that they were winners. That's what's truly amazing about your dad. It's what made him a truly amazing hockey player, what made him a good soldier, and what makes him a great father."

Everyone was quiet. Alice could tell when grown-ups didn't want to talk about something. They looked at their feet or they looked right past you. They made funny sighs or grunting noises. They played with the buttons on their shirts or the rings on their fingers. Bobby Bixby and Mr. Roberge did all those things.

Then Mr. Roberge slid out of the booth. "Good story," he said.

"Yeah," Bobby agreed. "Good story."

Without saying anything else, they went back to their own tables. Alice knew why. It was one thing to talk about the great and legendary Buzz Dingwell, hometown hero. It was another thing entirely to talk about Buzz Dingwell, the man who left his wife and daughter behind.

Ashley returned with a huge bowl of spaghetti and meatballs. "I expect that cleaned out before you go, Donny Dingwell," she told him.

"Consider it done," he said. He was still smiling, still glowing, like he hadn't even noticed what had happened with the other men.

He served Alice and her mom big bowls of spaghetti, then helped himself, heaping scoop after scoop.

"But what about the moose?"

"Yeah," Alice's mom said. "Where does the moose come into this tall tale?"

Uncle Donny grinned. "Nearly forgot that part. Well, your dad's team won, of course, but in the record books, it would've had an asterisk. We never finished the game."

"Why not?"

"Just as they scored their last goal, Alan picked up the puck and threw it toward the woods. He never was much of a sportsman. Next thing we hear is this awful moaning sound. No one moves. Then out of the woods comes Clem. That's what we called the moose. Clem. And he's got the puck in his mouth."

"No way!"

"Yep. He walks it over to us and just drops it on the ice. And he stares at us. He's got these big brown eyes like marbles, and I swear he looks at each of us in turn. None of us moves a muscle. So Clem, he lifts up his big front hoof—those things are mammoth, I tell you—and nudges the puck toward us."

"Then what?" Alice asked.

"Your dad got the puck," he said with a twitch of a smile. "And you know what happens when your dad gets the puck."

"He scores."

"That's right. The point didn't count, of course, but we're pretty sure it's the only time in history that a moose had an assist."

Alice settled back into her seat. "That's amazing," she said.

He smiled at her, a meatball poking his cheek out like a chipmunk's. Alice, though, was realizing something else: here was another story her father told her that was mostly true. Just like the stories about her mom and Henrietta Watanabe. An exaggeration, sure, but the basic facts were there. Could that mean the Story Web was real, too?

When they finished eating, Alice shrugged on her coat. The birds, the bear, the moose—could they all be trying to tell her something?

She was so lost in her thoughts that she didn't see Alan Sykes lurch toward her on the way to the door.

"This here is the little girl that kept me from bagging my first moose," he announced to the men standing around him.

"This little slip of a thing?" one of them asked.

Alice had never in her life been called a little slip of a thing. She was strong and powerful. She was bold, brave, and fierce.

"That's not how you wanna bag a moose, Alan," said Jimmy Roberge. "Some poor, confused bull out in the middle of the street. Not much of a story there."

"I'd say saving the town from a rabid moose is quite the story," Alan shot back.

"Way I hear it, it was Alice who saved the town. And the moose," Uncle Donny said.

Alan turned toward Donny, a thin smile on his lips. It was hard for Alice to see any of Brady there. Or any of the Brady she used to know.

"That park keeps going up, it's only going to get worse," he said.

"How's that?" Uncle Donny asked.

"Animals don't have a place to go," Mr. Sykes said.

"That was weeds and garbage before," Donny replied.

Alan shrugged. "I guess I'm just confused why you're suddenly against hunting."

"I'm against shooting harmless animals in front of children."

"Oh! Of course. It's all about the children." He smirked. "Why do you think I was ready to shoot the darn thing? Someone's got to step up to protect this town now that the great conquering hero is gone."

"Enough, Alan," Frank said. He put a hand on Mr. Sykes's arm, but Mr. Sykes shook it off.

"What? I'm not afraid to say it. Town worships those Dingwell boys, and what have they done? That run-down rink is all they've got to show for themselves. Can't even win a state championship."

Alice stepped forward, but her mom tugged her back.

"And if that park goes in, who benefits?" Mr. Sykes asked. "People go to the park, and they go to the rink. The Dingwells reap the profits. Get some real business in there and the whole town can benefit."

"Those stores never help the communities they're in,"

Alice's mom said, managing to keep her voice calm. "Taxes go up, and the wages aren't enough to live on."

"So we get that in whatever deal we cut. A certain tax rate. A certain wage. We can even get them to build us a park in a more central part of town. Heck, maybe we can get them to get the library up and running again. Who knows? All I know is they're sniffing around, and if we don't ask for anything, nothing is what we'll get."

"We don't need that kind of business here," Alice's mom said.

"Sure," Mr. Sykes scoffed. "We'll stick with blights like that rink."

"Watch it—" Donny said at the same time that Frank said, "Enough."

But it wasn't enough for Mr. Sykes. "You watch yourself, Donny. You don't have Buzz here to get your back. He's gone off and checked himself—"

"Enough," Alice's mom said. Loud and clear. "We're going home."

She took Alice's hand and pulled her out of the restaurant into the driving rain. Alice looked back over her shoulder. Through the window, she saw Uncle Donny. His jaw was set and his hands in fists. Part of her wanted him to punch Mr. Sykes, but only part of her, and she was glad when Uncle Donny just shook his head and came outside.

They were all soaked as they sat in the cab of the truck. Donny turned the heat way up, and none of them said a word the whole ride home. She went straight into her room and flopped onto her bed. It was several moments before she realized that her bedroom door had been open. Dare was gone.

Chapter Twenty-Two
MELANIE

If Alice wishes just a little harder, Melanie thinks she could disappear.

Mrs. Zee would say, in her matter-of-fact manner, "Well, that was unexpected."

But it would not be unexpected to Melanie. Melanie has been watching Alice, and disappearing is perfectly in character.

Alice, in general, holds as still as a bird eyed by a cat. Sometimes she forgets and makes a sudden movement, as if she is about to fly. Sometimes, it seems she almost remembers who she was. A hawk or a falcon, used to soaring fast and high, dazzling in flight. Like those birds, she could be cruel and sudden, diving to catch her prey. Izzy always broadcast her attacks with loud screeches—not that it gave her victim a chance to escape.

Melanie thinks that Alice attacked not because she wanted to but because she had to. Survival of the predator depends on defeating the prey. Of course, whether Alice meant to be cruel makes little difference to the victim.

Now, though, Alice is one of the frozen ones. Melanie knows all about that, but it doesn't make her any more eager to include Alice in the mission.

It's not up to Melanie, though. She has gathered evidence and is left with one conclusion: Alice is somehow necessary. There is the way that all the animals seem to be coming for Alice. First, the crow had landed at Alice's table in the cafeteria, and then the bear had been heading right for Alice until Melanie called it away. And the moose. Most of all the moose. Plus, there is the way Alice reacted when Melanie mentioned *The Story Web*. Alice *knows* something. Melanie needs to know what Alice knows.

Melanie writes two notes on plain white paper.

CLUBHOUSE

AFTER SCHOOL

URGENT

She folds them carefully and tucks them into Alice's and Lewis's lockers.

At recess she picks a daisy and plucks off its petals one at a time. *Yes, No, Maybe So. Yes, No, Maybe So.*

She lands on *Maybe So.* This is the best that she could hope for.

Chapter Twenty-Three
LEWIS

When Lewis arrived at the clubhouse, still clutching the note in his hand, Melanie wasn't there. Lewis figured she had to have been the one who had left it in his locker, since only Melanie and Alice knew about the clubhouse, and the note wasn't in Alice's handwriting. But no one was at the clubhouse. No people, anyway. There were, however, two squirrels, a chipmunk, three crows in the tree above, and a rodent-looking thing that Lewis thought might be an opossum, though he was fairly certain those were nocturnal animals. Sitting right on top of his crate of books was a small bird. It waved one wing at him as if in greeting. It looked just like the waxwing that Alice had rescued. That seemed impossible and yet, his understanding of what was and was not possible stood on shifting ground these days.

He sat next to the crate and looked at the bird that hopped

excitedly around. It swished one wing, quick and strong like a slap shot, all the while chirping to him. "I don't speak bird," Lewis said.

The bird nodded and stopped chirping, though it did keep dancing around on top of the box.

Lewis heard footsteps approaching, but it wasn't Melanie who stuck her head into the clubhouse. It was Alice. She had her winter coat zipped to her chin and an old hat pulled low. It looked like she was trying to disguise herself, but she didn't need to worry about Izzy and the other girls finding her out in the woods. Izzy's mom was spreading the word about rabid wild animals. Parents were starting to keep their kids indoors. Lucky for Lewis his mom figured she had raised four girls to near adulthood and Lewis would get there, too, one way or the other.

"Hi," Alice said. She stood at the threshold to the clubhouse. When they'd first built it, the door was above their heads, but now they needed to duck to get in.

"Hi," he said back.

Next to him, the bird started hopping and chirping frantically.

"She's not here?" Alice asked, waving a piece of paper.

"You got a note, too?" he asked, more than a little surprised.

"It was from Melanie, right?" she asked.

"That's what I figure." He looked at his hands in his lap,

wishing he knew the right thing to say. Instead he said, "I'm not sure why she gave *you* a note."

"Me either," Alice replied.

Bzeep. The bird chimed in.

"Dare?" Alice asked.

The bird hopped to the edge of the crate, jumped, uselessly flapping one wing, and hopped over to Alice. She crouched and held out her hand. The bird hopped right in. "What are you doing here?" she asked it.

"Is it really the same bird? You kept it?"

"She was at my house, but when I got home on Saturday night, she was gone. I can't imagine how she got out or how she got all the way here."

"Alice—" Lewis began. There was so much he wanted to ask her about. He wanted to ask her what had happened between her and Izzy and Sadie at the social. He wanted to ask her about her dad. Most of all, though, he wanted to ask about them. That was the hardest question.

Before he could, they heard a crashing sound outside. Melanie appeared around the corner with leaves in her hair and followed by a field mouse and what Lewis thought was a pheasant. Dare strained her neck to look at the newcomers but seemed put at peace when she saw Melanie.

"Good," she said. "I wasn't sure you would both come. With three of us, we should be safe."

"Safe?" Alice asked.

"Was I not clear about the danger? The urgency?"

"You weren't clear about anything." Alice's voice was icy, like a villain in a movie.

"All these animals, they're trying to tell us something very important. That's why they keep showing up," Melanie explained.

Lewis asked, "What do you mean they're trying to tell us something?"

Melanie looked at Alice when she answered. "I've seen the birds coming to you. The crow at lunch. The starlings in the woods. This little one," she said, pointing at Dare.

"To me?"

"And then the moose. That's how I know it's a problem. The birds, they're always talking, but moose are quiet, and when they want to talk, then you know it's serious. He came to you, and you have to listen."

"He came to you, too," Alice said.

"Because we both have a part in this. You and me. We're the ones connected to the web. I thought it was just me, but you have the connection, too."

"Connection?" Lewis asked. He was trying to keep up with the conversation. Melanie was right—there did seem to be something calling both girls, like what Mrs. Zee had been talking about. The call to action.

"The book," Melanie said. "You definitely know about the book, Alice. What about the web? Have you seen it? I think you have."

Alice said nothing. She just closed her eyes, and Lewis knew that she was going to refuse the call. He glanced over at Melanie. She was ready to go. So was he. Only, he hadn't been called. At least, he didn't think he had.

"We have to do something—" Melanie began.

"You're not making any sense," Alice told her.

"It's all very simple," she said. "The animals are communicating, and—"

Alice said, "Show it."

"What?" Melanie asked.

"If you can really talk to animals, then show us."

"Everyone can talk to animals." Melanie crossed her arms across her chest. "The real talent is making animals understand you. And understanding them. I'm not so good at that. But I can do a little." She bent over the bird in Alice's hand. "That's how I knew this was your bird. Also, she thinks that you are sad because your dad is far away."

"Anyone could've guessed that," Alice said. "Don't try to mess with my head." Her face was pinched. Lewis knew that wasn't a good sign.

"Melanie, maybe—"

Melanie interrupted him. "It's not magic or a trick. It's just being more attuned to nature." Melanie looked to Lewis like she wanted him to say something. But nothing he said to Alice these days came out right. It was like he had forgotten how to talk to her. Still, if there was even a chance, even one little thread still connecting them, maybe he could reach her. "I saw the web, Alice," he said. "It's bad."

Alice shook her head. "No," she said. Lewis could tell she didn't believe him. Had things really gotten so bad between them? He wished he could go back to that night. He wished he could've said the right thing or asked the right question. He looked at her and tried to catch her gaze. He could communicate his sorrow and guilt better that way. Looks and actions were so much easier than words. She wouldn't meet his eye.

Melanie said, "The moose came from the deep woods to warn us that the Freezing is coming. The first thing you need to understand is that there is far more to the world than most people see. The way the world is related. It's all connected to the Story Web."

"It's just a story," Alice insisted. "It's not real."

Melanie backed out of the clubhouse. "It *is* real. I can show you."

Alice, though, shook her head. "It's not real," she said again.

"You've been there—"

"I haven't!" Alice cried.

"Alice," Lewis said softly.

Alice crawled out of the clubhouse with Dare on her shoulder.

"The web is broken, Alice," Melanie said. "We have to fix it."

Alice's eyes narrowed. Lewis rocked forward, trying to put himself between her and Melanie, but it didn't do any good.

"I don't even know why I'm listening to you," Alice said. The words came easy to her. It was Izzy's language—and now it was hers. "I don't even know why I came. You're nothing but a witch in the woods."

For a second, Lewis caught something like regret cross Alice's face. She swiped at her eyes.

"Alice," Lewis said. He leaned toward her. His voice wasn't angry. It was soft. It was an invitation.

She clenched her fists. "Just leave me alone!" she cried. Before he could say anything else, she turned and ran from them as fast as she could.

Chapter Twenty-Four
ALICE

Alice wasn't sure she believed Melanie. What she did know was that if the Story Web was real, it was something that connected her to her dad, and she didn't need Melanie, or even Lewis, mucking it up. She had to figure out what was real and true and what was not.

At home, she searched her family's bookshelves for the book her dad had always read to her. She could picture it perfectly: blue cover, gold lettering, the edges of the pages ruffled. It had a ribbon for a bookmark built right in, yellow and frayed. They would sit together, she on his lap, the book in hers, and he would read the stories to her while she carefully studied the watercolor illustrations.

She checked the shelves in the living room, the ones in her bedroom, even the ones in her parents' room. She checked them twice. Nothing.

"Are you looking for something?" her mom asked. She sat in the middle of a sea of papers on the floor. Sometimes it seemed their house was being overtaken by paper.

"It's a book," Alice replied. "Dad used to read it to me. I think it was just called *The Story Web*."

"Oh! I remember that. Somewhere I have a picture of the two of you reading it. It's one of my favorite pictures. You've got pigtails in—back when you still had some curl in your hair. Dad's got one of his beards. A scruffy one that you used to like to tug on. You'd had a Popsicle that day, and the whole front of your shirt is stained red. But it's the look on your face . . ." Her voice trailed off, and she smiled. Alice's dad called that soft look the smile that launched a thousand ships.

"But have you seen it?" Alice asked.

"Not recently," her mom said. "You know your dad was bringing a lot of his stuff to the Museum. He saw that documentary on how we all have too much stuff."

"It's not there," Alice said.

"Did you ask Henrietta? I got the feeling she was holding on to some of those things for when he realized he likes having a lot of stuff around."

Alice nodded, although she hadn't actually asked.

"I wish we still had a library in town," her mom said. "I guess you can check in school tomorrow. If not, I can drive you up to the college over the weekend." She smiled. "Although, if your dad is to be believed, there were only a hundred copies ever printed."

Alice remembered the little number 47 stamped into the back side of the front cover. A hundred was a lot of copies, though. Surely she would be able to find one of them. Her mom was right. Alice needed to go to the library. Even if the library didn't have the book, Ms. Engle would probably know about the Story Web. She knew about everything.

"What are you doing, anyway?" Alice asked.

"Getting organized," she said. The papers around her were bills and pay stubs and some of her father's military papers. There were stacks with Alice's school reports and forms that Mrs. Zee had sent home.

"Whoa," Alice said.

"Yeah, whoa is right. I'm a little behind on my filing."

Her mom sighed and pushed her bangs out of her face. "I feel like I just did this, but these bills go back a year. I guess what I really need to do is shred them. I wonder if they're going to have one of those shred days at the bank."

"How long have you been doing this?"

"Past couple of hours. I was streaming that show where the inventors pitch their ideas, but then I just got depressed that I didn't have a great idea to make us millionaires."

"I'm sure you have lots of good ideas, Mom."

Her mom stopped and looked at Alice. "You're the best idea I've ever had." She smiled, and it was almost a real smile.

The next day, when everyone else traipsed into the cafeteria, she went to see Ms. Engle. Alice found the librarian perched on a high stool eating soup out of a thermos. She put her thermos on the counter and spun around on her stool. Before Alice could ask about the book, Ms. Engle said, "Are you here to help? Come on back here with me," she said. "Help yourself to a cookie." She pointed at a bag of chocolate chip cookies. "I need these books stamped so we can put them into circulation. Now, remember this stamp is a little tricky."

Alice nodded. She had stamped books before. Sometimes Alice wondered if Ms. Engle kept little odd jobs so the kids who didn't feel like going to lunch or recess could hide out in the library and feel like they had a purpose.

Alice picked up the stamp and pressed it into the inside cover of a book about sharks. As she reached for the second book, Ms. Engle held a new picture book up for her to see. "This is the most gorgeous book I've ever read," she said. "It made me all misty."

"Every book makes you misty," Alice said.

"Fair enough," Ms. Engle agreed. "I do love a good book and a cry."

Alice stamped another book and said, trying to sound casual, "Have you ever heard of a book called *The Story Web*?"

"I have," she said slowly. "But I'm surprised you have."

"My dad used to read it to me, and I— Well, I was just

thinking about it and about that Story Web. I remember a lot of the stories but not so much about the web itself." She paused. "Could you, I mean— What do you know about it?"

"Only all about it," Ms. Engle said. She handed Alice a cookie. "When I was in library school, I took a storytelling class. We had to do a big presentation, and I was tying myself up in knots trying to figure out which story to tell. My professor told me that some storytellers start each session by telling a story about stories. Where they came from, who tells them, all that stuff. She brought me to her office and gave me this ancient book called, can you guess?"

"*The Story Web?*"

"*The Story Web,*" Ms. Engle confirmed. "Are you going to eat that cookie or what?"

Alice took a bite. "So you'll tell me about it? About the Story Web?"

Ms. Engle smiled. She leaned back against the workroom counter. "Of course I will." She cleared her throat. Ms. Engle had the best voice for telling stories, second only to Alice's father. She began:

"A long time ago, when the world was new, or mostly new, there was no distinction among the humans, the land animals, the insects, and the sea creatures. Spiders and humans were especially close. Nearly every home had a web in it and a spider to live cozily inside. The humans brought the spiders food, and the spiders spun out the silk that the people needed. Silk for clothing, for bedding, for rope—all of it the spiders provided. Have you ever heard that you'll have seven years' bad luck if you kill a spider?"

Alice nodded.

"Well, it's based in truth. You kill a spider and you lose miles of silk and rope—enough to set you back seven years. Anyway, the world grew larger and the people grew farther and farther apart. Continents shifted, and we were not so close anymore. Wars began, and fear, and cries in the dark. The spiders wanted to bring the people back together with the animals—and with one another—and so they created the web. The web cuts through the earth but is also around it like a blanket—one we can't see but can certainly feel. It sounds impossible, but it is as it is. Most of the time it is invisible, but sometimes it shows itself. No one knows why it picks the places to show itself, but in forests and deserts and jungles and prairies all over the world there are glimpses of the web. One of those places is right here in Independence. Personally, I've always believed there's a little bit of magic in this town, lots of good stories to be told. I can't prove it, but I felt it the first day I set foot here. It feels like a storybook place."

Alice wasn't sure what Ms. Engle meant by that but felt her father was somehow tied up in it. Whether the magic came from his stories or whether the town somehow fed his magic, Alice couldn't say.

"No one knows for sure when the web started or who the original weavers were. The silk is strong and pure and has lasted for centuries. There are stories from every culture woven through. Those places where the strands intersect, those are the stories we share. Like the stories of the Great Flood. Or the world-beginning stories. These stories are the strands that move outward and hold it all together.

"What we do know is that the spiders couldn't do it alone, and so they recruited Story Weavers, people whose stories could bind the world. You know some of their names. Homer, of course, and Virgil. Some you don't know. Women mostly. Seems women are the ones who get cut out of stories—or in trouble for weaving them like poor Arachne, dear child. Of course Athena was quite the tale spinner as well. Sappho, I quite like her. Anyway, there are countless nameless Story Weavers who've done their parts over time. The griots of West Africa sang their tales while playing their story gourds. Buddhist monks used the stories to hold their messages and faith. Poets telling tales of heroism in mead halls in Anglo-Saxon times. All of them are Story Weavers. Your dad was one of those."

Is, Alice thought, but she didn't correct Ms. Engle.

"Later the authors added their tales, those that were

written down and spread around the world. Those are powerful strands of the web. Authors are a special type of Story Weaver.

"Others of us are Storytellers. We don't create the stories, but we tell them over and over. We watch over the webs and keep the stories alive. All of us work together: the Story Weavers, the Storytellers, the spiders. We keep the web intact. We keep the earth as one. At least, that's how the story goes."

As Ms. Engle completed her recounting, Alice remembered walking back from the Story Web with her father and what he'd told her: "You're very lucky to be able to see a Story Web. Not everyone can. Even fewer can see a single thread, but you followed it right from the house."

Her father was always telling her how special she was. How magical. What if those hadn't been just stories? What if it really was up to her?

"Oh dear." Ms. Engle's voice cut through Alice's thoughts. "I'm the crier, not you." She handed Alice a tissue.

Alice shook her head. "That's kind of what my dad told me," she said.

"Buzz knows all the best stories." Ms. Engle handed Alice another tissue. "I'm sorry, Alice. I truly am."

Alice snuffled into the tissue, glad that none of her friends was there to see her wet eyes and runny nose.

Ms. Engle said, "Your dad knew how important stories are. How magical."

"Magical?" Alice asked.

"Oh yes!" She took a deep breath. "You know, sometimes when I'm reading to kids, they get so quiet and lean in toward me. I've caught them, and it's like I'm wrapping them up in the story with me. I don't know any better magic than that."

Alice nodded. Her nose had stopped running, but she still reached for another tissue to blow it one more time.

Ms. Engle went on: "I like to think of the stories as real, living things. When I read the story it flutters out, and each kid—each of you—takes the story and carries it with you."

"Does that only work with books?" Alice asked, thinking of the stories her dad told her.

Ms. Engle thought about the question for a moment. "I think books are one way to hold stories—one of many. But stories are slippery things, Alice. The ones I share, those are ones I hope will help you in some way. But other stories aren't. And once they're out, they get all over the place like sticky, dirty goo."

Alice looked at Ms. Engle for a moment. It seemed the librarian was trying to tell her something, to talk about something without actually talking about it. Alice wasn't sure what she meant. They just looked at each other a little longer, and then Ms. Engle stood up. "I'm going to look for that book for you," she said. "When I find it, I'll bring it straight down. Until then, chin up, young person. You don't have to carry the world, you know."

Alice, for once, wasn't sure if that was true. Maybe she was the hero of this story. If that was the case, she had work to do.

Chapter Twenty-Five
ALICE

When they were supposed to be doing research about heroes, Alice instead typed the words "The Story Web" into her laptop's browser. All she found were a bunch of educational websites. She added the word "book" to her search and thought it was more of the same, but as she scrolled to the very bottom of the results, she found a website called simply Rare Books Found.

At the top of the page for *The Story Web* was a picture of the book, blue as she remembered it. The title was in gold, and there was a golden web that stretched over the whole book. No author was given. The description read:

A most curious book. Only a hundred copies of this story were ever printed. There is no author or editor given. The publisher is listed as Pallas Athene Productions, but there is no record of this publisher ever having existed. Attempts to determine where the books were printed and sold have also proven fruitless. In short, this book seems to have appeared out of nowhere. The book has gained something of a cult following for its unusual grouping of stories and watercolor paintings. Though none of the illustrations is signed, art historians have made connections to some famous illustrators of the day. A second strand of collectors are doomsdayers who have latched on to the book's prologue, which predicts a frosty end to the earth itself. This event is known as the Freezing, and there are those who believe the book's description is an accurate prediction of the end of the world.

Most copies found are well loved and in poor shape. A high-quality first (and only) edition might fetch tens of thousands of dollars.

Tens of thousands of dollars? Maybe her father had sold it. Times were tough, after all, and he had all the stories in his head.

Alice checked the clock. Just five minutes to recess.

She scrolled down. The site gave a table of contents for the book. Alice recognized most of the stories listed, but she realized her father had left some of the stories out. *The Steadfast Tin Soldier,* for example, she had never heard, which seemed strange, since it was about a soldier.

She scrolled some more and found listings for auctions

of the title. There were only three, and the cheapest one was four thousand dollars. There was no way she was going to be able to buy one. She had to find her father's copy.

Mrs. Zee started the clean-up music, and Alice logged out of her computer and put it back on the cart. As she headed for her cubby, Mrs. Zee stopped Alice and asked her to come sit at her teacher table. The rest of the class filed out for Music.

"How are you, Alice?" Mrs. Zee asked.

"Fine."

"I've been meaning to check in with you more. I know this has been a tough start to the year for you." Alice squirmed in her seat, but she didn't say anything. Mrs. Zee tried a different tack. "I heard you ran into a moose."

"Yes. Melanie, Lewis, and I did. It wasn't really a big deal."

Mrs. Zee tutted her tongue. "I will tell you this: moose in Independence are nothing new."

Alice nodded. "My uncle told me a story about how this moose came and played hockey with him and my dad."

"I remember," Mrs. Zee said.

"You do?"

"My kid brother was playing. With your dad."

Alice shifted in her seat. "You're Dale Zelonis's big sister?"

Mrs. Zee nodded. "Truth be told, I brought my skates that day. Boys didn't think as much about asking girls to play back then. I don't think it even occurred to them. I'm glad your dad and Donny have seen the light on that one."

"So you saw the moose?" Alice asked.

"It was the strangest thing," Mrs. Zee said. Her cheeks were pink, and she looked past Alice toward the doorway, like she was ready to run right back to the ice. "The moose brought the puck back and dropped it. He tried to nudge it toward the boys, but then his hoof went through the ice. He got stuck."

"Wait, what?" Alice asked. This was not how Donny had told the story.

"Your dad and Donny skated over to him, slow as can be. Your dad was talking the whole time. Like, *Hey, moose, what's happening? Are you stuck there? We're just gonna help you right out.* He squatted, and he and Donny started chipping away at the ice until the moose could get free. The moose looked at them, lowered his antlers as if he was bowing, then ran off back into the woods."

"He didn't actually play hockey with them?" Alice asked.

"No. Maybe he was trying, but moose and ice aren't the best match."

Alice worked over this in her mind. Her uncle had lied to her? But was it a lie, exactly?

Mrs. Zee's face and her tone changed. "Alice," she said. Alice's name hung like a weight in the air, a balloon in the split second after it popped. "I know you don't like to talk about your father. About his situation."

This whole conversation was dizzying. She was in the classroom, but also in the strange building where she'd gone to say goodbye to her father when he deployed. He was dressed in camouflage, stiff and uncomfortable looking. He was going to Afghanistan. They had found it together on a map. He told her he was just going there to help keep the base running, to help the supplies come in and go out where they were needed. He said he would be perfectly safe.

But she had seen what he had packed. She saw the rifle he had to carry. You only carry a rifle if you think you might need to use it.

He was gone for seven months.

Then he came back, and it was like he had never left. He coached her hockey team. He made waffles on Saturdays and sat in his special chair with Jewel in his lap.

Maybe there were some differences. Small ones. Like how he jumped when a car door slammed or when Alice dropped a pot in the kitchen. Or the way he got locked in his head sometimes and Alice's mom had to put her hand on his chest and say his name over and over to get him to come out. Or the nightmares.

She remembered the time he said, "I'm just so very angry almost all the time. Angry and sad and on the edge of losing control." He said this to Alice's mother as they sat on their bed. Alice watched through the crack in the doorway. Her mom pulled him close, and he put his head in her lap. She stroked his hair, which had grown back as full as ever.

Alice never saw that anger. He kept it locked away. His

sadness, too. It was his fear that showed up from time to time. That lack of control.

"I was in your father's class. I used to tutor him in algebra. I think that's when I first thought about being a teacher. He was so kind about it, you know? He made me feel like I was really valuable, really helping him."

"You probably were," Alice mumbled.

"He was very popular, your father. I was not especially."

Alice herself had been popular once. Now she was nothing.

"I concentrated on school and activities. I was editor of the yearbook." She shook her head. "Anyway, I didn't really feel like I missed out on anything."

"Thanks, Mrs. Zee. I'll keep that in mind."

"Sorry," she said. "That wasn't actually the point of my story. My point was about your father. He didn't see me as the unpopular girl or the nerdy girl. I was just Emily to him. The girl who helped him with algebra. Dale's big sister. Someone who also liked *The X-Files*. He didn't see any of the silly stuff. He just saw what mattered." Mrs. Zee's cheeks grew pink. "I asked him to Sadie Hawkins. He already had a date, of course, but told me Donny would go with me. And he did. They were both kind like that."

"Okay," Alice said. She stood up.

"The point is, whatever your father is going through now, it doesn't change that he's a good man. In fact, I would hazard a guess that it is in part his goodness that is making things so hard for him. Don't listen to what other people say. That's a hard lesson to learn, but the sooner you learn it, the easier life gets. People have their own stuff, their own baggage—don't let their stuff change what you know is true."

Alice started to back away. "Okay," she said again, though she really wasn't sure she understood what Mrs. Zee was talking about.

"If you ever do want to talk, Alice, I can be a good listener."

Alice nodded as she kept backing out of the room. As she got to the doorway she blurted, "I'm going to Music!" She shut the door behind her before Mrs. Zee could say anything else.

※

Henrietta dropped a box onto the counter. Clarice, the mannequin, jumped from the impact. Clarice was dressed in a raincoat for the cold, wet weather they'd been having.

"What do you want with that book?" Henrietta asked. Her head was bent over a piece of jewelry she was inspecting.

Ms. Engle was looking for a copy of *The Story Web*. In the meantime, Alice knew her best bet was to ask Henrietta.

"My dad used to read it to me," Alice replied. It was a truthful response, just not the whole truth. "Did he ask you to sell it for him? I heard it was valuable."

"Is that what this is about? You want to make some money off the book?"

"No!" Alice exclaimed.

Henrietta looked up. She had her monocular wedged over her eye, giving her a fish-eye appearance. "If you and your mother need money—"

"No," Alice said.

"Donny? The rink?"

Alice shook her head. "I just want the book."

"For your dad," Henrietta said.

Alice nodded.

"I understand. The things people own, the things they cherish, it's like having a piece of them when you have those objects." She held up the ring she'd been looking at. "This ring?" she said. "Beautiful. Valuable. But no one really cared about it." She put the ring down and took the monocular off her eye. "But this," she said, holding up a simple broach made of pewter and shaped like an anchor, "this piece has things to say." She held it to her ear. "A sailor gave it to his wife. She wore it whenever he was out to sea. She's his anchor."

Alice understood. Her mother was like that for her dad. Even when things were really bad, when he seemed to not be there at all, his mom could always bring him home. Sometimes Alice thought that if her mom had been there that day instead of her, then maybe her dad would still be home.

Henrietta shuffled into the back room. "These are the

boxes I have from your dad. I haven't sold any of it, and I won't. I don't think there are any books in here, though. He's not one for giving up books. But you take a look. Keep anything you want."

Alice pushed through the beaded curtain into the back room. Her dad's boxes were neatly marked with his name in his perfectly straight handwriting. There all the time, but she had never known.

She took down the first one. There was a baseball trophy, a miniature hockey stick, a glass paperweight with blue inside that looked like a jellyfish. She hadn't remembered ever seeing any of this stuff, which, she supposed, was how it had ended up here. At the bottom of the box, she found his dog tags. His name was printed on them, along with a string of numbers and letters that didn't mean anything to her.

She was surprised he hadn't brought them with him. The hospital had a lot of soldiers in it but also people who had gone through rough experiences other places. Her mom had fought to get him into that hospital. Alice thought that he would have wanted his dog tags so he and the other soldiers could identify one another and keep one another safe. She slipped them over her own neck and felt the cool metal against her chest.

The next box had trading cards, baseball and hockey, mostly, but also some for a game called *Magic*. All the fantastic creatures on the cards seemed to be glaring at her, ready to pounce. She tucked them back into the binder where she had found them. She dug deeper into the box and found a pennant from Boston University as well as his team jacket from his time there.

The book wasn't there.

Henrietta popped her head in. "Hot chocolate?" she asked. Alice shook her head.

"Cinnamon toast?"

"No, thanks."

"I take it the book wasn't there."

Alice walked across the room toward Henrietta. "No," she said. "I guess it's just lost."

"Did you find anything you wanted?"

Alice didn't answer. "Do you think he was a hero?"

"Your father? The greatest."

Henrietta backed up through the beaded curtain to the sales desk. She took a seat on the high stool and pointed to the chair beside it. Alice sat. "Because he went to war?" Without meaning to, she touched her chest, feeling the dog tags beneath her shirt.

"Eh," Henrietta said. "He would've been a hero even if he didn't go to war. Some people are just like that. This town—it never had a lot. It used to have enough, back when the mill was running. They'd go twenty-four seven sometimes."

Alice knew all about the mill history. They learned about it in school, visited the old buildings. Alice had never been sure why they had celebrated such failure.

"When your dad was in high school, the mills were shutting down. This town that had never had a lot suddenly didn't even have enough. People were fighting. Businesses were closing. They thought they might have to close the school if more kids moved away. People were stressed, Alice. Add to that the things that were going on in the world—sicknesses people hadn't heard of before, wars built on threats and bigger and bigger arsenals. We could've collapsed."

Alice thought maybe she understood. "There were animals back then, too, right? Coming into town?"

"Yes, that's right. Your dad and Donny found a dozen raccoons behind the diner one day, looking for all the world like they were holding a den meeting. There were strange, tough times all around this town. People needed something to rally around. Your dad was that something. No one missed his games. When he went down to Boston, we'd listen to the games on the radio, all gathered together at the Spaghetti Shed or Fitz's Pub. And when the games were on television—woo! You would've thought James Dean himself was from Independence."

"James Dean?"

"Handsome, tragic actor. Looked great in a leather jacket. The point is, your dad gave us hope. He gave us things to talk about, stories to share. He gave us something to be proud of." She pushed up her sleeves and regarded Alice closely. "That's a lot to take on, Alice. All the hope of one town on one young man's shoulders. That's why he's a hero. Because he took it. He took that on, and we were all the better for it."

Alice felt a hollow spot in her stomach. He had been that thing for all those people and still managed to be a hero for her. Until she had messed it all up and finally caused him to pop. The town still needed him, and her mom needed him, and Donny, and Henrietta, and Lewis—everyone needed her dad, but he wasn't there. Because of her. If the town was coming apart, then that was on her, too. She could practically feel her father's hand on her shoulder. *Be bold. Be brave. Be fierce.* It was time for her to act.

Luna Moth

Luna perched on a branch of the willow tree. Her pale green coloring was nearly the same as the tree leaves, and it would take a very careful observer to notice the purplish piping along the edges of her wings. Her long tail matched nearly perfectly the tendril-like leaves of the tree. She was not trying to hide per se, only wanted a safe place to observe.

The wind stung her delicate wings, but she had taken it upon herself to watch over the web. The other animals had their plans, their conversations, but Luna simply watched, being sure to stay far enough away from the web itself. An insect can get caught in a Story Web just as easily as it can in a regular spiderweb. She didn't want to do the web any further damage, nor did she want to harm her own beautiful wings.

She watched for the spiders and cheered them when they

decided to weave, less and less often as the days wore on. She watched the wind and rain knock strands loose.

She watched the events unfold one cold evening, and, when she could watch no more, she went to find the boy.

Chapter Twenty-Six
ALICE

Alice's mom was asleep on the couch when Alice got home from school. She wasn't supposed to leave the house without asking, but she didn't wake her mother. She whispered, "I'll be back soon. I'm going to fix this." Then she slipped out the back door with Dare on her shoulder.

It was harder to follow the thread this time, covered in ice and broken completely in some places. Alice had to pace back and forth among the trees and stones before she found it again. Dare tried to help, cheeping and chirping in her ear, but Alice couldn't understand the bird's messages. She walked and walked, her feet slipping at times on the ice. Carrying the box of letters under her arm didn't help.

Her toes and fingers began to burn, and she thought for a moment about turning around. Then she saw it. She recognized the willow. She dropped to her knees and crawled under the swooping branches and their tiny leaves that brushed her hair from her forehead back the way her mom did on lazy mornings.

Alice watched one loose strand of the web swing back and forth, back and forth. It made her ache for her father. If she could follow this strand back, it would lead her to him. She crouched, and Dare hopped off her shoulder. She took the end of the thread in her beak and looked at Alice as if she were telling her to grab hold of it, to see where it led her.

Alice's eyes, though, were drawn to the center of the web. It was empty. Alice knew what it meant that the web was weak and the strand to her house was gone. She supposed she'd known all along. Her father was a Story Weaver and a hero. He was both the spinner and the star of stories. Now he was gone, and the threads could not survive. He was the center that held the web and the town together, but he was trapped on that island far away, unable to help.

"I've brought him to you," she said to the web.

She opened the box and spread out the letters carefully on the ground in front of her. Eyes closed, she picked a letter.

Her voice shook as she read the words.

SEPTEMBER 23

DEAR ALICE,

HOW HAS THE START OF SCHOOL BEEN? IT'S HARD FOR ME TO BE AWAY ON SUCH IMPORTANT DAYS. I AM CERTAIN, HOWEVER,

THAT MRS. CARMICHAEL WILL BE DULY IMPRESSED BY THE
WORLD'S SMARTEST THIRD GRADER. IS LEWIS IN YOUR CLASS
THIS YEAR? PLEASE REMIND HIM AT EVERY OPPORTUNITY TO
KEEP HIS HAND DOWN ON THE STICK. HE CHOKES UP TOO MUCH.

    I THOUGHT WE WOULD BE COMING HOME SOON, BUT I'M
AFRAID THAT IS NOT TO BE THE CASE. YOU SEE, ON MY TRAVELS
I STUMBLED UPON A BRONZE ISLAND RIGHT IN THE MIDDLE OF
THE DESERT. AN OASIS, I THOUGHT, BUT AS I DREW NEAR I
HEARD VOICES AND SINGING. A BOY NOT MUCH OLDER THAN YOU
INVITED ME TO THE MOST MAGNIFICENT CASTLE. INSIDE I MET A
KING. HE NEVER LEAVES THIS ISLAND, AND HE LONGS FOR
STORIES. AS A STORY EATER MYSELF, I CAN CERTAINLY RELATE.

Alice looked up from the letter. "Story eater," she whispered. The phrase was unfamiliar, but she knew it was true. Her father liked to hear stories as much as he liked to spin them.

A spider emerged on the web and started lazily to weave. Alice kept reading, her voice stronger now.

    I TOLD HIM MY STORY. HOW I HAD NOT WANTED TO GO TO
WAR AND LEAVE YOU AND MOM BEHIND, BUT WE ALL HAVE OUR
OBLIGATIONS. ONCE IN THE WAR, I HAD NEW OBLIGATIONS: TO MY
TEAM OF FELLOW SOLDIERS. WHEN I FINISHED, HE GAVE ME A BAG
FULL OF WINDS. HE SAID THEY WOULD SEND MY SHIP HOME.
I TUCKED THE BAG UNDER MY ARM AND BROUGHT IT BACK TO MY

BARRACKS. I TOLD ONLY ONE PERSON, BUT AN ENEMY MUST HAVE
HEARD, FOR IN THE NIGHT THE BAG WAS OPENED. WIND WHIPPED
UP AROUND OUR CAMP, SWIRLING SAND THROUGH ANY CRACKS IN
THE BUILDINGS. OUR BEDS FILLED WITH SAND. WE STUMBLED
ABOUT LIKE BLIND MEN . . .

BUT ENOUGH OF THAT.

THE CLEANUP HAS BEGUN. WE SHALL BE FINISHED SOON AND
THEN, PERHAPS, WE SHALL BEGIN OUR JOURNEY HOMEWARD. LOOK
UP TO THE STARS AND PERHAPS YOU WILL BE ABLE TO TRACK
MY PROGRESS.

BE BOLD, BE BRAVE, BE FIERCE.

LOVE,

DAD

Alice refolded the letter and held it in her lap.

Most of her father's stories she did not know the truth of,
but this one she did.

A windstorm had come upon his camp. At the same time,
enemy insurgents came through. Three of the men in her
father's unit were lost. Her father had been injured but not
badly. The phone call came in the middle of the night. Her
mother answered and Alice picked up the other line. Her heart
had leapt at the sound of her father's voice, until she heard the
true story.

On the web, a second spider had joined the first, but they still wove slowly, far too slowly.

Alice sighed. She took out the newer, harder letters and spread these along with the older ones. "I suppose you want these stories, too," she said, not sure who she was speaking to.

Eyes closed, she chose another letter. The worst letter, from just two weeks before.

NOVEMBER 4

DEAR ALICE,

I TRY TO WRITE EVERY WEEK, BUT THEY KEEP ME BUSY HERE. I'M JUST BACK FROM SEEING MY CALYPSO. SHE SAYS IT IS GOOD THAT I WRITE YOU THESE LETTERS. SHE SAYS IT IS HEALING FOR BOTH OF US. IS THAT TRUE? I HOPE SO.

TODAY SHE AND I TALKED ABOUT THE LAND OF THE DEAD. DID I EVER TELL YOU THAT STORY? NO, OF COURSE NOT. YOU WERE TOO YOUNG THEN. NOW, BECAUSE OF ME, YOU ARE OLD. SO HERE GOES.

I VISITED THE LAND OF THE DEAD. I VISIT IT OFTEN, IN FACT. CIRCE TAUGHT THAT A SACRIFICE MUST BE MADE TO CROSS OVER TO ATTRACT THE DEAD. SHE SAID TO DIG A TRENCH AND FILL IT WITH MILK AND HONEY. IT IS THE BLOOD, THOUGH, THAT ATTRACTS THE DEAD. FOR ME IT IS DIFFERENT. I MAKE NO NEW SACRIFICE. I AM SIMPLY WALKING AND THEN THE LAND THAT SHOULD BE BEFORE ME IS GONE AND IN ITS PLACE IS THE

LAND OF THE DEAD. I KNOW IT BY THE SWIRLING MISTS THAT
SURROUND IT AND THE SMELL OF SULFUR. THE PEOPLE THERE
ARE GHOSTS, BUT THEY TALK TO ME. THEY TELL ME THEIR
STORIES. THINGS I KNEW OF THEM AND THINGS I DID NOT KNOW.
I SEE THE MEN I FOUGHT WITH. I HEAR THEIR HOPES. THEY TELL
ME I AM THE LUCKY ONE. I KNOW I AM, AND STILL . . . THE THING
OF IT IS IT'S NOT THAT THEY FRIGHTEN ME, THESE GHOSTS, IT'S
WHAT THEY REMIND ME OF THAT IS SO TERRIFYING. I WISH I
COULD THROW OFF THAT FEAR, BUT THEN, WHAT KIND OF
PERSON WOULD I BE?

THIS IS NOT A GOOD LETTER, I DON'T THINK. I WANT THE
LETTERS TO MAKE YOU FEEL SAFE. BUT I ALSO NEED YOU TO
UNDERSTAND WHY I AM NOT THERE WITH YOU.

Alice's throat tightened, and she couldn't speak the rest of
the letter. She squeezed her eyes shut and tried to swallow. She
remembered the day her father left.

Alice's parents had sent her over to Lewis's. It was the day
after the fifth-grade social, and the last person she'd wanted to
see was Lewis. She'd gone upstairs with Linda, who had grilled
her about who she had danced with. Alice said she'd danced
with Brady, which was true but also not true.

It had all been her fault, that's what no one would believe.
She'd tried to tell them a million times, but no one listened.

It had been fire-safety week at school. The firefighters
came and talked to them about what could happen in a fire,

why it was so important to have smoke detectors. Alice had gone home and put batteries back into all the smoke detectors. They didn't go off that often, she reasoned, and her dad sitting in the car was better than them all dying in a fire.

The day of the social she was making cookies. Her mom had signed up to bring some to share, but then she'd been called in last minute, and Alice had to make them. It was okay. It was just the tube of cookie dough. She'd sliced them neatly, put them on the pan, and gone to get ready for the dance.

Izzy had said they needed to braid their hair into crowns that encircled their heads, a trio of queens. Alice's fingers tangled in her hair trying again and again to get her braids to look like Izzy's. She braided her hair almost every day for hockey but couldn't make it bend around her head in the elaborate style Izzy had chosen. She had just about given up and was ready to ask her dad for help when the smoke alarm went off. She ran to the kitchen. Smoke puffed out of the oven, and the alarm blared and blared and blared.

In the center of it all was her father, stock-still and wild eyed. "Get down!" he cried.

She didn't move.

"I said get down!" He lunged toward her, grabbed her around the shoulder, and pulled her roughly to the floor.

"It's just the smoke alarm, Dad," she'd told him. "We just

need to open the window." She moved toward the window, but her father held her shoulders tightly.

"Stay down!" he ordered. He pressed her into the floor. She felt the ridges of the linoleum on her cheek.

"Dad," she said, struggling to breathe under the weight of his body. Then she yelled it: "Dad!"

He looked right at her. He closed his eyes tightly. He ran from the kitchen to his bedroom and locked the door.

Alice hadn't known what to do. She opened the window, then turned off the oven. She threw the burned cookies out into the lawn and finished getting ready. She never managed to get the braids in.

Lewis knocked on her door, and she met him in the party dress she had bought at the mall down in South Portland with her mom. Lewis said something stupid like, "Can't stop many goals in that."

Alice replied, "I can stop anything that comes my way."

Lewis's mom drove them to the social, and when Alice got out of the car, she said, "You know, my dad wasn't feeling so well. Do you think you could go check on him?"

It was Uncle Donny who had come to pick her up at the dance. "Where's Mom?" she asked.

"Busy," he'd replied. "Your dad is still feeling sick." Donny brought her to his house instead of taking her home. In the morning, Donny brought her to Lewis's house.

Her dad was gone.

When she opened her eyes in the clearing, she saw the spiders working more quickly. The sky had grown darker with clouds, and the strands of the web glinted silver.

A few light drops of rain fell on Alice's face and onto the web. The spiders kept going. Alice kept the story of what she had done locked behind her lips.

The rain came faster and then, all at once, the sky opened into a huge downpour.

Alice snapped around toward her letters. Already they were pressed into the mud. She fell to the ground beside them and tried to gather them up. They were wet and gritty in her hands, flopping like broken fish. She watched the ink seep through the paper.

Gone. All her father's letters, all his stories, were gone.

No, came a sweet voice in her head. It sounded like Ms. Engle, soft and warm as fresh cookies. *You still have his stories in your heart. You can tell his stories.*

But then it turned harder, to a voice she didn't recognize: *There is only one story you have that matters. You need to tell the truth of what happened.*

Alice swallowed hard.

It wasn't magic, these voices in her head. It was just what she knew to be true. To save the web, she had to tell the one true story she knew that really mattered.

"Alice?"

It was Lewis, peering at her from under the willow branches. He looked at her, caked in mud. He looked at the letters in her hands and on the ground. A luna moth flitted around his shoulder.

"Come on," he said.

"You shouldn't be here," she told him. Her voice cracked. Her chest ached.

"I know," he said with a shrug. "I went by your house, and you weren't there."

"Does my mom know?"

He shook his head. "She was sleeping. I didn't wake her up."

They kept close to the ridge line of the ravine. It led straight back to his yard, and from there she could go home. The ice covered everything and rain still fell, but there was enough light that they wouldn't get lost.

"How'd you know where to find me?"

He shrugged. "I just did."

That made sense, Alice thought, in the way that only things that didn't make any sense at all seemed to be happening these days.

Their feet crunched in the ice. When they got to the hill, they held on to tree branches to keep from falling.

How many hours, Alice wondered, had the two of them spent in these woods? Days? Weeks? Years, even? It seemed possible. So much time romping and playing and joking. Now everything was different. It looked different, covered in ice, but worse than that, it *felt* different. The air between them was tight and hurt her lungs.

They walked past his clubhouse, closed tight against the storm.

When they reached the edge of the woods, he stopped. "Alice," he said. "I'm sorry."

"It's okay," she said.

"Do you even know what I'm apologizing for?"

She looked at her feet.

"I should've asked about your dad," he said, his voice cracking. "I should've asked what happened and if he's okay."

Alice looked up at him, her eyes watery. Then, without really thinking about it, she lurched at him. She wrapped her arms around him and squeezed. Not like an after-a-big-win hug, which was halfway to a tackle. This was a real hug. The kind your parents give you when things are really bad.

Chapter Twenty-Seven
ALICE

Alice told the school nurse to call her uncle instead of her mom. "My mom has a night shift," she explained.

She met Uncle Donny in the front office. Ms. Barton laughed this funny high-pitched laugh, and Uncle Donny smiled along. Alice's mom said Uncle Donny was cursed with women, and Alice guessed that's why he wasn't married yet, even though he was the nicest adult she knew and also had a handsome smile.

"Just tell me straight up," he said to her when Alice came out of the nurse's office. "Was there any actual barfing?"

Alice shook her head. She wasn't sick exactly, unless guilt was a sickness. She'd felt it mounting and mounting and mounting. Lewis's concerned looks only made it worse. It felt like cold wet blankets and ants with itchy feet and a siren going off out of key all at once. It felt the way her dad's letters had looked in the mud. Unlike her dad, she broke easily. She'd practically run straight to the nurse's office.

"Do you foresee any actual barfing in the near future?" Donny asked.

Alice hesitated. If she said no, they might make her stay at school. "Anything is possible."

Uncle Donny turned to the school secretary. "Julie, could I please trouble you for a plastic bag of some sort? I just got my truck detailed."

Ms. Barton smiled and dug around in her desk drawer until she came up with a plastic bag far too small to capture Alice's potential vomit. Luckily, Alice was pretty sure she wasn't going to need it. "Thanks, Ms. Barton."

"Feel better, Alice," she said.

Uncle Donny put his hand on her shoulder and led her out of the office.

Outside, ice fell in spiky drops that stung Alice's face. She and Uncle Donny skated toward his red truck as if they were at the rink.

"You can drop the act, kiddo. I won multiple Oscars for my performances as 'Child Too Sick for School.' You've done a solid job here, but you can't fake a faker."

"I'm sorry you had to come get me," Alice said.

"You want to tell me what's up?"

Alice didn't reply.

"Okay," Uncle Donny said. "For now. But since you're not

really sick, I'm putting you to work." He paused. "Is that a bird on my truck?"

The gray bird with the yellow tail called out *bzeep*. "Dare?" she asked and trotted over to the bird. Dare raised her good wing in a wave.

"You know this bird?" he asked.

"Sort of," Alice replied.

Bzeep! Bzeep!

"Seems to know you."

"She kind of adopted me. I found her at the rink. She was hurt. I brought her home, but she keeps getting out." She extended her hand, and the bird hopped right in.

"Really, Alice? You're a bird tamer now?"

Dare looked up with her gray eyes. "I've been thinking about keeping her."

"Your mom thinks this is okay?"

"Not exactly. It's not like the bird is a pet or anything. I'm just helping out."

"You're getting really slippery with language, kid," he said. He glanced over at her. She turned away. Uncle Donny had the kind of gaze that could look right through you, and Alice didn't like disappointing him.

"I'm trying to do the right thing."

He scratched the top of his head. "You're putting me in a tight spot here, Alice. Faking sick, sneaking birds—if your mom finds out I aided and abetted, I'll be in big trouble."

"Please, Uncle Donny."

Uncle Donny smiled and frowned at the same time. "You kill me, kid. You know I can never say no to you, not when you sound so pitiful. Here's the deal: you help me out today, you keep the bird at the rink so if your mom asks we can plausibly say that it's *our* pet—"

"She's not a pet."

"It will stay at the rink. And you won't ever, ever, ever fake out sick again. Deal?"

Alice hesitated. She looked at Dare, who hopped back and forth and nodded. "Deal."

"Good." He tugged his cap down.

He opened the door to the truck and swung himself in. Alice sat with Dare in her lap beside him. "Bird's got fierce eyes," he said. "What do you call it?"

"Dare," she said.

He nodded. "Seems about right. Well, Dare, welcome. I think you'll fit right in."

Dare could barely contain her excitement.

☀

Uncle Donny told Alice to clean up the supply closet. She figured she'd be on her own, but he went into the small room with her. The walls were lined with hockey sticks and bins of tape and hockey pucks. Donny hummed as he started straightening up.

"I was talking to Mrs. Zee about you."

"Ms. Zee," Donny corrected.

"What?"

"She's not married, so she's not a Mrs."

"Okay, well—"

"I think maybe she had a little crush on me back in the day."

"That's not what we talked about," Alice said, though she couldn't help but think of the way Ms. Zee's face had gone all soft and dewy like a honey-glazed doughnut when she talked about Uncle Donny. "You didn't tell the truth about the moose and the hockey game. She said that the moose got stuck in the ice, and you guys helped him out."

Donny stopped with a loop of tape in each hand. "Huh," he said. "You know, I think she's right. That's how we told it all these years, so I guess I forgot that's not really what happened."

"So it's not true?" Alice said.

"There's a difference between true and factual," Donny said, and went back to gathering loose rolls of tape and tossing them into a plastic tub by the door.

"You sound like those politicians on TV who never answer the questions. That drives Mom crazy."

He twirled a roll of tape around his finger. "A true story is true at its heart, even if all the facts aren't exactly right. It's honest."

Alice tried to hold that idea in her head, but it was having trouble sticking.

"You need to be able to suss out the truth. The honest stories. That's what matters."

"But if things can be true and not true— How do you ever know what's really true?"

Uncle Donny scratched his head. "Man, I wish your dad were here. He's much better at explaining this stuff." He grabbed a hockey stick that was leaning against the wall and spun it in his hands as he spoke. "It's like all the stories about him. They're all based in fact. He really was the best hockey player this town has ever seen. And a good man. And a hero. All that builds up into myths and legends, and you throw his big personality on top of that—" He stopped walking and took a deep breath. "It's hard to tell the difference between honest and true, Alice, but you need to learn how. You need to figure out what's honest and believe in it with all your heart. That's what's really true. And that's how it lasts."

Alice tried to let this all sink in. She thought she understood what her uncle was telling her—or starting to. She got that people could manipulate facts in a dishonest way. But something still bothered her. Maybe it was an honest story that her dad had scored a goal off a moose—if anyone could get an animal assist, it was her dad—but something else had actually happened that day.

"What really happened—how you guys rescued the moose—that's a much better story."

"A better story than getting an assist from a moose?"

"Yeah," she said. "It's more like him. More what he cared about." She paused. "It's more true. And it's the whole truth."

"I suppose you're right about that," he said. "I guess it's hard to know the truth even when you're the one it happened to."

Alice considered that. There were only two people who'd been there the day her dad had to leave: her father and herself. Would she ever be able to tell the whole truth? She wasn't sure, but she did know it would be honest to say he had never meant to hurt her. She cleared her throat. "Ms. Zee said Dad was a leader. That he made space for everyone."

"Yep, that's your dad. One hundred percent."

"Do you think I'm like that?"

Uncle Donny twirled the hockey stick in his hand.

"I don't think I am," Alice said. "I want to be—" Her voice cracked.

"I know, hon."

She hung her head and looked at the bin of loaner skates: worn, dull, their laces tangled like vines in Minnow Pond. "Sometimes it feels like too big of a risk, like putting in your weakest player when you only have a one-point lead in a championship game just so everyone gets playing time. Only a thousand times worse."

Uncle Donny nodded. "So you put the player in. He fouls up. What do you do?"

"Lose?"

"And then what?"

"I don't know."

"You sulk about it. Maybe throw your gear into your locker a little too hard. Maybe smack your stick. And then what?"

"I don't know," she said again.

"You take a shower. You go to bed. The next day you get up, and you go to practice with the kid who fouled up. Because you're a team. Because really it wasn't just his mistake. Because if you had gotten a bigger lead, one little mess up wouldn't have mattered. That's how a team works."

"But these are just kids in school. They aren't my team."

"Yes, they are. This whole town is a team. That's the way this works. We look out for one another. We invite everyone in. We forgive and move on."

Alice thought of the Basic Becky dinners Izzy's mom held that Alice's mom was never invited to. "Some people. But not everyone."

"Not everyone. And maybe fewer every day."

Uncle Donny hung rolls of tape on a peg board. "Listen, I am in no place to tell you what to do. I only took Emily Zelonis to the dance because your dad offered to give me his signed Bobby Orr picture. But you asked if you were like your dad, and if that's what you want, well, making everyone feel like part of the team is key."

Alice squatted to grab loose pucks to throw into the bin.

They worked in silence.

"Alice, this is looking pretty good. I feel like you've repaid your debt of fake illness."

"Thanks, Uncle Donny." She hesitated. "Can I ask you a question?"

"Shoot."

"Did you ever regret bringing Ms. Zee to the dance?"

"Officially, she asked me." He smiled. "And no. Not for one single millisecond."

Chapter Twenty-Eight

LEWIS

Lewis lifted the heavy knocker on the Bird House door and let it fall. Inside, the owl hooted. A moment later, Melanie pulled open the door. She looked him up and down. "You don't look ready to go to the web."

"Yeah," he said. "It's just that I have practice." Lewis never skipped hockey practice. Coach Donny had a rule: you cut practice, you didn't skate in the next game. Missing a game wasn't just about him. He would never let his team down like that. "I thought maybe we could do more research and work from here."

Melanie pointed to the bushes that flanked the door. The stems and orange-red winterberries were encased in ice as clear and shining as glass. "It's happening."

"It's just an ice storm," Lewis said. He shoved his hands into his pockets. He looked at the berries. It looked like each one had been carefully dipped in the ice. His eyes traveled down the line of shrubs. An evergreen's branches hung low, heavy with the ice. The spikes of the holly leaves tried to break free but couldn't. The ground shone like nothing Lewis had ever seen in a rink or on a pond. The ice was perfectly clear, and he could see each pebble beneath it.

Melanie stepped aside to let him in. "It's what the book said would happen. The Freezing." She closed the door behind him. "You can't go to practice. We have to do something about the web."

"We still don't know what to do."

"We have to tell stories."

But what stories? Nothing had worked so far. He thought of Alice out in the woods with those letters from her father. His stomach twisted as he remembered how Alice had hugged him then, and he wished she were with them. Whatever was happening, they needed her.

Melanie led him toward the back of the house.

"Maybe we should call Alice," he said.

Melanie's face darkened. "She doesn't want to help."

"I think she does. Yesterday—" But he stopped himself. Alice had been a wreck. Maybe it wasn't his place to tell Melanie. Maybe Alice deserved a little bit of privacy. He wasn't really sure where his loyalties lay. Alice had been his best friend forever, but Melanie was his friend now, and they had a real, live mission.

"Yesterday, what?"

"Nothing," Lewis said. He had never imagined not knowing what to do when his adventure came calling. "I just think she's coming around." He paused. "I think it all ties back to her dad."

"Maybe," Melanie said. She took a cloak off a hook by the back door.

"Where are you going?" he asked.

"To the web."

"You can't go alone," he told her. It was never a good idea to go into the woods alone, but especially not on an afternoon like this.

She clutched the cloak to her chest and looked at him with her pale blue eyes that always looked like they were ready to fill with tears. "The web needs saving," she told him. "I'm going to go save it, and if I'm the only one who can or who will— Well, maybe that's the way it's meant to be."

Meant to be. Like the Hero's Journey. But maybe this was his journey, too. Was this the part where he was rejecting the call? He shook his head. If this was a hero's journey, he was the sidekick. But that didn't mean he didn't have a role to play. "Okay," he said.

"Okay, what?"

"I'll go, too."

She smiled. "Good."

"Where's your aunt? Should we tell her we're leaving?"

"She's out on one of her walks."

Lewis glanced through the window of the back door. Icy rain continued to fall. "In this weather?"

"She thought she saw a golden eagle yesterday. This isn't one of their nesting areas, so it would be a big find."

Lewis figured if Melanie's aunt felt okay with going out in the storm, then they would probably be okay, too. "We should leave a note," he said.

Melanie agreed and wrote a short note to her aunt, which she left on a small table just inside the door. She placed a smooth rock on top so it wouldn't blow away.

Melanie swung the cloak over her shoulders. She pulled the hood around her face, throwing it into shadows. She took a leather satchel, too, and hung it across her body. She looked like something out of a fantasy novel, so at least it felt like they were on a real adventure. At least it seemed like they were doing something.

It didn't make Lewis feel any better about skipping practice.

They found the web more easily this time, coming at it from the side.

It was worse.

The spiders had continued to rebuild the one corner, but long strands were falling. Pearls of ice clung to each strand, weighing them down and threatening to snap them. The spiders were nowhere in sight.

Melanie took a deep breath. She held out a hand toward the web. "It wasn't supposed to be like this."

"Like what?" Lewis asked, confused. They'd known there was something wrong with the web all along.

"My story," Melanie said. She closed her eyes. "That's it," she said after a moment's hesitation. "I think I have to tell you my story. The story of how I got here." Her face had gone pink and tight. Whatever the story was, it didn't look like she was eager to tell it.

"You don't have to do that."

Melanie gestured toward the web. "Yes, I do. Look at it. If we're going to tell stories, they have to mean something."

An image of Alice clutching the letters filled his head. Those stories mattered. Had the spiders been on the web then? He hadn't noticed because he'd only paid attention to her. He looked at the web now. There, in the upper right corner, was one section of the web that looked new and stronger. Maybe Alice's letters had done something after all. "Maybe you should," he said.

So she began: "A long time ago in Istoria, the king and queen welcomed into the world a princess. Princess Melanie Amber Azalea Blossom Finch. The princess had golden hair and silver-blue eyes, and all in the kingdom welcomed her arrival as a good sign. Each of the Story Weavers wanted to dazzle her, so one by one they came and shared their tales. As she heard each tale, she traveled all around the kingdom to each realm. Each one was more beautiful than the next. Her favorite stories were the ones the animals told. In Istoria, animals and people understand each other perfectly. She loved their funny stories and their tales of adventures. But all the while, her parents were sad. The princess never knew why. Each night her mother whispered in her ear:

Hold me closer, hold me tight,
Listen to my tale,
Each day you grow and fill with light,
But some day you must sail.
A world beyond is dark and drear
And filled with so much fear.
To this land you'll go,
By sea and snow,
And bring the people near.

Melanie sang beautifully until the very last note, when her voice cracked. She sniffled and kept going with her story. "When the princess was nearly nine years old, full of laughter and starting to tell her own stories, that dreaded day came to pass. You see, the king and queen had made a deal with a sorceress who lived in the land of earth to share a child full of stories. The land of earth needed someone to protect them from the Freezing. Istoria needed the sorceress to keep their own realm safe. The king and queen knew it would not be fair to send the child of one of the people of the land. They would have to send their own child. They were good and honest people like that. They promised her she would be loved. She was promised there would be true friends to help her when she needed help. Queen Beatrice removed a necklace from around her own neck and placed it in the hand of her daughter. It was an ancient spider captured in glass the moment after it had spun its last web, a reminder to the princess of her origins and of her responsibilities.

"The sorceress came and wrapped the princess in a blanket made of wool. The strands came from all over the kingdom and were woven together just for her. When the blanket was spread out, it told a story: her story. The sorceress strapped the princess to her back, and together they flew over Istoria. They left behind the ocean and flew over the mountains. On and on they flew. The princess fell asleep. When she awoke, the sorceress was gone. She was still wrapped in her blanket and utterly alone."

She was crying as she spoke. It was hard to tell because raindrops had also gathered on her cheeks, but Lewis knew they were mingled with tears. "That's when my aunt came to get me," Melanie said. "I've been with her ever since." A spider had emerged while she spoke and worked to reattach a long radius that had fallen, carefully weaving it back into the frame of the web. Together they watched it work. "She used to tell me that story. When I first got here." In her hand she clasped the pendant of her necklace.

"Your aunt?" Lewis asked, surprised.

"She's not as bad as she seems. She just doesn't like children very much. She likes stories, though, and—"

"Don't do that," Lewis said.

"What?"

"Make excuses."

"She's rough around the edges, it's true. She's not used to talking to people." Melanie stared at the web. "When I first got here, every night she would make me a cup of warm milk. I'd never had warm milk before. It gets sweeter, somehow. Sometimes it was plain; sometimes she added vanilla, or maple syrup, or cinnamon. She'd bring it upstairs, and I'd sip it in bed. She sat in a rocker, and she'd tell me stories. All kinds of stories."

"Like that one?"

"Yes. They were all about this land where stories lived. Where I was the princess. I think some she made up and some she cobbled from other stories. I've never really had any friends, but I had those stories, and I had my aunt." Melanie wrapped her cloak tighter around her. "I know she's not usual, but I'd rather be at home with her than at school where I have to admit that no one likes me very much."

"I like you, Melanie," Lewis said. "I like you a lot." He blushed.

She smiled, but only for a second, because then the spider stopped. It regarded them for a moment, as if waiting for something. "I think it wants another story," she said.

Lewis opened his mouth, but nothing came out. He felt queasy and embarrassed. "I don't have any stories," he finally admitted.

"Everyone has stories," she replied.

He shook his head. That was his whole problem. He wanted adventures. He wanted to be like Buzz, where everyone had a story about him. But he hadn't had a chance to do anything wonderful yet. "I have games," he said. "Big games. Good games."

She didn't look impressed, so he quickly said, "My mom told me a story the other night. About a moose and—"

"Not a summary." She leaned in closer to him. "Tell it."

"Once when my mom was a girl, she and my aunt went to stay at their grandparents' house. My great-grandparents. I only met them once, but I know where their house is—on that road that goes out by the marshes to the ocean. That old white house? Anyway, they were there, and this big storm came up."

As Lewis told the story his mother had told him, a second orb weaver emerged onto the Story Web and started weaving.

"They waited for the game wardens to get there, and my mom just sat with the moose."

Melanie watched the spiders. Their yellow-and-black backs barely moved.

"And when they revived him, he stole my aunt's apple and ran into the woods!" Lewis said. Then he added: "The end."

"Wonderful!" Melanie clapped her hands together.

Lewis, though, frowned. "It's not enough."

"It's a start," Melanie said. "Let's keep going. What stories do you know? You must know some stories."

He supposed he did. They took turns telling them. Melanie told fairy tales and fables and poems about old knights fighting monsters and stories about trickster animals. Lewis told the story of the 1980 Olympic hockey team. He told Buzz's stories. He told a story about a boy who had been lost on Mount Katahdin and survived. They racked their brains and told every story they could remember.

The spiders did their job. But the web was huge and the spiders so small.

Eventually, they decided they needed to go back to her house. It was getting dark, and the ice was falling in heavier and heavier sheets. They walked in circles, he was pretty sure, though any footsteps they left were filled up by the falling ice. On and on they walked.

Chapter Twenty-Nine

ALICE

Uncle Donny always answered the phone the same way. *Hull-oh!* Like no matter who it was, he was grateful to be talking to them. Alice barely even noticed when he pulled his phone from his pocket and answered it. They had just come into his log cabin. Her mom was stuck at the hospital because of the ice storm, and so Alice was going to stay at Uncle Donny's. She was taking off her boots and thinking about what they were going to have for dinner when he said, "Wait, slow down . . . *slow down.*"

Fear had crept into his voice. The last time Alice had heard that was the night of the social when he'd come to pick her up. *Your dad is still feeling sick*, he'd said in that tight voice. What was going on now? Was it her dad? Was he okay? The questions came as fast as her speeding heartbeat.

"It was canceled . . . Yes, we called. I spoke with Laurel."

Alice, still bent over her own boots, froze.

Lewis.

"We just left the rink. No one was there . . . Okay, okay. Hold on. Have you called the sheriff's office?"

Alice lifted her head. The sheriff's office? What was going on? Where was Lewis?

Uncle Donny turned so she couldn't see his face.

"Yes. Yes. I'll go right back. I'll turn on all the lights. I can go out in my truck or I can . . . Okay . . . Yes . . . Yes, of course."

He clicked out of the call and held the phone in front of him, staring at it.

"What happened with Lewis?" she asked. But she supposed there was a part of her that knew.

"He never came home," Uncle Donny said. "He's missing."

He marched toward the kitchen. She followed right behind. He yanked open the freezer. "I'm getting you some dinner and then I'm going out looking. You'll stay—"

"No," Alice said. "I'm going, too." She felt topsy-turvy, like the ground had ceased being solid. *Lewis? Missing? Gone?*

Uncle Donny tugged at his hair. "Alice, I can't deal with this right now. One of my guys is missing. I can't be worrying about you, too. I need to know you're safe, okay?"

"I can help," she said. She *had* to help. She'd done nothing when her father needed her, and now here it was, crisis time again, and she was expected to just sit still?

"You can help by staying here. Man the phones."

"Is he with Melanie?"

"Who?"

"Melanie Finch. Has anyone seen her?"

He held his phone out to her. "If that's a friend of Lewis's, can you call her?"

"I don't know her number. She lives in the Bird House."

"I'm calling Officer Tibble. I'm making you a pizza, calling Officer Tibble, and you're going to stay here."

Alice knew she couldn't win this argument. So she just watched as Donny left the room, dialing his phone. She sat there. Useless. Her dad would know what to do. Even when he was her age, he would've known. How could she possibly think that she was anything like him when she couldn't even help her best friend?

She thought of how Lewis had just shown up when she'd been alone and scared out by the web. He'd known what to do, too.

She stood, ready to act. Just as she was reaching for her boots, Uncle Donny came back in with his heavy Carhartt jacket on, an orange hat pulled over his head.

"Someone's heading up to the Bird House. No one answered the phone there. Do you have any idea where they might be?"

Alice shook her head.

Which was a lie.

She knew where they were.

They were in the woods. They were trying to fix the web. They had not given up.

"Pizza's in the toaster oven. It will be done in five. Eat it and stay by the phone. Do not leave this house."

"Okay," Alice said.

Donny stopped his frantic movements. He placed his hands on her shoulders and looked right into her eyes. "Alice, I am serious. Do not leave this house. I absolutely could not handle it if anything happened to you. Do you understand? Promise me you won't leave."

She nodded, and then, without really thinking about it, she threw her arms around her uncle's waist.

He squeezed her back. "It's okay, Allie. We'll find them."

"Maybe . . . ," Alice began. "Maybe check the woods."

"His clubhouse? His mom already checked there."

"Maybe check beyond there. They both really like to explore in the woods."

"On a day like this? And with all those animals?" Uncle Donny shook his head. "I'm sure Lewis has more sense than that. But I'll let them know." He kissed her on the top of the head on his way out the door.

The toaster oven dinged. Alice took out the French bread pizza, being careful not to singe her fingers.

Dare stood on the counter. Alice broke off a piece of the bread. Dare danced around it before pecking at it and putting it into her mouth.

Alice found she wasn't very hungry. "I have a room here, too," she said. "Wanna see?"

She hefted her backpack onto her shoulder and took the receiver of Donny's house phone upstairs with her. Her room was at the back of the house. It had been her dad's room, when he and Donny lived here together before her parents got married. It still had his posters of old hockey players and classic rock bands. In the closet were boxes of things from her grandparents' house before they sold it and moved to Florida.

Alice sat on the bed. Ice pelted the window sounding like tiny bullets, one after another, unrelenting.

They're out there, she thought. Lewis and Melanie were out in the storm trying to stop whatever was happening. But how could they do that without her?

She stood. Dare rushed to the edge of the bed. *Bzeep-zeep!* Her call was urgent, like she knew what she was thinking of doing. "I can't just leave them out there. I think I can find it."

Bzeep!

The bird and Alice stared at each other.

"I promised," Alice said.

Dare stilled and sat next to her. Alice stroked the top of her head.

"Sometimes I feel like I have a broken wing, too. But it's something deeper inside me, you know?" she said. "Everything I want to do, everything I think I should do, I go to move, and I can't." She lay back with her head on her father's old pillow. "Like hockey. I still want to play, but I can't get my feet into my skates. I mean, I can. I could do it. But my brain or my heart or something—the broken thing—it won't let me."

Dare gave a soft, sympathetic *bzeep*, and Alice almost believed the bird really understood.

She stared at the ceiling. Her dad had hung an M. C. Escher print there. It was one of the tessellations where the designs morphed as they repeated: birds into fish and fish into birds. It felt like metamorphosis to her, and she wished she could dive right in. How would she change?

Too much thinking! she told herself. Her dad used to say that she would get too much in her own head on the ice sometimes. She needed to clear her thoughts. Stop thinking about herself. Stop thinking about Lewis.

In the closet was a box full of old comics that had belonged to her dad. He liked the Avengers best of all. "He told me he likes when all the heroes come together," she explained to Dare as she hefted the box out of the closet and placed it on the bed. "He said it's like a hockey team. Like you figure out everyone's strengths and you make the team better by playing up those strengths. Better than the sum of its parts." Dare looked intently at the drawing of the Falcon on the cover.

Alice smiled. "You'd make a good comic character," she told the bird. She held up both hands. "Waxwing!"

She picked through them. "It's funny, you know," she said to Dare. "Some superheroes want to be heroes. Like Batman or Captain America. They make it happen. Other ones don't really have a choice. Like Spider-Man. Ms. Zee would probably say those ones are part of the Hero's Journey, but I don't know. I mean, are you really a hero if you don't want to be?"

Dare didn't get a chance to respond because, for the first time ever, Alice had made it close to the bottom of the box. There she found a red spiral-bound notebook. On the cover, looking like they'd been written by erasing away the red, were the words *Andy and Donny's Awesome Comics.*

Alice hesitated. Then, she pulled out the notebook. She turned open the cover and sighed. There was her father's handwriting. A little messier than it was now but still straight and tall.

The adventures of Andy and Donny, AKA Hat Trick and the Penalty, two hockey-loving kids who save the world. Often.

The word "often" had been added by someone else, probably Uncle Donny.

The comics were silly. Her dad and uncle rescued cats from trees and kids from bullies and, in one particularly long string, stopped the Russians from sending over a nuclear missile by beating a group of Russian kids in a game of pond hockey. It ended with Hat Trick and the Penalty going out for pizza with Ronald Reagan and Mikhail Gorbachev.

Alice turned the page and froze. There was a drawing of a web. A big one that stretched across the whole page. The lines were thick and gone over again and again. The only problem was the center was gone, replaced by a big question mark.

Alice traced her fingers over the lines. She was certain her dad had drawn them. What was supposed to be in the center of that web? She leaned in closer and closer as if, if she got near enough, an answer would appear.

She looked at the comics spread over the bed. There was the Justice League: Batman, Superman, Wonder Woman standing tall, the Flash and Aquaman hovering in the background. Next to them was an *Avengers* comic, the cover crowded with heroes. *Like a hockey team.*

"Oh, Dare," she whispered. "I've been so stupid. He's been trying to tell me all along."

The focus on the team, whether it was Independence Youth Hockey or the Avengers or the 1980 Miracle on Ice team—her dad had drilled it into her. Some people got the glory, but you couldn't do it without your team. She thought about what Uncle Donny had said earlier that day—if a teammate messes up, they didn't blow the game. The team blew the game. Her dad had stressed that, too.

And who was her number one teammate? Lewis. Lewis who had asked for her help with Melanie's quest, even though he hadn't really understood it. She had rejected them. She had tried to do it all herself.

She hung her head.

That's when she saw it.

It was at the very bottom of the box, peeking out from under an old piece of newsprint: *The Story Web*.

Carefully she took the book out of the box. There was a spine label, and inside was stamped: *Property of Independence Community School Library*. Her dad had stolen a library book!

The pages were yellowed around the edges, and when she opened it, it had that old-book smell: not bad, but like the stories had been locked inside for ages and straining to get out. She flipped through, looking at the pictures without reading any words. On the inside back cover was a pocket with an old-fashioned library checkout card. Alice pulled it out. People had written their names in neat cursive or crooked letters.

Nadine Alegernon
Sam Pelletier
Emily Zelonis
Abby Clark
Andrew Dingwell
Henry Green

Alice ran her finger over her father's name. He had written in shaky cursive, carefully forming each letter of his full name. He had checked out this book. This very book. She went back through it. All those old stories, the kinds told over and over again so everyone knew them. Stories of great floods, like Noah's ark, but also the Gilgamesh tale and another from the Hopi Indians, and one from China. There were stories of epic heroes, of great battles. There were princesses and knights, and sometimes the princesses were knights. Then she found herself back at the beginning. There was more to the prologue than she'd remembered. It explained what would happen if the Story Web broke. The picture showed the world covered in ice. *The Freezing.*

She had the book, now she needed the team. But they were lost in the wilderness. *Lewis* was lost in the woods. A sick, bitter taste filled her mouth as her throat tightened. She rocked back on the bed and curled into a ball.

Outside, the ice pelted.

There was only one thing Alice could do. "I'll be back, Dare," she said to the bird, and went downstairs to put on her boots.

Chapter Thirty
MELANIE

Melanie wraps her cloak around her tightly. Her purple gloves are frozen and stiff. Each drop feels like a tiny knife, poking, poking, poking.

She remembers that the night of the car crash it rained, too.

The story her aunt told wasn't completely true.

They weren't a king and queen to anyone but her.

They didn't send her away. They would never have made that choice, even to save the whole wide world. The story still makes her feel better.

She tells herself the ice hitting her face is stars. She is traveling at warp speed. She has shot through the stratosphere, the mesosphere, the thermosphere. Up and up and up. She will keep going until she reaches them.

What will she say when she gets there? That she failed?

She found the web, but she couldn't save it. That she couldn't stop the Freezing.

"Just a little farther," Lewis says to her.

But he is wrong. Neither of them knows where they are.

No one knows where they are.

Her pendant is against her chest, cold as the sky. *Maratus volans. Maratus volans. Maratus volans.* The spider's name is her mantra. It was her mother's favorite spider, the peacock jumping spider, because people are usually scared of spiders, but this one was so beautiful. "You have to find the beauty in every little thing, Melanie."

"Just a little farther," Lewis says.

They walk and walk and walk.

Her parents would have to understand that she tried, wouldn't they?

Their feet crunch over dried and frozen leaves. Maple, elm, birch, oak. The icy rain pelts them over and over. They walk and walk.

Nothing. No one. Nowhere.

Emu

Living as she did in a world between the humans and the animals, Emu felt she had much to prove. Emus were very proud to begin with, of course, and, at the same time, a trifle self-conscious about their inability to fly. Not merely the inability to fly but the fact that they were so often overlooked. Say "flightless bird" and people think of ostriches and penguins. They may also think of turkeys, which isn't quite true. Turkeys *can* fly, just not very well. The point being that people think of turkeys before they think of emus, and that made Emu defensive. Taken altogether this meant that Emu was always trying to prove herself. Sometimes it came across as showy—the stiff-legged walk, the long neck curved just so—but it all stemmed from a deep need to be seen.

The cold gray sky had sent Emu into the shed, so she saw her girl and the boy walk into the woods. She watched their footprints fill with ice as they disappeared among the trees.

Not so strange those humans going into the forest.

But the sky turned darker and darker, and the night crept in.

Emu paced back and forth in the shed. She wished the woman would return. If the woman came back, Emu would tell her—somehow, some way—that the children were in the woods.

Then the other girl came crashing through the forest, the one all the animals were so concerned about.

Emu nodded one time, her long neck bending in that graceful way the other birds so admired, though they'd never admit it. She kicked one leg out in front of her and began her walk into the forest. She had to catch that girl in order to save her own girl.

Chapter Thirty-One
ALICE

Getting across town was the first challenge. Alice slipped over the ice, twice falling right to her knees. She didn't give up, though. She stepped into the woods by the Bird House. The emu sidled up beside her and made a strange grunting sound. "You know where they are?" Alice asked.

The emu nodded.

"Then show me."

Her backpack was heavy. She had two blankets, a thermos of hot chocolate, and the book. Its edges dug into her back as she walked.

"Is it far?" she asked.

The emu didn't respond. Deeper and deeper, they went into the woods. Alice had her warmest mittens on, but still her fingers started to burn. How much longer could she stand being out here? How much longer could Lewis and Melanie?

She searched the ground for any sign of the web but saw nothing, only ice crystals forming over the leaves and pine needles on the forest floor. The emu kept swiveling its long neck to look back at her, making sure she was still there.

Finally, the emu stopped. Alice wasn't sure why at first, and then she saw them: Lewis and Melanie, curled together under a tree. "Lewis!" she cried.

He looked up at her, blinking ice from his lashes. "You came," he said.

"Of course," she replied, and forced a smile.

She dug out the blankets and wrapped them around Lewis and Melanie. "Do you know how to get back?" Lewis asked.

"I think the emu does," Alice said. "But I have it. I have the book."

Melanie finally looked up then. "*The Story Web?*"

"Yes!" Alice replied.

Melanie and Lewis looked at each other. "We can't," he said. "We already tried."

"We have the book now," Alice said. "Don't you see? You couldn't do it alone, and I couldn't do it alone." She was talking so quickly she could barely catch her breath, but she had to get it all out. "I know what we have to do. At least I think so. Remember in the movie Dad always made us watch? The one

about the 1980 hockey team? How they had all been on different teams, all rivals, and they had to come together into one
team? That's how they won?"

Melanie looked a little confused, but Lewis nodded.

"And, like, the Avengers and the Justice League."

"Sure," Lewis said. "But—"

"That's the message," Alice said. "Ms. Zee keeps talking
about *the* hero. But there's never just one."

"That makes sense," Melanie said.

Lewis pursed his lips, which Alice knew meant he was trying to get his head around something.

"Henrietta told me about how when she was in World
War II, she was part of a team of translators. A lot of it was just
work. It wasn't one person finding this one important docu-
ment and, like, ending the war. It was all of them just doing
their jobs that saved things. My dad said that, too. That most
of the time being a soldier isn't big movie-style heroics. It's
showing up, doing your job—that's what makes a hero."

"Like Cal Ripken?" Lewis asked. Cal Ripken, Alice
knew, was Lewis's favorite non-hockey athlete. He set a
record for the most baseball games played in a row: 2,632
games! He always said his job was baseball, and he was just
doing his job.

"Yes. But not one person. All of us." Alice wrapped her
arms around herself. "I was trying to do it alone, but I can't.
That's not the way it's supposed to be."

Lewis stood up. He still had the blanket over his shoulders, which almost looked like a cape. "So what do we have to do?" he asked.

"We have the book, and we have our team." Alice said. "Now we just need to go out to the web and read the stories and—"

"We're freezing, Alice," Lewis said. "Let's go home and warm up, and we can come back tomorrow—"

"No!" Melanie interrupted. "Look around you, Lewis. It's happening. The Freezing. It's happening now, and we need to stop it."

"It's just an ice storm," he said.

Alice and Melanie shook their heads. "We have to go," Alice said. "And I need you."

"Fine," Lewis said. He tightened the blanket over his shoulders. "Let's do this."

❁

Emu led the way back to the web. It was just up and around the bend.

"We must have been walking in circles," Lewis said. "Everything looked so different with the ice on it—we couldn't find our way."

"My dad once told me about a windstorm that came through his camp. He said he didn't know which way was which. Places he'd gone a thousand times, he couldn't find

261

them." They approached the willow tree. Alice lifted the branch so Melanie and Lewis could crawl under. "He said when it was over, he honestly wasn't sure if it was the same place. There was part of him that wondered if he'd been picked up in the storm, like Dorothy in *The Wizard of Oz*, and dropped down someplace new."

Alice remembered how he'd said it: *It certainly wasn't Kansas, and it sure as heck wasn't Oz.*

When he'd told the story to her, he'd always left out the part about the soldiers attacking, the part she'd heard in his phone call to her mom. She took a deep breath. "During the storm, insurgents came. That's how my dad lost his friends. That's how—" She paused. Melanie put her hand on her arm. Alice looked at the long fingers, wrapped in soft purple gloves. "I mean I don't know for sure, but I think that's part of what happened with him."

She felt Lewis looking at her.

"I think being so confused, losing his friends like that. On the day it happened— I mean, the day of the social. When he—" She couldn't quite bring herself to say what he had done. "He was protecting me. I knew that the whole time."

"Look!" Melanie exclaimed.

On the web were three spiders, busily weaving even as the icy rain fell around them.

Alice's heart rate quickened. She pulled the book from her

backpack. "It says we have to tell the stories," she said. She flipped through the book to get to one of her favorites and began reading. "Once upon a time . . ."

She read clearly, loudly, with great feeling. She was trying to sound just like Ms. Engle who was so wonderful at reading aloud. But, as she read, no more spiders appeared. In fact, the three on the web slowed down, lazily spinning out their lines and loosely connecting them. The rain was strong enough to break the threads, so any work they did was immediately undone.

Melanie took the book from her and read a story. She read with her voice filled with emotion. Nothing. Alice crawled up the web, the mud seeping in at her knees. "Weave," she begged the spiders. "Please, just weave."

Lewis took the book next but with the same results. He slammed it shut.

"What's going on?" Alice cried. "Why isn't it working?" She'd been so certain they were going to solve this. She'd found the book. She'd had the big realization about working together. What more did this stupid web want from her?

"Maybe it already has these stories," Lewis said. "Maybe—"

"The book says to read them! To keep telling them!" Alice's voice cracked. She blinked away hot tears. How could the book be wrong? "We're doing what it tells us to do, so why isn't it working?"

"I don't know," Melanie said. Her voice was so soft and broken, Alice barely heard her. "I just figured if we had the book, if we did what it said . . ." Her voice trailed off.

The spiders slowed even more. One of them let a strand fly out into the wind.

"You see that strand right there?" Alice asked. "The one just flopping around?"

All three looked at it.

"See that little spruce needle caught in it?"

The spruce needle was not even half an inch long, dead and orange brown. It flopped up and down, tugged about by the wind and battered by the rain.

"Ever since my dad left, that's how I feel."

Melanie and Lewis nodded.

"Like any minute, I might disconnect and fly off and never be seen again." She snapped the book closed. "I thought if I could figure this out, if I could save this stupid web—" She shook her head.

"I know," Melanie said.

"I'm not even sure if this story is true, if this web is holding our whole world together. I just thought I could save it because that's what my dad would do if he were here. But he's not. Because of me."

Alice dropped to the ground and hugged her knees to her chest. She'd failed. The icy rain fell harder. It pelted her face and drenched her hair. Her clothes were soaked through. She shivered, cold to the bone. "It's going to come," she whispered. "The Freezing."

Melanie shook her head. "No," she whispered. "It's already here."

Waxwing and Owl

Waxwing, who had come to love the name Dare, hopped from the bed and jumped, flapping her useless wing the whole way. It took a while longer to cross the room, and there was a struggle to climb the curtain. Once in the window, she tapped the glass two times, then three, then two again.

Maybe she hadn't been able to get her message to the girl. Maybe she had a broken wing. But the girl needed her. The girl was out in those woods, along with the other two children. Dare couldn't go find them, but she could send help.

BZEEP! BZEEP! She tapped on the window as she cried.

A moment later, Owl appeared. Dare told him about the other children, lost in the woods, and how the girl had gone to find them.

Owl nodded and took off, filling the air with his low hoot.

The night creatures heard the sound and set off looking.

Owl circled over the forest. Listening, listening, listening. Humans were so very loud, he thought certainly he would hear them. The storm, though, muffled sounds.

Below, the other animals searched as well. Raccoon and Skunk sniffed the earth. Porcupine climbed trees and peered through the falling ice. Owl kept track of them as well. On and on they searched until the sky began to lighten.

Crunch!

Owl's attention quickened. He dove down, down, down and landed right at the feet of the three children who sat, defeated, in front of the web.

Whooo! he called.

For once, the humans seemed to understand.

Chapter Thirty-Two

LEWIS

"You have given me the scare of my life, Lewis Marble."

His mom squeezed him so tightly he thought he might stop breathing. Part of him thought that might be her plan. He sat on the exam table in the emergency room wrapped in a blanket and wearing his dad's old college sweatshirt. He didn't need to be here. He was fine. The owl had rescued them.

The owl.

Maybe he wasn't all right after all.

"Are you okay? Are you going to faint?" his mom asked. It was strange to see her so high-strung.

"I'm fine," he told her.

After the stories hadn't worked, they had just stayed at the web. What else could they do? They just sat there, still as rocks.

All of a sudden, there was the owl. It hooted at them,

and they had followed. It flew low so they could see it, and soon they were joined by an army of nighttime animals, all leading them home.

He rubbed his forehead.

That's how he remembered it, so that's how it was. The animals had led them to the Bird House. Melanie's aunt ran out the back door. She wrapped them in cloaks that smelled of mint and lavender and hurried them inside. She put them in front of the fire where they had thawed out like old mittens after a snow day.

The ambulance came, and everyone was all over the house. They tramped their wet feet on the antique rugs and left angry, muddy bootprints. Nocturne, the owl, had dashed down at one of the EMTs and been brushed off.

They hurried Lewis and Alice into the ambulance. Melanie stayed behind with her aunt. He saw her in the window before they closed the doors of the ambulance. She waved and he tried to wave back, but an EMT pressed his hand and said, "Shh, you're okay now. We got you out of there."

In the window, one last glimpse, Melanie's aunt placed both hands on Melanie's shoulders and pulled her close.

The doors shut, and Lewis realized he had been wrong about everything.

Beside him, Alice sobbed. He wanted to reach out to her, but his arms were under a heavy blanket.

Then they were at the hospital, all bright lights and beeping machines. Alice had been pulled away from him, ushered into some other room.

"You can take him home," he heard a voice say. Alice's mom. She was the nurse in charge of the floor.

"Where is she?" he asked.

"Alice is fine," her mom answered. "Better than you, actually. You've got frostbite, my friend, on two of your toes."

"Are they going to have to come off?" he asked.

She laughed. "No, Lewis. It's not that bad."

Would he be able to skate? But that was a foolish question. Whether he could skate or not wouldn't matter as the earth splintered apart.

"Can I see her?" he asked.

"I've got her set up in a room upstairs. There's another bed. You can spend the night if you want."

His mom said, "Maybe we should go home. Your dad's down in Portland tonight, Lew. The girls are home alone."

"The roads are truly terrible," Alice's mom told her. "Even Donny said so, and you know how stubborn he is. We can have a bed for you, too, Shiloh. We've got room in the nurses' lounge."

"I want to be with Alice," Lewis said.

His mom smiled, but it was a sad sort of a smile like he had never seen before. "Okay," she said. "Okay, we'll stay."

Alice's mom leaned over and kissed him on top of his head. "I'm glad you're safe, bud. Buzz would be, too."

He looked at her, but she had turned away, gathering up his chart and his things. He saw his muddy pants and the blanket Alice had brought for him.

Alice's mom wheeled him down a long corridor and into an elevator. The pediatric ward was quiet with the lights dimmed. Lewis realized he had no idea what time of night it was. She stopped the wheelchair in front of a room marked Dingwell. His mom helped him from the chair.

Alice slept in the bed closer to the window. Clutched in her arms was the book. The stupid book that hadn't done them any good, but still she hung on to it.

His mom fluffed a pillow on the bed and pulled back the sheet for Lewis to climb in. She kissed him on the cheek. "I love you," she whispered.

Then he and Alice were alone in the room. Ice pelted against the glass. This storm, he knew, wasn't just weather. Worse than that, he knew he and Alice and Melanie had failed.

❄

"None of this would have happened if she'd just taken some responsibility!" The voice jolted Lewis awake. He didn't recognize it, and for a moment in that groggy state between asleep and awake, he thought it was a dream. Then he heard, "Someone needs to go up there and talk to her."

"Patricia, please—"

Lewis blinked. The yelling was coming from out in the

hall. He folded back the thin blanket Alice's mom had spread over him and let his bare feet drop onto the cool tile floor. In the bed next to his, Alice slept soundly, her chest going up and down. Lewis tiptoed to the door.

As he reached for the door handle, a booming voice echoed through the hall: "This is unacceptable!"

"He's right. Those kids went to her house first. Any other reasonable adult wouldn't have let them outside. Not in this weather. Not with those animals out there." It was Donny's voice this time, not yelling but edged with anger. "But she wasn't home. She didn't even know they were missing until we'd already been searching for more than an hour."

Lewis opened the door a crack so he could look out. Donny was there, with Alice's mom, his mom, a nurse, and Officer Tibble. Brady's dad was there, too, along with some of the other hockey dads. Lewis figured it was Mr. Sykes who'd been doing the most yelling, a theory confirmed when he started up again: "Half this town out there looking for them! A thousand things could've gone wrong. What if someone else got lost? What if someone got seriously hurt? We're lucky only Jimmy put his truck in a ditch."

Lewis realized then that Mr. Sykes's arm was in a sling. Had he been hurt out looking for them?

"What do you suggest?" Officer Tibble asked. He wore a sturdy-looking raincoat and held his hat in his hands.

"Charge her!" Mr. Sykes roared.

"With what?"

"There ought to be something," Donny said. "She's that girl's guardian, right? Isn't that negligence?"

Lewis slipped out of the room and made himself a shadow against the wall.

"I'm not sure I can," Officer Tibble said. "There's no law in the state saying how old a kid has to be to be left alone."

"Can't even question her?" the nurse asked. Her cheeks were pink. "That witch isn't fit to—"

"Patricia," Lewis's mom interrupted.

Witch. They were talking about Melanie's aunt.

"What?" Mr. Sykes demanded. "That's what she is. Living up there all by herself, not letting anyone in those woods. No hunting. No trespassing."

"None of that is illegal," Officer Tibble said.

"This town is a shadow of what it was. We've got animals in the street, and that Hammersmith woman won't do anything about it. We've got people like Anastasia Seersie endangering kids, and you won't do anything about it. I'm calling a meeting."

"A meeting for what?" Alice's mom asked. It sounded like she was trying to hide the disdain in her voice, but she didn't do a very good job.

"A meeting to get this town back on track. A meeting to get that woman—"

"I'm as angry as anyone," his mom said. Her voice was

quiet and sad. "She should have been there. She never should have let them go out into the woods. They could have—" Her voice cracked.

"Exactly!" Donny said.

"Who are you mad at, Donny?" Alice's mom asked.

"What do you mean? This is Anastasia Seersie's fault."

"You were watching Alice," Alice's mom said. She wouldn't even look at him.

"So you blame me?" Donny's cheeks had turned pink, his eyebrows knit together.

Alice's mom shook her head. Her face, her shoulders— her whole body slumped. "I can't blame you. I can't blame her. I can't blame Buzz—"

"Jo—" Donny interrupted, but Alice's mom shook her head.

"So you go up there with your pitchforks and you bring her in. What good will it do?" she asked.

"What good will it do?" Mr. Sykes demanded. "It will let people know you can't live that way, can't avoid responsibility—"

"She hasn't done anything illegal, Alan," Officer Tibble said.

All the voices were so shrill, so angry, so uncertain. Lewis wanted to yell at them to just stop and listen to how foolish and scared they sounded, but then he'd be yelling, too.

"If you won't take care of it, then I will," Mr. Sykes said.

He had said the same thing about the moose. What was he planning to do?

"She's got a child up there with her. What happens to Melanie?" Alice's mom asked.

"Probably best for her to get out of that rickety old Bird House anyway," Mr. Sykes said. "My kid says she's as crazy as her aunt."

"Stop!"

The voice came from behind Lewis. Alice. She still held on to the book.

Alice's mom moved toward her.

"All of this is my fault," Alice said. "All of it. It's not Melanie or her aunt or Lewis or Dad or Donny. It's me."

"That's not true," her mom said. Her arms were out and open, as if she wanted to wrap Alice up in a hug.

Alice clutched the book more tightly to her chest. "I just want to sleep," she said.

"Me too," Lewis agreed.

His mom came over and gave him a kiss on the head. "Okay," she said. "Okay, come on." Alice's mom, glaring at the men, put her arm around Alice and led her back into the room. Lewis came right behind.

Their moms stood there for a minute or two as Alice and Lewis each got into their beds. It was like no one knew what to do or what to say. Maybe that was part of the web falling apart, too, when people who loved each other couldn't find the way to speak to each other. Like him and Alice.

Their moms left, and the room grew still. Lewis thought Alice had fallen asleep again, but instead she got out of bed and went to the window. He stood beside her. There was nothing to see outside, not with the clouds covering the moon and the stars. "What do you mean it was your fault?" he asked.

"I burned the cookies," she replied.

He thought back to the night of the social. There was a bake sale: brownies, cookies, that sort of thing. Alice hadn't brought anything.

"The smoke alarm went off. He—" She breathed in. "He didn't mean to hurt me, Lewis."

Lewis gripped the windowsill in front of him. He couldn't quite believe what Alice was telling him, but he didn't say anything. He knew his job right now was just to listen.

"He sent himself away," she told him. "I wanted to tell you, but—" She sniffled in hard.

"There were no words," he said.

"Not that I could find. All I wanted to do was disappear. So I did."

Lewis leaned forward. That's what it had been like in the end. Alice had just faded. If he had reached out to her, would it have helped?

He couldn't go back in time, he knew that, but he could

reach out now. He held out his hand to her. It's funny, in all the years they had been friends, they had never held hands. Never run through the forest or down the beach with their palms pressed together or fingers intertwined. The closest they'd ever come was when they'd helped each other up, like if one slipped on the ice or if they were climbing up a big rock in the woods. They grasped hands like that—like a handshake only firmer. Like teammates. He reached out to her, and they held on to each other, tight as chains.

The clouds parted and, for a moment, the moon shone onto a field behind the hospital, and there, sitting, waiting, watching, was a crowd of animals. Moose was in the center.

Chapter Thirty-Three

MELANIE

Ice falls all night long.

It falls in sheets that cover the earth.

It falls like glass shattering, like marbles cracking, like her tears falling.

It covers Melanie's castle, the house everyone calls the Bird House but she calls home.

It is happening, she thinks. *The Freezing.*

In the morning, she cannot open the front door.

Her aunt tells her to stay. To sit by the fire. To stay warm, to stay close. Just stay.

But Melanie needs to go to find her friends. She knows just where to look for them. She goes where the stories live.

Chapter Thirty-Four
ALICE

When Alice awoke, Henrietta sat in a pink armchair at the foot of her bed. She was wrapped in a turquoise scarf and wore a purple fez-styled cap tilted to the left side of her head. Lewis was still there, sitting up in his bed and eating a bowl of cereal.

"Look who decided to wake up," Henrietta said.

Alice didn't answer. The ice still fell outside. She could hear it crackling and saw the ice crystals on the windows. She couldn't see if the animals were still there.

"I am taking you two home," Henrietta announced.

"I guess when my mom was sure I'd be okay, she went home to check on my sisters. She's usually not a worrier, but there was a bad accident on the highway, and my dad couldn't get up here. She didn't want to leave them alone." Lewis shrugged.

"So she sent me," Henrietta said. "And your mom has a

couple of more hours in her shift, so, lucky you, you're coming with me, too."

Alice felt her stomach drop. She had almost died, and the world was ending, but still her mom needed to work.

So it was that Henrietta ended up bringing both Alice and Lewis to the Museum. Neither of them was very surprised to see Melanie waiting in the shelter of the locked doorway with Dare cupped in her palms.

Once inside, Henrietta made them all cinnamon sugar toast. She wrapped her scarf more tightly around her neck.

"That's a beautiful scarf, Mrs. Watanabe," Melanie said.

Alice thought it was so strange, Melanie making this small talk while the earth was being covered with ice. This was not how Alice had expected to spend the end of the world. She had planned, in giggling games with Izzy and Sadie, more laughter, more dancing, more antics. Maybe she would kiss a boy. The world would be ending, after all. Instead they sat in Henrietta's shop, Alice on an old chair from a beauty parlor, the hair-drying dome flipped up above her. Dare sat on her lap, eyes closed.

"Do you know why I like scarves so much?" Henrietta asked. She held out the end of her turquoise scarf and rubbed it between her fingers. "The way they are woven. I like ones like this where you can see the strands." She let it fall, and it fluttered down like a leaf in autumn. "Do you know what a text is?"

"Like on a phone?" Lewis asked.

Henrietta shook her head.

"Like a book?" Melanie replied.

"Yes. A book. Words on paper. Do you know what the word means? Where it came from?"

All three kids shook their heads.

"It has to do with weaving. In Latin it means 'thing woven.'" She coughed. "In college, I studied classics. That's the greats, you know, the ancients. There was a Roman scholar named Quintilian. He wrote about writing speeches, and he said, after you have chosen your words, they must be woven together into a fine and delicate fabric." Henrietta smiled and rubbed her fingers along her scarf.

Alice was used to Henrietta having her own way of saying things, but this was making no sense at all. "This is really interesting, but I'm not sure where you're going."

"You weave a story; you spin a yarn. Athena was the goddess of literature, but she was also the goddess of handicrafts, especially weaving," Henrietta said.

Alice thought of the story of Arachne.

"And war," Lewis said. "Athena was also the goddess of war."

"Well, there you go," Henrietta said. "That's it exactly."

Alice, Lewis, and Melanie looked at her totally confused.

Henrietta rearranged her hat on her head. Unsure what else to do, Alice nibbled on her cinnamon toast. She thought of her father. He was a storyteller. He was a soldier. And she supposed he was good with his hands. He fixed stuff around the house, and he was the one who always sewed buttons back on things and patched the knees in all their pants. He had gray eyes, too, just like the goddess. Was Henrietta saying that her father was like Athena?

Henrietta stood up and began walking around the store. She picked up objects as she went. "See this chalice?" she asked, holding up a bronze goblet. "It came from a church up near Rumford. Imagine how many lips have touched it, how many fingers." Next, she held out an antique iron. "People used to put these in a fire to get them warm and then they'd set to work. Imagine that? Imagine spending your time heating this up and pressing the clothes. Imagine the girl who did." Next, she pointed at her strange purple hat. "This hat belonged to Eudora Van Eckles, original occupant of the Bird House. She was the wife of the mill's first owner. That's how things worked back then. The mill workers lived in town. The owners lived on the hill, away from it all. It was a marvelous house, perfect for parties. Oh, Eudora threw the most wonderful parties. Here, look, I have an invitation to one right here somewhere."

Henrietta dug through an old shoebox and pulled out a weathered piece of heavy black paper. *You are cordially invited to a masquerade ball* was written in looping golden script.

"She spent most of her time traveling or throwing parties,

but she could be very generous, too. She funded the first library in Independence and made sure that every child had a library card. She paid for dance lessons at the community center for any child who wanted them. She had beautiful flowers planted all around town. Then, Eudora went on a trip to England. She visited all the sites and spent days and days in the museums. She had a head filled with ideas for new artwork for her house—and a little museum for Independence. She wrote it all down in a letter that she sent to her husband, including directions to start purchasing the art and plans for the building. For her trip home, she was excited to be on the maiden voyage of a brand-new, state-of-the-art ship. I'm assuming you've heard of it. The *Titanic*."

"Oh no!" Lewis exclaimed.

"'Oh no' is a mighty understatement," Henrietta told him. "When the ship sank, it is said, she gave up her seat in a lifeboat. I don't know if that is true or just a tale that's told to make those left behind feel better. But the long and short of it is, she perished at sea. Her husband was heartbroken. He closed the house and moved to Portland and ran the mill from there for the rest of his days. The house was abandoned for years and years and years. That's when the spiders moved in."

Alice shivered. "Creepy."

"Spiders aren't creepy," Melanie said. "They're lovely." She grasped at something at her neck, but Alice couldn't see what it was.

"Then, maybe thirty years ago, someone came along and bought the mansion from the Van Eckles's family trust. She fixed it up and moved in. She wanted a place where she could see the ocean and where she could do her work in peace. She came to town from time to time to go to the library or the hardware store or put in her grocery order. But as the days went on, she came less and less. That's when the stories started. People said she was frail or that she was sick. Those were simple stories, though none of them true. She was in perfect health. Then the stories about the birds started. People seemed to forget she was a scientist. *What's she doing with all those birds?* The story changed: she was an enchantress, and the birds were under her spell."

Alice looked at her lap. She had believed that about Anastasia, too.

"From there all it took was a little twist from an enchantress to a witch. People would go up and peek in her windows. Teenagers would go into the woods behind her house to scare each other with séances and spells. People left things on her doorstep."

Alice and Lewis exchanged a quick glance. They hadn't meant to do any harm. The truth was, they hadn't even thought about her as a real person living inside that house. She was a story. A fiction, not a person.

How many other people had done things like that to Anastasia, she wondered. All she had ever wanted was to be alone, not bothered day after day. No wonder she never came to town.

No wonder the web was falling apart with all these twisted stories twirling around. Stories that she had let swirl and steam and fester.

Alice looked around the store. All the items that had become so common to her, she didn't even see them anymore. All of them, every single one, had a story. Ms. Engle had said that books were only one way to hold a story. These things were story holders, too. What else, she wondered. People held stories inside them. Towns did, too, passed down from person to person, a thread tying generations together, a line from neighbor to neighbor.

Like a web.

Could it be that simple? Was that what the web needed? For her to let her story go?

She turned to Melanie and Lewis. "Do you think it's too late?" she asked. "Really and truly too late?"

Lewis looked toward the window. Outside the icy rain continued to fall and coat the earth. "What are you thinking?" he asked.

Alice wasn't entirely sure. The thought was still forming in her mind. "We did what the book said. We read the stories. But that was wrong."

"Okay," Lewis prompted.

"The web is still broken."

"It's unweaving," Melanie said.

Henrietta watched them, holding an old letter opener in her hand. The handle was dotted with tiny emeralds that glinted in the scant light.

There were the dark, untrue stories that people told again and again, not caring who they hurt. Then there were the stories that people didn't tell but maybe should. Could it be that easy? Was that what the web needed? For her to tell her story?

Of course, there was nothing easy about Alice's story. It was the thing no one talked about, least of all Alice—where her father was and why. But why was it so hard to tell? Why did it get stuck in her throat?

"Alice?" Lewis prompted.

"What if we've been telling the wrong kinds of stories to the wrong people?" Alice asked.

Melanie and Lewis exchanged a look, and Melanie was just about to respond when they heard the roar.

Bobcat

Bobcat slinked around the outer circle of the animal council while Moose recounted the steps they had taken and where that had gotten them. The answer, anyone could see, was that they had not been successful. The web hung limp from the tree. Strands drooped into the icy mud. Time was nearly up.

Crow cawed that it was already too late. He urged his fellow birds to take to the sky, to see if they might save themselves.

Moose told him to be calm, that he was frightening the skittering mice and chipmunks.

Bobcat admired Moose's thoughtfulness. She herself was a very patient, thoughtful creature, skills necessary to be a hunter. Indeed, Bobcat had been carefully observing the proceedings from the start. She had studied, most of all, the children. Children, she believed, were ruled by passions. The girl had broken from her stupor when Moose was in danger, not before.

Perhaps, Bobcat thought, more danger was needed. Perhaps, she thought, the children needed a greater sense of urgency.

She opened her mouth and roared. The single word silenced the other animals: "Come."

The animals followed her from the forest into town.

Chapter Thirty-Five

ALICE

Pacing back and forth on the sidewalk was a bobcat. It stopped when Alice emerged. All the hairs on its ears seemed to stand up. Dare dug her claws into Alice's shoulder. The bobcat let out a sound somewhere between a moan and a growl. Alice rocked back. The bobcat started walking. When Alice and the others didn't follow, it cried again. Alice wailed back.

"Are you okay?" Lewis asked.

Alice nodded. This time, she understood the animal. "Come on," she whispered. Dare gripped her shoulder more tightly.

A heron emerged from the road leading to the marshes and ocean. Then a beaver, a skunk, and a red-tailed fox had joined the progression. Even the emu came along.

They took up all of Minnow Lane. Cars stopped, and the army, for that's what it felt like, marched around the vehicles.

Alice knew what story she had to tell. The most important story she had. The truth. That's what the web needed. That's what would help her father. But she also thought about what her uncle had told her about true stories and honest stories, and as she walked, she thought about what she was going to say.

They turned onto Main Street, which was lined with cars.

A row of cars and trucks was parked outside Town Hall, Alan Sykes's big white truck among them. Bobcat hissed at it.

Together they marched up the stairs of Town Hall. Melanie and Lewis held the doors open, and Alice and the animals streamed in. Alice led them right down the hall to the big auditorium where they held square dances and elections. Alan Sykes stood at the podium, gripping it with the fingers of his good arm. "What we have in this town is a failure of leadership. Everyone's been counting on Buzz Dingwell for so long, we don't know how to do anything for ourselves. We've got animals running wild through town. We've got grown-ups sending kids into the woods. We're building a playground when we should be creating jobs."

He pounded the podium with his fist. A group of men behind him chorused their agreement.

"What we have here—"

Roar! The bobcat interrupted. It strode toward the podium with its ears back, tail twitching.

Mr. Sykes stumbled backward. He pawed at his waist, beneath his sling, his fingers fumbling over something.

"People! People! Stay calm," Officer Tibble yelled.

The animals kept their steady pace forward with the bob-cat in the front and the moose right beside it.

"Piper!" Donny yelled from the doorway. He had arrived behind the children and the animals. He grabbed on to Piper Hammersmith's arm. "Piper! The animals!"

"I know!" she yelled back.

It would have been funny, maybe, under other circumstances, watching the adults scramble about, unsure what to do.

"Alice!" Donny yelled again. "Stay away from the animals!"

But the animals were everywhere. Bobcat paced back and forth in front of the podium. Moose moved toward the rear door where he could survey the scene. Crow and Owl made lazy circles in the air while the starlings huddled together in the rafters. Baby Bear was fascinated by a bundle of cords near the door. The porcupine waddled, sniffing the ground for good eats. A snake wrapped itself around the legs of Becky Clancy's chair.

Alice knew she was safe with the animals. It was the grown-ups who worried her.

"This is unacceptable!" Alan Sykes yelled from the front of the room. He lurched toward the podium, like if he could get back on the microphone, he would regain control. Bob-cat, though, disagreed. It picked up its paw and swiped at the podium, toppling it and sending it sliding across the floor toward Moose, who bent over and prodded it with his nose.

This was too much for Alan Sykes, who once again started grasping at his waist. It was so curious. Alice could not figure out what he was doing. Bobcat, though, seemed to understand.

Chapter Thirty-Six
MELANIE

The animals are too large, too frenetic, too true for this space. Moose, especially, looks uncomfortable.

All the yelling doesn't help. Yelling like raising voices makes them more right. Yelling like you can make someone hear who doesn't want to listen.

Melanie scans the room for stillness. She finds it in her aunt. Anastasia is perched on a chair beneath a cracked window. Her face is drawn. She looks tired. She is tired.

The stillness is shattered by the man—Brady's father. He is thrashing and yelling loudest of all.

Then the clattering.

Then the *bang!*

Then silence.

Chapter Thirty-Seven
ALICE AND LEWIS
AND MELANIE

The gunshot reverberated around the old room. It rattled the metal folding chairs. It echoed off the huge lights that hung like bells above them. The starlings lifted up slightly, then landed again in the rafters. That was the only movement.

Mr. Sykes stared at the gun, mystified. It was his gun that discharged. He hadn't fired it. He'd dropped it, and it went off. The bullet flew the length of the room just above the floor and left a small hole in the cinder-block wall. A pile of dust settled on the floor.

And then, chaos. Yells from the people and squawks from the birds. People kicked over their chairs as they started to make for the door.

"Wait!" Alice yelled.

The people still hurried toward the door. The animals moved to block them.

"Wait!" Alice yelled again.

No one seemed to hear her. At the front of the room, near the stage, was the old clock tower bell. It had been saved when the tower was torn down. She marched toward it and gave it a big shove. The bell swung slowly away from her and then, on its pendulum, swung back, letting out a low, heavy *dong!* Everyone, people and animals, froze.

Alice stepped into the silence. "We have stories to tell," she announced.

The people of Independence took their seats. The animals guarded the perimeter. Alice looked at the crowd. Mr. Sykes had managed to gather most people from town for this impromptu meeting, even with the terrible weather. There were some kids from her school. Izzy sat in the front row, with her mom beside her. Becky Clancy clutched a stack of papers, probably all about how dangerous animals were. Brady sat near them, his arms crossed over his chest and his chin down. Ms. Zee was there in a seat near the back with Ms. Engle beside her. Mr. Cleary, Bobby Bixby, Sadie and her parents, Jimmy Roberge, Ashley from the Spaghetti Shed—she knew them all, and they all knew her. Uncle Donny stood by the door. He almost eclipsed Alice's mom, who stood slightly behind him. She must have come straight from work. Piper Hammersmith had her hands on her hips, ready to act. Lewis's mom walked in with Henrietta, who took off her hat. Sitting by herself in a chair below a cracked window was Anastasia Seersie, who didn't seem at all surprised by the animals.

Mr. Sykes, knocked out of his stupor, said, "Now listen here, Alice Dingwell—"

The crow cawed at him, and Lewis said, "No, you listen, Mr. Sykes."

Alice looked over at Melanie. "You go first?" she asked.

Melanie stepped forward. She wore the strange cloak and a hat shaped like a bell. Alice thought she saw Izzy snickering, but Melanie only smiled at her aunt and pulled her pendant out from beneath her shirt. The spider inside, long dead and preserved, shimmered in the bright lights. Melanie wondered why she had kept it tucked away for so long.

"Once, a long time ago," Melanie said, "but not so long ago that it can't be remembered, a woman moved into the woods. She had all the things she needed in her house. She had books for reading. She had food for eating. She had the woods to explore. She had the birds for company. People wondered about the woman in the woods. Some of them said she was a recluse. Maybe she was a poet who needed solitude. Or maybe she was a wealthy old heiress who wanted peace after years of society life. As the years went on, the stories grew and twisted. Sometimes children chanted that there was a witch in the woods. But the woman didn't mind, because she wasn't around to hear them."

Some people in the audience shifted uncomfortably in their seats.

Melanie continued her story. "She lived in the woods on her own. She kept herself hidden away. Then, one day, another tragedy struck. Amid this loss, a young girl arrived on her doorstep. Her niece. This girl was far from the kingdom where she had been born and where she had been loved. She was far from all she knew. The woman never wanted to be a mother and had grown quite accustomed to being alone. Still, she took in this child."

Lewis grasped Melanie's hand in his. He did it without thinking, just as he had done the day of the lockdown, before they'd known it was only a bear. "The girl heard the stories," he said, "because none of us bothered to keep them quiet."

Melanie watched Lewis as he spoke. When he finished, she said, "Each day she went home to her aunt, to the woman in the woods. The woman did not come down the hill to the town. But each day she made the girl cookies or scones with jam. Each day there were books to read and the woods to explore. Each day the girl was loved."

Anastasia clutched her hands to her chest as Melanie spoke. People stared at her, but it was not the way they used to: sideways and with a glare. They looked at her as Melanie saw her.

Lewis looked at the hockey boys. They all there—Mr. Sykes must have spent all morning calling around town. All of them were sitting together in a row with three empty chairs. One for him. One for Alice. One for Coach Donny. All Lewis had ever wanted was to be a hero, but he was realizing he knew less and less what that meant. Maybe being a hero didn't mean you were always the all-star. Sometimes, maybe being a hero meant stepping back.

The room stayed silent, and all eyes turned to Alice. Or maybe to the bobcat at her feet. Either way, Alice knew what she had to do. She had to tell the most honest story she could, but that didn't mean she had to tell the whole set of facts exactly as they had happened. She needed to tell a story so that the people of Independence could understand the truth.

She cleared her throat. She closed her eyes and took a deep breath. "There once was a mighty warrior—a giant actually. This giant was known throughout the land as Buzz. He had a younger brother—a very handsome and daring younger brother—who served ready at his side, and together they kept the land happy and wealthy in victory."

Melanie gave Alice's hand a good squeeze, and Alice kept going. "Like all good heroes, he went to seek his fortune in foreign lands. There, a maiden stepped out of a roaring fountain. She, too, was strong and powerful, and they fell deeply in love. They had a child. The daughter wasn't a giant. She was just a regular-size girl. He could pick her up in his hand, and he carried her from place to place in his front pocket."

Alice wasn't sure if she was telling this story the right way.

Her father had always felt bigger than life, more magnificent. She wanted people to know that he was all that but also a fragile, imperfect person. Just like everyone else.

Alice's voice cracked, but she kept going. As she spoke, she could feel the guilt lifting off her like balloons drifting into the sky. "He traveled to far-off lands where sand blew into his eyes rather than the wind off the ice. There he faced greater terrors than he could ever describe. The people there had never seen a giant before, and they set upon him with weapons and flames. They threw him to the ground. They plucked the whiskers from his beard." The words spilled out of her, bubbling up from some place deep within her. It was like all the stories her father had told her were seeds now blooming into flowers. But it was also something else—something just her. Maybe she was a Story Weaver after all. "They tied him up with thick ropes and ninety-seven knots. They rolled him into the ocean. In the ocean he almost despaired. He thought his days were done. But then an image of his daughter came into his mind. He saw her waiting at home for him, alongside his fierce wife. He untied all ninety-seven knots, and the ropes floated away. He swam to the bottom of the ocean. He dug deep, deep down. He dug until he popped out of the earth on the other side of the world. He strode across the land, stepping from mountaintop to mountaintop, until he made his way home just in time to tuck his daughter in for the night."

Tears were starting to stream down Alice's face, and it was

getting hard for her to talk. Lewis took over for a moment, giving Alice a chance to catch her breath. "The townspeople rejoiced at the return of their giant. They held a parade in his honor. All this they did for the giant but not for the woman in the woods."

"What people didn't realize," Alice said, "was that Buzz had indeed met an evil sorcerer, not here in Independence but far away. The sorcerer put a spell on him. He was still brave, loyal, kind, and fierce. None of this had changed. The curse was that he could not tell true threats from false. Chiming bells and ringing alarms sounded to him like the calls of war. And so it was on one fateful day when his daughter was getting ready for a ball that smoke filled his kitchen and an alarm rang out. He could smell the burning buildings and feel the heat of the desert. He rushed to save his daughter, realizing only too late that there was no real danger. So he put himself into exile. He sailed to Calypso's island, where he now rests. But he will return. One day, he will return."

Donny squeezed the brim of his hat in his hand. Alice knew she had gotten something close to the truth. Alice saw Ms. Zee sitting with her hands folded in her lap, a thoughtful expression on her face.

Lewis thought about stories, about who got to tell them, and what kinds of stories people told. He cleared his throat. "The giant and the woman, they lived side by side in the same town. Everyone made Buzz into a hero. That's who I wanted to be. But I don't know if I could live up to that, not the way everyone here sees him. I don't think I could carry what he carried. I'd be so afraid of making a mistake—" He glanced over at Alice. "I don't know if any of us ever really saw him as he was. I don't think we see either of them."

"My dad always told me to look up at the stars. That's how I'd know I was home," Alice said. "Maybe home isn't just *where* we are; maybe it's *who* we are." Alice thought of all those nights with her father, him pointing up at the stars. *That* was home. *That* was what mattered. She could almost feel her father behind her, urging her on. *Be bold*, he would tell her. She continued talking. "We tell this one version of our town, with giants and heroes who vanquish evil witches. But it's not the truth. We have to be more honest," Alice said. "We can't hide things away, because that makes them seem scary or bad when they aren't. We can't pretend things didn't happen. And making stuff up—we have to be careful with that, too."

Melanie nodded. "We have to think about the kinds of stories we tell."

"We have to," Alice said. "Or else we shatter." Melanie took Alice's hand. The three of them stood without moving. The story was done. The crowd was silent.

Alice had never heard so many people be so quiet. She could hear the bobcat snoring, the rustle of bird wings.

It was the moose, though, that had the last word. He tilted his head back and let out a long, low, cowlike call. The other animals stood at attention. The moose tipped his head to the children, then left, clomping through the open door at the back of the hall. The rest of the animals followed.

After a moment, Alice, Melanie, and Lewis ran to the door.

The sky, finally, was clear, and the moonlight rained down on the animals, casting them in silver like they were all in a black-and-white photograph. Beyond the animals at the edge of the woods stood the moose. He swung his antlers into the sky.

Alice and her friends stepped out. Alice held up one hand. "Goodbye," she whispered to the air. It was like breaking a spell. The animals all turned and dashed into the woods.

An owl lingered behind. It let out its hoot and flew into the air. Up and up before it swooped toward the forest.

"Look," Alice whispered.

"I see it," Melanie said.

It was the web, spreading out and over the trees, the strands so thin they wavered with each soft puff of air. If you weren't quite sure, if you didn't quite believe, you might not see those strands at all.

But Lewis and Melanie and, most of all, Alice, they believed.

Chapter Thirty-Eight
ALICE

They woke early to drive to Massachusetts. Alice's mom and Uncle Donny sat up front. Alice rode in the back seat. On her lap was the bird, Dare, in the small cage that Donny had bought for her. In the trunk was the elaborate habitat Donny had built. Officer Hammersmith had looked the bird over and said that it might still be weeks before Dare could fly, and anyway, she had become too accustomed to people.

Alice lifted the blanket and peered in at Dare. She sat quietly on the floor of the cage, silver-gray eyes staring right back at her. "My dad will like you because you have the same eyes," she whispered. The goddess Athena had gray eyes, too, penetrating and pure. Athena, the goddess of war and literature and handicrafts and the protector of Odysseus, who only wanted to get home to his family.

"Did you bring his stick?" Alice's mom asked Donny, even though she had seen it placed into the trunk of her car.

"Yes. And his jersey. The one all the kids signed for him after the championship last year."

Alice's mom nodded. She checked her side mirrors and the rearview mirror, catching Alice's eye. "He might seem different," she said. "But he's still your dad. He'll always be your dad," she said.

"Is he taking lots of medicine?" Alice asked. "I heard that's what they give people when they're sick like Dad. Like antidepressants and things and they make them seem different. Like they aren't really there?"

"Who told you that?" Donny asked.

It had been Izzy, back when Alice's dad had first been sent away for treatment. Alice had heard Izzy whisper to Sadie that doctors would likely drug her father until he was zonked and then leave him in a room alone. "It doesn't matter," Alice said.

"He is taking some," Alice's mom said. "I've been talking to his doctors the whole time, honey. They are being careful. It can be hard to get the dosage right, but what they have now seems good. It's kind of a constant monitoring thing. I know that meds that work on your personality can seem weird and scary, but some people really need them. Like we wouldn't look down on someone for taking acetaminophen for a headache, right? These meds are the same. They treat a problem that needs treating. They treat the symptoms, and your dad is doing the work to make himself healthy again. That's all."

Donny reached across the center console and squeezed Alice's mom's shoulder.

"I see," Alice said, although she really didn't know if she did.

She wished she had a person in the back seat with her who could reach across and give her a hug, a person like Lewis or Melanie. Instead she had Dare, who seemed to think this moment was the perfect time to go all quiet. Or maybe the car ride just bothered her. Alice let the sheet drop and hoped the bird would fall asleep.

They drove on down the highway. There were so many more cars here, and they were still in Maine. There were license plates from Massachusetts, New Hampshire, Connecticut, and New York. She saw one from Arkansas, which seemed impossibly far away, and another from Illinois. All driving south at speeds that made her dizzy.

They passed over a huge bridge and into New Hampshire. From way up on the bridge she could see all the houses and cars and churches and cranes down below, small and perfect. They went under huge tolls that they didn't even need to stop for, and then, as quickly as they'd arrived in the state, out they went again. *Massachusetts Welcomes You* a sign read, alongside a picture of a chickadee. If they were in Massachusetts, they couldn't be far from her father.

She stared out the window. There were even more cars here, going faster and faster down the three lanes of highway. Cars weaved from lane to lane, and Alice's mom gripped the steering wheel more tightly. Uncle Donny fiddled with the radio until he got a classic rock station to come in. "Sweet Caroline." Alice tried to relax. It was one of her dad's favorite songs. He'd taken her to see the Portland Sea Dogs play a game one summer, and they played that song during the seventh-inning stretch. He promised he'd take her to Fenway to see the Red Sox play and hear that song in all its glory. He'd promised her, too, that he'd take her to see the Bruins play. They'd never gone.

Uncle Donny sang along and said, "Come on, Alice! Let's hear you, JoJo!" But Alice and her mom stayed silent.

Alice's mom moved into the right-hand lane and got off the highway, easing down the exit ramp. Alice felt her skin grow tight all over her body, tight and itchy. She thought her breath was coming too quickly, her heart beating too fast. "I have to pee," she blurted.

"We're almost there," her mom told her.

"I can't wait," Alice said. "And I don't want to run to the bathroom as soon as I see Dad. I need to go now. Please. I need to go now." Tears welled in her eyes.

"Okay," her mom said. There was a gas station ahead. "I guess it can't hurt to fill up now, anyway," she said.

"I'll get some snacks. You know how your dad loves those Hostess fruit pies."

"Apple," Alice's mom said.

"I know," Uncle Donny replied.

Her mom pulled up alongside the pump. Alice put Dare on the seat beside her, fumbled with her seat belt, then fled from the car.

Never had she been so happy to be inside a gas station bathroom.

She stood over the sink and let the water, cold, run over her hands as she looked at herself in the mirror. Would her father even recognize her? Her hair was longer, bone straight, and parted on the side, because that's how Izzy had wanted it. She raked her fingers across her scalp and pulled her hair back at the base of her neck, then she nimbly braided it. She had a ponytail holder jammed into the pocket of her jeans and twisted it around the base of her braid. This her father would recognize. It was how she wore her hair under her hockey helmet. She could do nothing about the circles beneath her eyes or the sadness in them.

Her hands turned cold from the water. She splashed some on her face then patted it dry with one of the brown paper towels.

Donny and her mom were waiting for her in the car when she slipped into the back seat. After buckling, she put Dare back on her lap. "Okay," she said. "I'm ready to go."

They drove the rest of the way in silence. It was a pretty enough town, she thought. Once you got past the convenience stores and fast-food restaurants right off the highway, there was a nice little downtown with a coffee shop and a library and a big field with a bright white gazebo. They took a left turn and drove along a winding road, past cow farms and apple orchards until they got to a driveway with a large stone at the end. *Hemlock Center* was engraved in the boulder. Her mother turned up the driveway.

If it was possible to become more silent, they did.

The driveway took them over a bridge that crossed a thin river, and then they were on her father's island.

The main building was old, large, and brick, but welcoming. The front door was painted a cheery blue, and the steps leading to it had white railings laced through with Christmas lights.

Alice's mom stopped the car.

It was Alice who moved first. She unclipped her seat belt with a loud *snap*, and then opened her door. The damp air was heavy with the smell of pine trees, the cow farms, and maybe, Alice thought, maybe even a hint of the sea salt of the ocean. She hugged Dare's cage tightly in her arms and listened hard. Birds called from tree to tree: warblers and sparrows and crows. She heard cars rushing by far away. She heard the wind. Then she heard the sound she hadn't even realized she'd been waiting for: skates on ice.

She moved toward the sound, around the main building along a path paved with gray stones and lined with hedges no higher than her knee. In her cage, Dare twittered excitedly. Behind her came the clunk of her mother's clogs and the thud of Uncle Donny's boots. They came around a bend and there, at the bottom of the hill, they saw the pond. It wasn't much of a pond, not even twenty yards across, and there was a tree growing right out of the center of it. Alice's dad skated around that tree, around and around and around. His body was straight and tall, and he glided without any effort. He was exactly as Alice remembered him.

☼

Buzz Dingwell coasted to a stop. Alice, still holding the bird-cage, scurried down the hill to him and nearly fell into his arms, cage and all. He sighed into her hair. "Alice."

"Dad," she sobbed.

He looked right into her eyes with his gray ones, made shiny by his own tears.

"I have your bird," she told him.

"My what?"

"Your bird," she said. But by then her mother and Uncle Donny were down the hill, too. Buzz pulled Alice's mom into the hug, too. Then he stepped over and hugged his brother.

"I didn't expect you for another half an hour," he said.

"She drove like a demon," Uncle Donny said. "You should've seen her, weaving through traffic, laying on the horn, cursing like a sailor."

"None of that happened," Alice's mom said.

"It really didn't," Alice agreed.

"I know," Buzz said, and he kissed Alice's mom right on the lips. "Let's go inside."

They waited for him to unlace his skates and slip on his boots before they walked back up the hill. "There was a moose in town and a bear and a bobcat came and we all went to a meeting," Alice told him. "Izzy's mom wanted to have the animals all trapped and killed and Alan Sykes wanted—"

"Slow down, Alice," her mom said.

"You don't have to tell him everything right away," Donny added.

Alice's dad reached down and slipped his hand into Alice's. It felt smaller than it used to. "Oh, but you do," he said. He squinted against the sun. "I need to hear it all."

Her father opened the blue door for her, and she went into the building in front of him. It smelled of cinnamon and cleaning products, homey and antiseptic all at once. A woman hurried toward them. "They found me first, I swear, Carlie," Buzz told her.

"Welcome," she said. "I'm Carlie Templeton, Buzz's case manager. We just need to get you signed in."

"I'll take care of this, Alice," her mom said.

Alice's mom and Uncle Donny went with Carlie, the woman who had been holding her father captive all this time. She and her dad were left alone.

They walked across a scuffed black-and-white tile floor. He brought her up a set of stairs that led to a narrow hallway lined with doors like a hotel. They walked to the very end of the hallway where her father turned the knob on one of the doors and led her into a small room. A single bed was neatly made, the pillow stiff in the center. There was a small desk with a neat stack of her father's letter-writing paper, and, by the window, an armchair. "That window looks due north, right to Maine," he told her. "Right to you."

Alice sunk onto the edge of the bed. She put the birdcage down in front of her. Her father hesitated but then came and sat next to her. "So," he said. "Tell me everything."

Alice twisted her fingers together. She licked her lips, ready to tell him what she had done, how she was to blame. He looked down at her with those familiar eyes, and she couldn't do it. Not yet. She couldn't tell the truth and risk losing him. So she did her best to tell the story of the web. She told about the crow, the bear, and the moose. She told about Dare. She told about his letters and getting lost in the woods. The words spilled out of her like thread unwinding from a bobbin. Her father was so entranced that neither noticed the tiny house spider making a web in the corner of the room.

"I always knew you were a special girl," he said. "From the moment you were born. And the day you found the Story Web for the first time—you certainly were one of the chosen few."

Alice shook her head. "I'm not sure it works like that," she told him. "Magical births and refusing the call and all that hero's journey stuff. I mean, that makes for good stories, but I like teamwork better."

A smile spread across his lips. "You've been listening all these years."

Dare bzeeped in her cage. "There's something else you said that is the most important thing. We have to pay attention to the kinds of stories we tell."

He nodded, but then his face went soft and sad again. He looked out the window. "There are lots of stories about me. Not everyone knows them all."

"But I told people, Dad. I told them so they would understand."

He wrapped his arm around her, warm and familiar. "There's one I never told you. One I'm still embarrassed about." He coughed. "It's about Anastasia."

"Okay," she said.

"When Donny and I were kids, we'd always hear these stories about the witch in the woods. No one would go up there. Well, to me, that was a challenge. I wanted to show everyone how brave I was. So I told anyone who would listen that I was going to confront the witch."

Alice's stomach flip-flopped.

"I made Donny come with me," he said. "I, the conquering hero, and my loyal sidekick—"

"Dad," Alice interrupted. "Tell it true."

He looked at her with his gray eyes, right into her. "Okay," he said. "I will. We weren't brave at all. We were terrified. We snuck up there, and we knocked on the door. No one answered. I thought I heard an owl hoot, but that was it." He shifted on the bed. "So we went around back, and I saw a trellis. Donny dared me to climb it. Back then, I never turned down a dare. So up I went. I was peeking in the windows. It was a pretty amazing house, but nothing witchy."

Alice nodded.

"Next thing I knew, I heard a yell and then a loud *bang!* It startled me, so I let go. I just—let go." He opened his hands to show her. This wasn't the way he normally told stories. His voice was flat, and there was no light in his eyes. "Fell flat on my back. I heard the snap. It was my leg."

"Oh no!" Alice said. At the same time, she was thinking about things people had said about her dad. Like Mr. Roberge saying something about the Dingwell brothers falling off a building.

"She was there in an instant. Anastasia. She brought me to her car, drove us to the hospital. I got my leg set. I was out for the first two weeks of the season."

Alice put her hand on her dad's. "Lewis and I did something like that, too," she confessed. "We went up with milk to see if it would sour."

"I'm sure people brought all sorts of things up there. Said

all manner of unkind things to her." He looked at his hands. "I know they did. After I got hurt, people blamed her. Some said she'd shot at me with a real gun. Then there were others who said she was a real witch, and she cursed me."

"People make up terrible stories."

"It's just as bad letting the stories live," her dad replied. "I knew the truth. I knew she had shot up a flare, like a warning. She didn't know we were just some stupid kids. We could've been burglars or worse. And I knew she wasn't a witch. But it served me to have people think she was. So I let it go. I let it grow wings and fly." He took a deep breath and let it out.

"How many times did I hear people calling her a witch and I could've told them—"

"You told me now," Alice said. "That's a start."

Silence washed over them. Alice noticed a small vase on her father's desk with a single red carnation. She thought of Henrietta's beautiful flowers, of Anastasia's birds, all beautiful and fragile. Like her dad.

"When Melanie came, I brought Anastasia some of your old clothes. I guess I was trying to say sorry. But I never said sorry, so I never felt like I had made amends."

Amends. Alice had her own mistakes to amend for. The clock ticked. Someone in the hall coughed.

Alice scuffed her foot on the rosy pink linoleum floor. "I'm sorry," she whispered. She had to tell him. He had been honest with her; now she needed to be honest with him.

"You've got nothing to be sorry for, kiddo."

"I do," she insisted.

He scooted closer to her. "So tell me."

He looked at her with his silver eyes not blinking once. She remembered sitting next to him, looking at the stars, learning about myths.

"I put the batteries back in the smoke detectors," she whispered. She rubbed her hands against the quilt on the bed as if she were trying to wipe away the guilt.

He didn't say anything, and all she heard was the sound of a heater blowing air between them.

"I put them in and then I burned the cookies. I'm the reason you're here."

His face crumpled, and he started to cry. Hard. Alice didn't know what to do. She sat ramrod straight. She had never seen her father cry like this, not even in his worst moment. "Oh, Alice!" he cried. "Alice!"

She had broken him; she was sure of it.

"Alice, none of this is your fault," he said. "It's not your fault and it's not my fault. It's the world and the war and the things I saw—not you. Never you."

Alice launched herself into his lap. They cried together, with him holding her tight to his chest. He smelled just the way she remembered him, and if he didn't feel quite as safe as he used to, that was okay. He was still here. He was still her father. Maybe she had learned some things about him that changed how she saw him. He wasn't perfect. He wasn't larger than life. But she still loved him. And he still loved her.

Eventually their bodies calmed, and he stroked her hair.

"I miss you so much, Dad."

"I know, kiddo. I miss you, too. Every millisecond of every day."

"Are you getting better?" she asked.

"I think so."

"Will you come home?"

"Yes," he replied. "As soon as I can. Now," he said. "Tell me about this bird you've brought."

She pulled the sheet off the cage, and Dare and Buzz stared at each other, each with a broken wing, each with silver-gray eyes.

"She's for you," she said. "She's yours."

Then she picked up her bag and took out her other gift for her dad. She'd asked Ms. Engle, and she said it was all right so long as it came back by the end of the year. She handed the blue book to her dad.

"*The Story Web*," he said with a smile. He hugged the book to his chest. "I love this book."

"You stole it from the library," she said.

"Well—" His cheeks turned pink.

"It's okay. Ms. Engle checked it out to me for the rest of the year."

Her dad opened the book, and they looked at the picture in the prologue together: the earth frozen and shattering. Alice shivered. "It's real," she whispered. "It's not just a story, and it almost happened."

He put his palm on the book, over the picture. "It's always happening, Alice. That's why we have to keep telling stories. The kind of stories that connect us, not the kind that divide us. No more witch stories."

Alice tucked herself into the crook of his shoulder. She used to fit better, but it still felt just right. "So let's do it," she said. "Right now. Tell me a story."

"Once upon a time," he began, "a girl was born under the light of a silver moon. No one knew it at the time, but one day this girl, and her friends, would save the whole wide world."

Epilogue

Alice, Lewis, and Melanie walked down the stairs of the library, each with a book under their arm. Most of the books came from Anastasia's library, carried over in a parade of townspeople after she made the donation. Anastasia had watched the books go from an upstairs window of the house and was grateful to shut the door behind them. The town had also raised money for new books and hired a friend of Ms. Engle's from library school to be the new town librarian. The three friends volunteered as pages mostly so they could get their hands on the new books first.

They walked together through the park. The town had decided not to call it Buzz Dingwell Park after all. When Alice told him in a letter, he replied that it was a relief, and he liked the name they gave it a whole lot better. The town had had a naming contest, and Melanie's choice won: Historia Park. It told the story of the town. At one gate, there was a statue of kids playing hockey—Donny insisted the boy was modeled after him. At the other gate was a statue of Eudora Van Eckles tending a flower garden planted by Henrietta and her canasta friends, who had formed a new gardening club. In the playground, one of the climbing structures was shaped like an old mill and another like the moose. The sea serpent bench was there with a perfect view of the whole park. The path was lined with bricks, each with a name. The children had all been able to press their hands into the cement that surrounded the basketball courts. There was a war memorial, too, and Alice noticed Henrietta Watanabe's name freshly carved into the stone base.

Ms. Zee had changed the hero project to focus on local heroes. Everyone had gotten to interview someone in town and present their story. The interviews were being archived in the library. Alice had chosen Henrietta, and once people knew her history, they'd decided to add her to the monument.

After their heroes project, they had researched animals in the area and had created new signs for the park that taught about them. Officer Hammersmith had helped, and Brady and Izzy liked it so much that they had become junior animal control officers. Maybe it was spending all that time with animals, but both of them had softened a little. Not enough that Alice wanted to be friends with them again but enough that life was bearable.

Lewis ran along the path ahead of Alice and Melanie. "It's

Lewis Marble on the breakaway. He's skating down the ice; he's got the puck!" He mimed a slap shot. "He shoots! He—"

"Is blocked by Alice Dingwell!" Alice yelled.

"Aren't we on the same team?" Lewis asked her.

They were, actually. The night before, Alice had decided to rejoin the team. Today she and Lewis were going to get back on the ice together, before her first official practice. Outside, the sun shone on them, but as soon as they stepped into the rink, coolness fell over them.

Alice tied her skates on while Melanie watched.

"You coming or what?" Lewis called from the ice.

Alice strapped on her goalie pads and dropped her helmet on over her head. Then, for the first time in months, she skated out onto the ice and to the goal.

Lewis liked the sharp noise of the hockey stop. He liked the way flakes of ice drifted up like snow in a snow globe. More than that, he liked the sound of Alice's skates roughing up the space in front of the goal.

"You think you still got it?" he called across the ice to her.

Alice grinned behind her hockey mask. Nothing had felt normal since her father left. Not one single thing. Except for this. It had taken her so long to discover it, but it had been here all along: the ice, Lewis, her uncle Donny watching from the office above. This was her father's world, true, but that didn't mean she didn't have her own place in it. It didn't mean she couldn't be here without him.

"Yeah, I've got it," she called back to him.

"Go, Alice!" Melanie called from the far side of the rink where she stuttered across the ice gripping the side wall for support.

"Hey, what about me?" Lewis yelled to her.

Melanie shrugged.

Lewis dropped the bucket of pucks and picked one out. He rocked it back and forth on the ice a few times before he started down the ice. He built up speed with each kick of his leg, racing toward Alice faster and faster and faster. But to her, he was in slow motion. She saw each stride, each tap of the puck from side to side. She saw his stick go back, saw it bend as it slapped into the puck, saw the puck lift into the air. Her glove was up. She was ready.

She was brave.

She was bold.

She was fierce.

All of them were.

Acknowledgments

When you are writing a book about stories, you think about the people who told stories to you. So, my very first acknowledgments must go to my mother, Eileen Frazer, with whom I read nearly every night, and to my father, Joseph Frazer, who made up stories to tell my brother and me, mostly about abominable snowmen. Thank you also to Jack and Matilda who listen to my stories and let me experience tales, both old and new, through their eyes.

Every book needs an editor, this book perhaps more than any other I've written. Thank you to Mary Kate Castellani for asking all the right questions and steering me and the book to the place it needed to be. Thank you, also, to the whole team at Bloomsbury: Beth Eller, Lizzy Mason, Alli Brydon, Claire Stetzer, Erica Loberg, Erica Barmash, Danielle Ceccolini, Susan Hom, and Cindy Loh.

Kids often ask me if I design and create the covers of my books. I don't! I'm so grateful to illustrators like Erwin Madrid who captured the story for the cover.

Thank you to Sara Crowe, agent and friend, who nurtures and finds homes for my stories and for so many wonderful tales.

Thank you to Lee Kantar, State Moose Biologist, Maine Department of Inland Fisheries and Wildlife, who answered all my moose questions, including how to get a moose out of a trench. Equally valuable was Carly Hippert explaining how nurses balance their schedules with parenthood. Thank you to all the other experts who answered my questions.

Thank you to all my families: the Blakemores, the Pikcilingises, the Frazers, the Tananbaums, and my Dyer family. Thank you for understanding when I need to lock myself in my office and not do fun things with you.

Thanks, finally, to Nathan, with whom I've written my favorite story.